PRAISE FOR

I remember when the author considered joining the FBI. This novel is a tribute to his continuing interest in complex investigations, intrigue, and international operations of law enforcement. Just have to keep telling yourself it's just a novel!

Thomas Kneir, Special Agent, Federal Bureau of Investigation (Retired)

SAC Jacksonville 1999-2001

ALL HAVE SINNED

MARCUS BUCKLEY

"ALL HAVE SINNED"

BY MARCUS A. BUCKLEY

Published by Area613 An imprint of 613media,LLC in partnership with LifeFilters,LLC. Ephesians 6:13.

This is a work of fiction. The characters portrayed in this book are fictitious unless they are historical figures explicitly named. Otherwise, any resemblance to actual people, whether living or dead, is coincidental.

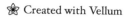 Created with Vellum

ACKNOWLEDGMENTS

Acknowledgements

Stories are most often credited to one person, but there are many who influence its progress and help bring it to fruition. Thanks are owed to so many for their help, but I need to point out a few in particular: Thomas Kneir for introducing me to the real world of the FBI; Chase Brandon for inviting me to Langley all those years ago; Mark Sutton and Bruce Hennigan for helping this book finally see the light of day; Mom and Dad, who always encouraged my imagination, and continue to; all of my friends in law enforcement, the Armed Forces of the United States, and the Intelligence Community who lent a hand when I was trying to figure this thing out; and most importantly, my wife, LeaAnn, and our kids, who have had to listen to me wrestling with this book for so many years now. Thanks for believing in me.

Cover Design by Jordan Hargrave

To the greatest gift God has given me other than my relationship with Him; my heart, my love, my inspiration, my everything—my incredible wife, Lea Ann. This one's for you.

CHAPTER ONE

Why do I even bother, Rev. Jim Isaac thought as he parked his Buick Lucerne in a parking space designed for a more compact vehicle. He opened the door, careful not to ding the sport utility parked next to him. Sweat began to form on his brow, under his dress shirt, tie and suit coat, a natural by-product of the fierce humidity found in Jacksonville, Florida in June. Each year it seemed the annual city-hopping Coalition of Christian Churches became more and more casual, and Isaac remained one of the few pastors who still wore a suit and tie to each of the sessions. Well, he *had* been going to the Convention in a suit and tie for a long time—longer than some of these new pastors had been alive —and he wasn't about to change now. *Let them be casual if they like*, he mused, *but I'm going to look like a pastor should.* Isaac didn't have an egotistical perspective or superiority complex; he simply believed that a pastor should look professional and should raise the standard for others. *Heaven knows the standards have dropped enough*. Even as the thought went through his head, a young family poured from a minivan. The father wore a solid colored t-shirt with a sport coat—a t-shirt! —while the wife had on a form-fitting shirt with hip-hugging Capri pants and sandals. Their teenage daughter appeared through the side door wearing a shirt that stopped just above the waistline of her not quite knee-length skirt. She stood three or four inches taller than her actual height, he noticed, elevated by the almost cartoonish platform shoes she wore. *What is the world coming to? That's probably a preacher's family, and look at how they're dressed!* Isaac sighed, realizing that the world was changing more rapidly than he liked.

The security system chirped as the family walked from their minivan, and Isaac stopped in his tracks. He felt for his coat pocket and let out a grunt of frustration. Once again, his all-important cell phone had been left behind in the car. It was hard for him not to chuckle at the irony of his thoughts: lamenting modern life and its rapid changes and simultaneously feeling undressed without his ever-present miniature computer that doubled as a cell phone. Isaac turned and walked back up the ramp to the spot where the Buick was parked. As he made his way to his car he noticed a utility van parked in a no-parking zone. He hadn't paid attention to it before, but then he hadn't looked up the ramp behind him either. With the phone stuffed in his inner coat pocket and the car door locked once more, the pastor looked at his watch and noticed the time: eight minutes past nine. There would be just over twenty minutes before the first session started, more than enough time to stop and get a cup of coffee, maybe see a few friends he hadn't seen since last year.

Isaac walked down the ramp, and he suddenly felt a twinge of regret about his thoughts from just a few minutes ago. *Life's too short to worry about dress codes*, he thought. *After all, Jesus wore a robe and sandals. Face it, Isaac, you're turning into the grumpy old man you always said you'd never be.* Smiling to himself, he took off his jacket and walked back to the car yet again. Loosening his tie and folding it, Isaac removed the cell phone from his pocket and put the tie in its place. *Out with the old, in with the new.* It occurred to him to call his wife and tell her the stodgy old man she was married to had abandoned his tie and coat for his venture into the convention hall. His bride had been after him

for years to loosen up, and she was right. *Might as well live a little.*
Tossing the jacket into the trunk of his car, Isaac dialed the
number to reach his wife at home and pressed "SEND". He
never saw or felt the explosion that ripped through the garage
structure, sending him to the place he had preached of and
believed in for nearly 60 years.

Everyone else in the country is burning up, and I'm trying to find a jacket.
This did not bother FBI Special Agent Thomas Hawkins in the
least. Although he had spent most of his life in Florida, hot
weather ranked at the bottom of his list of favorite things. He
had never cared much for the beach, but the mountains called
him the way they had called John Muir. It was this love of stone
and wood that led to the purchase of this mountain-top home in
Cosby, Tennessee. Most people had never heard of the tiny town,
a short drive from the more touristy Gatlinburg, which also did
not bother Hawkins. When vacation days needed to be burned
he liked to get away from the Florida heat, and Cosby lay close
enough to Sevierville, Pigeon Forge, and Gatlinburg that he
could always find something to do if he got bored sitting on his
deck looking at the Smoky Mountains. Most of the country
found themselves experiencing an unusually hot June, but the
mountains of eastern Tennessee were enjoying some of the
coolest weather on record, reaching into the mid-60s during the
day under overcast skies.

Hawkins pulled on a black leather jacket, one of several cool-
weather coats in his closet. The house was fully furnished with
any clothing and toiletries one might need, so packing wasn't
much of a requirement for these excursions. In the enclosed
garage sat his black Dodge Challenger Hellcat Widebody
Redeye, one of several performance cars he owned. The car was
an absolute brute, far and away the most powerful car he had
driven. The performance driver training courses at Quantico
were excellent, and Hawkins was an excellent wheelman, but this

car was no ordinary vehicle. The Redeye demanded respect—a careless right foot would send the back end of the car around before the driver knew what was happening.

With the press of a button the supercharged engine barked and crackled to life. A glance at the clock radio told him the time: 9:08 a.m. Big Wally's would be open for breakfast, and he could already taste the stack of crispy bacon, 4 eggs, and what seemed like half a gallon of grits. Wally lovingly referred to it as "Heart attack on a plate", and although it wasn't the healthiest of fare, he justified it by thinking of the five-mile run he had taken earlier that morning. Even now, running did not come naturally for Hawkins. He had never done much of it to speak of before the FBI began recruiting him, and then he had a lot of years of light workouts and lying about how many miles he ran on the treadmill to make up for. By the time he went through the Academy at Quantico, he had become the fourth fastest in the required 2-mile run out of his class of 31 Agents-in-Training. Hawkins kept up a 5-mile regimen at least three times a week so he would never have to work that hard again.

Hawkins paused at the end of the freshly paved, inclined driveway, and turned onto SR321 toward Gatlinburg, the satellite radio locked in on the 80's station. The mountains shut out almost all radio signals, and even the satellite radio would cut out from time to time as the Great Smoky Mountains swelled over the roads in the area. He listened to classic 80's rock most of the time, and if the TV was on there was a good chance it would be tuned to one of the myriad programs devoted to automotive restoration and performance. He would watch the cable news networks just to amuse himself, as they all had become driven by ratings over reporting. He hadn't gotten a satellite dish yet at the mountain house—no cable company served his neck of the woods—so he felt a bit out of touch with the world, but then he realized that wasn't an altogether bad thing. The world would wait, or it could go on without him.

As he accelerated hard up a steep incline he savored the cool wind whipping through his open window. The whine of the massive supercharger rang out above the engine's bellowing roar as it spun towards the redline. The computer-controlled transmission shifted more quickly than any human ever could, allowing him to focus on keeping the monster pointed in the right direction. Already the car had crested triple digits, so he backed off. He grinned like a kid on Christmas morning. The car settled into a comfortable 60 mph cruise for the remainder of the short drive. A few minutes later Hawkins walked in the door of Big Wally's Barbecue Pit and Diner, greeted by a number of head-nods and friendly "Hey!s."

"Top of the morning, Hawk!" The owner of Big Wally's, Rick Wallace, greeted Hawkins with the warmth of an old friend, his Australian accent standing out in the midst of the Tennessee drawls filling the crowded room. Hawkins still got a chuckle out of the thought: an Australian man running a country-style barbecue diner in the middle of the mountains of Tennessee. But the success of the tiny diner had been no laughing matter: people came from all parts of the country to eat at Big Wally's.

It amazed Hawkins how warmly he had been welcomed by everyone into the small town. He had inherited a sizeable amount of money from his family and used a small amount of it to purchase the large piece of property on which his log home now sat. He had been apprehensive about how the residents of this small mountain town would feel about some wealthy outsider moving in and buying up their land for a vacation spot, but his prejudicial thoughts had been blown away almost immediately in a pleasant breeze of good old Southern hospitality. The sweet little lady who lived down at the intersection of Highway 321 and the road leading up to his house—Marge Willard—drove up in her Jeep and brought him a fresh baked apple pie. The apples came from the orchard just up the road, she had said, as proud of her pie as Michelangelo had been of *David*. Apple pie wasn't his favorite—he tended to be a chocolate man—but he found himself touched by the sweet lady's thoughtfulness and thanked her for the pie. He had returned the favor by having her up for steaks on the grill, and she filled him in on the history of the area. Marge told Hawkins she'd keep an eye on the place for him when he wasn't there and, in her words, if anything needed doin', she'd do it. It was also his neighbor who told him about Big Wally's, where the good hiking spots were, the names of the folks one needed to know around Cosby, and other important facts. That was last summer, and although he had only been up a handful of times since, it seemed everyone in the small town knew of him and his profession, referring to him as "our FBI agent".

"Mornin', Rick. How's the bacon today?"

"Thick and crunchy."

"Sounds good. As long as that doesn't describe the scrambled eggs and grits, I'll have some of those, too."

"Heart attack on a plate, coming up", Rick replied, heading back towards the kitchen. A curly-haired blonde, whose name tag declared her to be "Sue", poured a cup of decaf on the counter in front of Hawkins.

"How are you today, sugar?" she asked. Sue got a little friendlier each time Hawkins came in. He didn't mind, of course, because she was a knockout. She appeared to be no more than 21 or 22 years old and had the look of the stereotypical farmer's daughter: angelic face, curly blond hair pulled up in a ponytail, and a great figure.

"Great, Sue. How're things going at your Dad's farm?"

"Goin' great. Sure would like for you to come out and see it sometime. I'd love to take you out and show you around the place." The look on her face told him she had some special places in mind for his visit.

"I don't have much time this trip, but I may have to take you up on that one of these days."

"I sure hope so", Sue said, smiling and glancing back at Hawkins as she turned and walked toward other customers longing for a cup of decaf and a closer look at Sue. She was attractive—*very* attractive in fact, but she just didn't ring Hawkins's bell. He had dated based on looks-first before, ignoring the little voice which told him "Not this one," and he swore he'd never do that again. Sue was likely a great girl, but he just couldn't get interested. Not in the right way, at least.

Hawkins passed a few minutes by reading the local paper. Published once a week, it contained news about the goings-on in the area: activities for the kids during summer break, who had caught the biggest trout so far that year, and special recipes from around Cocke County. The chirping of a cell phone interrupted his reading. His hand instinctively reached for the jacket pocket before he realized it wasn't his. He grunted to himself: the thing was still in the car. Although Hawkins was on a short vacation, he had told them at the Jacksonville Field Office his cell phone would be on the whole time. A decent radio signal was hard to come by, but several cell phone companies had just erected towers nearby, making cellular phone service not only acceptable but excellent through the mountains. His particular cell phone would have a good signal wherever he went, as he carried the latest encrypted cell phone in the Bureau's inventory. It operated on satellite as well as conventional cell towers to insure total service availability. In addition to satellites, the phones used special government cell towers strategically placed throughout the country and around the globe. A new wireless technology had been introduced in the new towers, and each cell had sufficient range to cover hundreds of miles. The technology would not be available to the general public for years, and it remained somewhat untested—hence the satellite back-up. If it continued to work as well as the first 6 months had, the new system, which had cost hundreds of millions of dollars and years to bring online, would guarantee secure communications anywhere in the world.

"Here you go, Hawk," Rick said as he set the plate down on the counter. "Enjoy!"

Hawkins stood just as the plate was set in front of him. "I'm sure I will. Don't take it away before I get started, though. I've got to go grab something out of the car."

"I'll put it under the heat lamp for you. Just come around and grab it when you come back in."

"Thanks." Hawkins walked out and reached into the Challenger, grabbed the phone out of the center console, and walked back in. He reached around the counter and picked up his plate from under the warming lamps. Sitting down on the counter stool, he felt the phone vibrate in his pocket: a message waiting. He fed himself with his right hand and tapped on the phone with his left.

"You Feds are an impressive bunch," Rick said from the pass-through window in the kitchen, his thick Australian accent making some words almost hard to understand. "Eatin' and dialin' at the same time. Just don't get confused which hand is doing what."

"Not much chance of that," Hawkins said as he placed the phone to his ear. "Besides," he said with a smirk, "I'm very good at multitasking." He pressed the necessary spots on the screen when prompted to access his voice mailbox, not quite hearing the comment Sue made as she walked behind him. The automated voice said: "Today, 9:26 a.m." A familiar voice followed: "Hawk, it's Bob Shear. Call me on my cell as soon as you get this." The automated voice returned, declaring the end of the message. Hawkins had expected it to be Mark Woodley, his partner on the White Collar Squad back at the Jacksonville Field Office. Woodley always called him after he had been gone 2 or 3 days, just to catch him up on the goings-on in Jacksonville. They had only been partners for a couple of years, but the two of them had hit it off famously. When the SAC in New Orleans invited Hawkins to come to Jacksonville with him, he agreed—if Woodley could also transfer. Hawkins had grown to like New Orleans, the food in particular, but Woodley had a family and while New Orleans is a great place to visit, it didn't always lend itself to be the most ideal of places in which to raise kids. Then again, what big city was?

Hawkins thought it strange Special Agent in Charge Robert J. Shear, head of the Jacksonville Division, had tried to reach him. It wasn't that Hawkins and the SAC weren't close; in fact, it had been Shear who had recruited Hawkins right out of seminary. Hawkins had been shocked at the time the Bureau would want a preacher for a Special Agent, but Shear told him his leadership experience, problem-solving skills, and intelligence would serve the FBI well. Having always harbored a desire to work for the Bureau, Hawkins applied. He had been surprised when offered a chance to take the Phase 1 exam, and even more surprised when he passed and was presented with a slot in the exclusive Phase 2 interview and written test. When he received notification a week later, he had been offered a conditional appointment with the Bureau, he cheered so loudly his neighbors were sure he had been attacked at the mailbox. A few short months later, three weeks after getting his Ph. D. from Gulf Coast Theological Seminary at the age of 26, he received his marching orders: report to the FBI Academy at Quantico, Virginia for 16 weeks of training. He told the small congregation at the church he had been pastoring he felt the Lord had opened a new door of opportunity for him, a chance to make a difference in a new way. Amid many tears and well-wishes, they gave him a going away party on his last night as pastor. The gift he prized the most came from the Chairman of the Deacons: an official FBI ball cap the deacon's friend had gotten for him on a visit to the base at Quantico. It was signed on the bottom of the lid by every deacon in the church—all four of them. They did it so that Hawkins would know someone would always be praying for him.

He dialed the preprogrammed code which connected him to the SAC's cell phone. After two rings, a familiar voice sounded over the line.

"Hey, Hawk."

"Hello, Bob. Wishing you were here?"

"You have no idea. I'm assuming you haven't seen this yet?"

"Seen what?" Hawkins heart sank a bit in his chest.

"Somebody hit the CCC Convention at the Orson Convention Center," Shear said, his voice conveying the seriousness of the situation. Shear never raised his voice, never got perturbed. Now, however, his voice contained something Hawkins had never heard before. "Looks like a truck bomb. Took out most of the new parking garage in the blast, then the rest came down about 5 minutes later."

"When did it happen?"

"9:11 a.m."

"That's not likely to be a coincidence."

"No. I need you back here. Effective immediately you and Woodley are on the CT Squad." Hawkins had wanted to get back to Counter-Terrorism, having done work on the squad for a short time in the New Orleans Field Office. There had been no openings in Jacksonville when Shear had transferred and brought him and Woodley along, so he had been content to bide his time. *This is not how I wanted to get back into CT*, he thought.

"I'll be there by dinner time."

"We'll meet at the FO at 1700. I'll have Woodley give you a buzz as we get more. Be safe."

"Thanks," Hawkins said, and the line clicked off. The realization he likely knew some of the people in the pile of rubble that had been a parking garage caused his breath to catch in his throat. Looking up, he noticed Rick and Sue looking at him as if he were about to pass out.

"You alright there, Hawk?" Rick asked.

"Gotta roll, Rick. Bad thing happened in Jax, and I need to be there." Hawkins reached around for his wallet and started to get out cash to pay for his half-eaten meal.

Rick held up a hand. "Uh-uh, mate," he said. "You know your money's no good 'ere. Get on down the road and do what you've got to do. You just be careful."

"Thanks. See you guys soon." As he headed for the door several people spoke toward him. Sue's soft twang cut through. "Be careful, Sugar."

"Wouldn't think of being otherwise," Hawkins replied, and stepped out of Big Wally's into the cool mountain air.

CHAPTER TWO

Special Agent in Charge Robert Shear stood at the perimeter of
the destroyed parking garage. Investigators had the ubiquitous
crime scene ribbon stretched around an area some 700 feet from
the actual pile of rubble and debris to keep onlookers and the
media from getting too close while leaving an opening for rescue
personnel to drive their vehicles through. The actual exclusion
zone extended to 500 feet, and only rescue personnel and EMTs
were allowed within. The next 200 feet out had been marked off
as the operations zone where a field command post had been
established. The FBI, Jacksonville Sheriff's Office, and Fire
Department already had representatives at the CP, and the
Florida Department of Law Enforcement was on its way. The
entire area had been shut down for over a mile, and the police
found themselves with their hands full rerouting traffic. Interstate 95, which ran directly past the Convention Center, slowed
to a crawl as people gawked at the destruction. The collapse of
the structure had suffocated the flames of several vehicles
ignited in the initial blast, although there were some small
secondary fires burning as vehicles outside of the garage had
been set ablaze by flaming debris thrown outward from the
explosion's core. The scene reminded him of other similar expe-

riences—the first World Trade Center bombing in 1993, the Alfred P. Murrah Federal Building in 1995, and the WTC and Pentagon attacks on 9/11. He had been in Washington that day, attending a meeting with FBI and Justice Department officials when the Pentagon was hit. Minutes later, he had been standing amidst the chaos about the same distance from the point of impact as he now stood from the destroyed parking garage. The same thought struck him as it had with the other bombsites he had been to: *what a waste. These people died because some arrogant fool wanted to make a point.* He contained his outrage, of course— it didn't do any good to kick dirt around like a ticked-off coach at a baseball game. No, it was better to present a cool head for the people working the scene. He had seen more than his share of Bureau leadership blowing their tops and running around like chickens with their heads cut off, and had likewise seen what that had done for the morale of the agents. They needed leadership, not tantrums, and he remained determined to do his job, regardless of the rage and sorrow which swirled in equal parts in his soul. He also knew the press had cameras trained on the site. He scowled inwardly at the fact that media personnel arrived almost before emergency crews did. *In a big hurry to start the rumor mill.* Of course, they would make speculations about who carried out the attack, who planned it, what had actually happened, and so on—that was what they were paid to do. But *he* was paid to do a job as well: find the people responsible for atrocities like this and bring them to justice.

SAC Shear did his job well. He had been in the Bureau for close to 30 years, starting out as many agents do by working as a clerk while in college. After graduating with a Juris Doctor from Yale, the FBI brought him on as a Special Agent. The handsome Shear had always looked the part of a G-Man: tall and lean, a skin tone which showed a propensity for outdoor activities, and dark hair that seemed always about to fly out of place but never quite doing so. After some 3 decades in Federal service his hair had turned much whiter, but the tan skin still covered the musculature of an athlete. At 6'3" he had been an intimidating figure to many on the wrong side of the law, but he always had a warm smile and firm handshake for a friend, fellow agent, or shady character he needed to win over. His engaging personality matched his success as an agent: he had arrested some of the biggest names in white-collar crime, as well as bringing several crooked politicians to justice. He had joined the Bureau right before Oklahoma City and worked the Cole bombing and 9/11, moving up through the ranks from street agent to Squad Supervisor. He earned a shot at an Assistant Special Agent in Charge, or ASAC, position in Albuquerque which he got, then became SAC when his predecessor retired. Usually ASACs would fill in when an SAC retired or otherwise moved on, but they weren't always promoted to the top position in their respective Field Office. Unusual or not, Shear was promoted to SAC directly, and proved to be an excellent top man—so much so he had been offered a position as interim Assistant Director over the Criminal Investigations Division in Washington. After 2 years in the bureaucracy that is FBI Headquarters, he took the SAC position which had come open in New Orleans.

It was there he had met Thomas Hawkins, a young man he felt had a huge future with the Bureau. Shear had received a call at his office one day from a young man-- a seminary student and pastor of a smaller church out in Metairie. The young pastor told him of a special service where they would be honoring people who served in government positions, and asked if Shear would attend. Intrigued, Shear agreed. Being a churchgoer himself, he would not be intimidated by the prospect of attending services in a church on Sunday morning. When he and his wife arrived, a young man in his mid-twenties greeted them. He stood a little taller than average—although not as tall as Shear—and was solid looking, like a guy that could handle himself if he had to. *Not many preachers would ever need to*, Shear thought, *but one never knew*. Shear had been impressed with the young man's easy demeanor and his natural way with people. He watched as the young pastor went to each person seated in the pews before the service started, called them by name, and took the time to find out the answer to his question of "How are you doing?" When the service came, Shear became even more impressed. The young man had been a natural public speaker, and seemed at ease addressing the crowd of 150 or so congregants. After the service, the preacher had thanked Shear for coming. Shear invited the young man to give him a call—they could get together and have lunch that week. Hawkins had smiled widely at him, saying he'd be in touch.

The next day Shear had pulled up what he could find on Thomas Hawkins. The young pastor had been a decent student, always in Honors or Gifted classes, and pulling A's and B's. He had attended Stetson University as an education major, and attended Gulf Coast Theological Seminary, where he had received his Master of Divinity degree and was almost finished with his Ph. D. Hawkins had never been in trouble, with only a couple of speeding tickets in high school. He came from good stock: Hawkins' father was an executive with a major financial investment company, and his mother was a physician. He had an older brother, Nathan, who had pursued a career in medicine and now worked as an administrator of a large medical center in Texas. Hawkins had no law enforcement skills, but that was fine. In fact, the FBI preferred it that way, so they could train an agent the right way and not have to waste time helping them to "unlearn" bad habits. Hawkins had the characteristics which had made for successful agents throughout the Bureau's history: a natural, easy way with people and a sharp mind. When Hawkins called a few days later, Shear had taken him to lunch. He found himself even more impressed with the young pastor after 2 hours of conversation, and so he asked: "Would you consider a career with the FBI?" Shear had been surprised at how quickly Hawkins had said yes. One 22-page application later, Thomas A. Hawkins' future rested in the pile of nearly 100,000 applications to be a Special Agent for the FBI.

A tap on his shoulder interrupted Shear's reverie. He turned to see his ASAC, Walter Simmons, standing with a tablet in one hand and a cell phone in the other.

"The local affiliates are all here and they want some news. A CNN van almost ran over one of our Evidence Techs coming over the Matthews Bridge, and Fox News is already putting up the broadcast pole." Simmons was a tall, muscular black man in his mid-40's who seemed to be in competition with his boss about which one would be best dressed. Shear found himself already sweating in the morning sun in his suit and tie, yet Simmons had not so much as a bead of sweat on his shaven head. There had been no competition between these two, however; they had hit it off from the day Shear took over as SAC Jacksonville, and he trusted Simmons to get things done. The ASAC had been onsite 15 minutes, and yet he had half a day's work done already. *And not even sweating*, Shear thought as he shed his suit coat and clipped his FBI ID badge onto his shirt pocket. "The Sheriff just said there was an explosion and that was all we know at this point. His press officer is trying to fend off the news hounds right now, but they want to hear from the Bureau. The Sheriff said he knew we were taking this, and anything you need from him, you've got". Shear had ridden piggyback on the good relationship Simmons had established with the Jacksonville Sheriff's Office over the last few years, and as a result the head-butting that often went on between law enforcement agencies had generally not been a problem with the JSO and the FBI.

"The Mayor's Office called and said he wants to come down as soon as the area is secure. I told them it might be a while."

"First things first," SAC Jacksonville said. "We need to get the sniffers to confirm for us there's nothing else about to go off somewhere in the area."

"They already have about 60% of the immediate area covered and expect to finish their sweep within the next couple of hours. Bogart is on the horn right now with Homeland Security, and is monitoring the big picture very closely down here,"

ASAC Simmons said. He referred to Charles Bogart, the Weapons of Mass Destruction coordinator and Crime Scene guru for the Jacksonville Field Office.

"Good. After that's done, I don't mind him coming down, but make sure he doesn't get into anything dangerous. Have you gotten Renee yet?" Shear hoped his lead press officer, Renee Cortez, would be the one to talk to the media. As good as Shear was about keeping his cool, reporters seemed to have a knack for finding his last nerve and striking it repeatedly.

"Nope. Been trying her cell for 30 minutes and haven't gotten through. She was supposed to be coming back from the Keys this morning. Her new secure cell wasn't working right, so the tech guys promised to work on it while she was gone. All she has is the old cell phone."

"And all of the cell systems will be messed up for hours with everyone calling to check on family members and friends," Shear said. "Call the Miami FO and see if they can raise her on her radio." Shear had come to be so reliant upon Cortez' excellent skills and working relationship with the media that he allowed the press officer to break the rule about using a Bucar for personal trips. He knew Cortez always kept her digitally encrypted FBI radio switched on. If they couldn't talk via cell phones, maybe they could get through another way. "In the meantime, tell them I'll come over in five minutes to give them a brief rundown," he said, emphasizing the word "brief". "And tell them this is a statement, Walt...no questions."

"Got it," and the ASAC jogged off towards the waiting media. Shear turned at the sound of a vehicle approaching and saw a dark blue Suburban with flashing strobes in the front window and grill pull into the restricted area—Evidence Technicians. Now that the ETs were here, they could coordinate with the rescue crews and help direct their efforts. It would be prudent to focus time and energy where people would most likely still be alive under the rubble. Shear prided himself on being an optimist, but the more he looked at the smoking pile of concrete and steel in front of him, the more he believed the crews were wasting their time.

"What in Sam Hill is going on down there?" David Hathaway, the President of the United States, asked as he hurried into the White House Situation Room. He saw before him several people he had seen only a short time ago in his morning Intelligence Briefing: the Director of National Intelligence, the National Security Advisor, and the Director of Homeland Security, now joined by the Chairman of the Joint Chiefs of Staff, and the Secretary of Defense, the Secretary of State, the White House Chief of Staff, the Director of the National Counterterrorism Center, and the Deputy Assistant Director of the FBI. The Director of the FBI would have been here as well but was already on his way to Jacksonville from another engagement.

"Best we can tell at this point, sir, is that we have a likely terror incident at a religious gathering in Jacksonville, FL," Director of Homeland Security said. "It wasn't a WMD, but a conventional explosive device demolished a parking garage at the convention center there."

"Religious gathering?" POTUS asked. "The annual meeting of the Coalition of Christian Churches is one of the largest religious gatherings in the country. That's like saying Disney World is a nice little theme park. There's likely to be thousands of people there, of all ages."

"Yes, sir, I realize that," DHS replied, then continued. "We have no estimates of casualties at this point. Local law enforcement and the FBI are coordinating."

The Director of National Intelligence, Jack Price, spoke next. "We don't have any indication of international chatter over the last few days, so this doesn't seem to be an ISIS thing. They tend to get real noisy before they try to pull something."

"Which is how we've been able to shut them down before they could," POTUS interjected.

"Precisely," DNI replied. Everyone in this room knew how many terrorist plots had been foiled in this country and abroad because of the diligent work of the agencies represented there. They all knew equally well the general public would never know of those successes but would hear only of their failures. It had been said that when the Intelligence Community did their job well, no one knew about it; when they screwed up, everyone did.

The National Counterterrorism Center Director, Alfred Reid, spoke up. "We've been running specific data analysis based on what we know right now, and nothing has come up that raised any flags." The NCTC was responsible for making sure that all the agencies in the United States Intelligence Community shared any and all relevant information with one another in the fight against terrorism.

DNI Price continued. "This is not to say that it couldn't be ISIS or one of their ilk, but we could have another Oklahoma City-type thing here."

"The militias have been laying low for a while, so it's about time they tried something," the Deputy AD for the FBI said.

"That they would hit another group of Christians is a little unusual for them, though," the National Security Advisor said. "They usually target racial groups, or those they see as a threat to their way of life."

Price spoke again. "I'm not very knowledgeable on comparative religions, but I know the Coalition of Christian Churches is diametrically opposed to most of what these militias stand for, racial equality being only one of many such things. That could make them a target."

"Well, whatever it takes, we need to get to the bottom of this and find out who's behind it," President Hathaway said. "Each of you has a job to do, so go do it. I'm meeting with the Senate Majority and Minority leaders after this, so I'm confident we'll have any resources available you need. No one's going to want to look partisan and petty on this."

"I can think of a few who would step up to the plate," the

Chief of Staff said. Nearly everyone in the room grunted in agreement.

"Regardless," POTUS continued, "I'll get my part done. You get yours."

Hawkins returned to the house just long enough to deposit his leather jacket back into the closet before heading to Florida. He climbed back into the Challenger and placed his blue LED flashers on the dash, then called the FBI operator back in Jacksonville and asked her to contact the various law enforcement agencies along his route. They would appreciate knowing that the black Hellcat Challenger roaring through their jurisdiction with lights and sirens wasn't some nut who had ordered a bunch of stuff off Amazon and was pretending to be a cop. It was a pretty long drive—8 hours when you weren't trying—but he figured by the time he arranged for a flight, and waited around to get clearance to take his ever-present gun on board, it would be quicker to drive. Especially if one had a 797-horsepower car with blue lights and sirens.

He had only traveled a short distance down the interstate before he heard the familiar voice of SAC Shear on the news radio station he had been able to pick up after coming out of the mountains of Cosby. Shear's voice sounded confident and reassuring as he spoke: "Less than an hour ago, an explosive device was detonated in the parking garage of the Orson Convention Center here in Jacksonville, FL. Shortly after the initial explosion, the parking structure collapsed as a result of the structural damage caused by the explosion. We do not at this time have any idea how many persons may be trapped in the wreckage, but rescue crews are hard at work searching for those in need of aid. We do not have any suspects at this time, and I will not speculate at this point as to the origin of the explosion or those who might be responsible. What I will say is that the FBI is coordinating with local and state law enforcement to investigate the

facts behind this morning's tragic event. As we have more information, we will keep you updated. Thank you."

Hawkins heard reporters shouting questions as Shear walked
away, and the radio commentator jumped back in to overanalyze
what Shear had said, and try to add some things the SAC
didn't say.

Five hours and a couple of gas stops later, Hawkins entered the
Jacksonville City Limits. He was still a good 20 minutes away
from the heart of downtown, however, as all of Duval County
had been incorporated into the City of Jacksonville years ago.
Twenty minutes at *normal* speeds—at better than 120, it would
take less than half that. He merged from I-95 onto 9A South, the
final stretch of the I-295 loop which encircled Jacksonville. He
crossed the Dames Point Bridge that connected the Northside
with the Arlington area, spanning the St. Johns River with its
many docks and shipyards. As he approached his exit, he killed
the strobes and assumed more reasonable speeds. Turning onto
Merrill Road, he hung a right at the next intersection, then
turned onto Fort Caroline Road. A short drive led to the long,
winding private drive which ended at his waterfront house. The
relatively modest medium-sized two-story brick home —small
compared to some of the mansions that reared like angry
sentinels on the water—stood peacefully in its exclusive location
overlooking the St. Johns River and the Dames Point Bridge he
had crossed only minutes before, expansive windows affording a
panoramic view. The feature he enjoyed most on the property,
however, was the massive garage. Bordering on the size of a small
warehouse, it contained a complete service facility for his vehicles. Once unable to identify a distributor cap, he had become
handy with automotive mechanical work thanks to a few adept
friends. Stored within the climate-controlled structure were his
various "toys": cars, trucks, a pair of Sea Doos, and a 31' Wellcraft
Scarab speedboat with a supercharged big block engine. His

parents had always been car aficionados, and the love of all things automotive found its way into his heart as well. He bought and sold cars continually, but there were a few he would not part with under any circumstances.

Hawkins pressed the button on his remote and one of the doors on the massive structure opened. He pressed the button on the dash to shut the engine off, walked through the enclosed corridor that joined house and garage, and ascended the stairs to his bedroom. He showered and grabbed a dark blue polo shirt with "FBI" in small yellow letters across the breast pocket and a pair of khaki pants from a shelf in the closet, then pulled on a pair of black Magnum Stealth side-zip boots—a zipper was far superior to dealing with that many laces. Hawkins placed his constant companion, a Sig Sauer .45 pistol with 10 rounds in the magazine and one in the chamber, into the triple retention holster. There would be a meeting at the office first, but a trip downtown was soon to follow. Suits and ties were not the 24-hour-a-day requirement they had once been under Hoover, particularly on an active crime scene.

Hawkins grimaced. The antiseptic phrase "crime scene" seemed somehow inappropriate in this case. Special Agent Mark Woodley had called him with what they had so far after only an hour into his trip home: a large explosive device, most likely a truck bomb, detonated at 9:11 a.m. in the newly built parking garage of the Orson Convention Center. The force of the blast resulted in several vehicles being blown out of the garage and into the surrounding parking lot. The main structure of the Convention Center had received only minor damage, leading Woodley to believe the point of detonation had been on the side of the garage facing away from the Convention Center. The damage to the garage had been sufficient, however, to bring the whole four-story structure down upon itself a few minutes after the blast. *He ought to know*, Hawkins thought: his partner had been a Navy SEAL for several years before joining up with the Bureau's HRT, or Hostage Rescue Team. SEALs spent much of their time blowing things up or figuring out how, so Woodley would be a good man to make judgment calls on explosives. The majority of Convention attendees for the morning session were already inside the convention center, but there remained a considerable number still in the garage, either having just parked or circling around trying to find an empty space. *One would be too many.*

Hawkins had been to several Coalition of Christian Churches conventions himself, and could visualize the people he had seen, people of all ages and ethnicities. Suddenly his mental picture was torn apart by his conceptualization of what had happened: innocent men, women and children, minding their own business, thinking of nothing but the events of the day, without warning being ripped to pieces, burned to cinders, and crushed beneath tons of debris. The image highlighted his own recollections of personal tragedy, something still far too vivid in his mind even after the passage of several years. He tightened the strap on the holster around his left calf which held a Sig Sauer P938 9mm that served as a backup pistol, and walked downstairs to the garage, picking up his satchel off the small roll top desk next to the fridge with his unencumbered left hand. He turned the handle and the electronic voice of his security system announced the garage access door had opened. Hawkins noted for the hundredth time that it said nothing when he closed it; after all, alarms didn't care when you closed a door, only when you opened one.

The FBI agent stepped into the garage and walked to another car, this one parked in a special spot with no other conveyance nearby: his Bucar—the jargon term for Bureau vehicles. There sat a black Dodge Charger Pursuit sedan, gleaming like a black jewel under the incandescent lighting. Every night when he came home he cleaned the car, regardless of how late the hour. The immaculate state of his car made it very easy for him to get whatever vehicle he wanted, including the newest car in the Division. Agents with years more seniority were relegated to 8-year old Ford Tauruses in some cases, but the agent in charge of the motor pool told them: take care of your car the way Hawkins does, and you'll get a better one. The garage door in front of the Hemi Charger opened and the black sedan rolled out, aiming for the Field Office a few miles away.

CHAPTER THREE

Hawkins had been able to tune in to various news radio stations on the drive home, and as usual the media leapt to conclusions just to have something to say. Each reporter seemed to be trying desperately to come up with some theory no one else had so they could get the notice of a bigger station or network and therefore move up the career ladder. *Not unlike some people in the Bureau*, he thought. The recurring theme under it all remained the same: terrorists had struck against the Coalition of Christian Churches, assumed by some to be natural target because of their outspoken evangelism toward Muslims and the fact that a number of Coalition leaders had spoken out against Islam in the days and months following September 11, 2001. The time of the explosion, 9:11, had been avoided by the SAC and Cortez, the press officer in Jacksonville. Hawkins remembered Cortez had been on a diving trip to the Keys, and thought with no satisfaction his wasn't the only vacation interrupted by bad news. And yet, someone had leaked this piece of information which seemed to be more than just a strange coincidence, and the press ran with it. Hawkins had to admit that calling the 9:11 explosion a coincidence was a reach, but a good investigation demanded allegiance to facts. A quote learned at the FBI Academy at Quantico came to mind: "A fact merely marks the point where we have agreed to let the investigation cease." Hunches and suspicions were helpful, but they could also be misleading. Jumping to conclusions too early in an investigation meant you would probably wind up wandering around in the wrong field.

He turned into the parking lot of a sturdy-looking office building squatting just off I-295. He knew as he did several hidden sensor arrays and video cameras told security personnel stashed away in the heart of the building everything there was to know about the vehicle and what it contained. Facial recognition software would instantly identify him. They would be able to determine the make and model of his car, running the tag to confirm its attachment to the correct vehicle. The weight of his vehicle would be compared to the correct weight of such a car when loaded with a certain number of occupants—in his case, one. Advanced computer programs would calculate that, according to the biomedical data of the driver, he was a 30-year-old male in excellent physical shape. They could tell if the vehicle contained anything which might pose a threat to security, such as firearms or explosive components, so they would register the two pistols he wore on his body, as well as the Remington Model 870 shotgun and custom 5.56 rifle in his trunk, along with an accurate count of how many rounds of ammunition could be found in the black Charger. Such things had seemed very James Bond-ish when he had first found out about the information gathering capabilities of the FBI, and he still found himself somewhat in awe of it. Not all the technological wizardry originated with the FBI. In fact, most of it originated from CIA headquarters—known colloquially as "Langley"—or from the Secret Service, who had their own division which specialized in advanced technology. All the bells and whistles of Bureau gadgetry served to greatly improve the effectiveness of law enforcement, and he had to admit he still loved to see what the tech guys around the Beltway would come up with next.

After punching in his access code on a recessed outer door,

he walked into a stairway which led up to the secure entrance to the Field Office. The main lobby featured a public entrance with a security checkpoint and a bypass check-in for agents, but the most personnel usually went in the back way. He walked into what would, at first, seem to be an ordinary workplace: portable dividers creating numerous cubicle workspaces, well dressed men and women walking to and fro, and phones ringing. The difference was nearly all the well-dressed men and women were wearing firearms and badges identifying them as Special Agents for the Federal Bureau of Investigation. Posters looking like items out of the OSS in World War II were attached to wall and cubicle alike, with phrases like "Loose lips sink ships!" and "National Security is YOUR Responsibility!" emblazoned on them. He walked to his cubicle, nestled amongst others in the White Collar Crime squad, and found an official letter from the SAC notifying Hawkins he had been transferred to the Counterterrorism squad until further notice. A post-it note lay next to the letter that read: "Lousy way to get back to CT, huh? See ya upstairs. W." He knew his partner, Mark Woodley, would be as excited as Hawkins to get back into a Counterterrorism squad. The White Collar work was great for a lot of agents, but Hawkins and Woodley preferred the energy and sense of accomplishment of CT. The joy of being placed in their area of greatest interest and aptitude, however, was tempered by the event that dictated their transfer. People had died today whose only crime was they were Christians.

He turned and walked to another stairwell which led to the third floor where the conference room waited. As he walked into the room, he saw SAC Shear seated at the end of the table, talking on a phone and writing on a legal pad. Several other agents milled about, looking at photos attached to a large mobile bulletin board. Various indecipherable notes were written on a marker board on the wall closest to the bulletin board, with CHURCHBOM written in large red marker at the top. A secretary brushed by Hawkins and handed a telephone message to the lead evidence technician—*what was his name?* Bogart came to Hawkins' mind just as he saw the man's ID. The evidence tech looked up from his laptop computer to receive the message from the harried secretary and waved at Hawkins when he saw him. *Charles Bogart, that's it.* Hawkins had not worked a case with Bogart before, but had worked out with the other agent at the gym after hours and found him to be an affable guy. Originally from Georgia, Bogart had a thick southern drawl and a quick wit. Although he was some 20 years Hawkins' senior, he could do 200 sit-ups and pushups at a clip and run circles around people half his age in a workout circuit. Bogart had been a Marine and, as he liked to say, still was: "Once a Marine, always a Marine." He remained a crack shot, and rarely missed his mark on the range. As sharp and intuitive as Bogart was, Hawkins figured he didn't miss much of anything.

"Care for a cold one, mountain man?" Hawkins turned to see his partner, Mark Woodley, holding out a can of cherry cola.

"Thanks," he said, popping open the soda and taking a sip. The body heat of a dozen agents in the small room made for an environment not unlike the humid air outside. "Anything new?"

Woodley was about to respond when the sound of a phone being placed into a receiver echoed in the small room. "Take your seats, folks, and we'll get started," SAC Shear said. The agents found a chair around the rectangular table and sat, Woodley taking the spot next to Hawkins. Cortez, the press officer, caught Hawkins' eye and shot him with her thumb and forefinger. "Welcome back," she mouthed without a sound.

Hawkins did likewise. "You, too." Cortez had been nicknamed "Renee Lo" because of her strong resemblance to the seemingly ageless Jennifer Lopez. Cortez would be a busy lady in the days to come. They would all certainly be busy, but an agent could not be found who would willingly trade jobs with Cortez. Agents almost universally agreed it was better to face an armed suspect than a reporter trying to make a name for themselves. Cortez just took it all in stride. She never got riled, always had just the right thing to say and, as a result, got excellent press for the Jacksonville Division.

SAC Shear leaned back in the leather executive-style chair. "Alright, we're at almost 8 hours post-event. Let's talk about what we know at this point. 9:11 a.m., explosion in the parking garage. Three cars blown through reinforced concrete retaining walls into the parking lot surrounding the garage. The explosion damage was sufficient to cause the structure to collapse at approximately 6 minutes post-event. Rescue arrived on scene as the structure collapsed, so no fire and rescue guys got hurt in that. They have recovered a couple of bodies and lots of parts, but no survivors within the structure. We have 3 confirmed fatalities from debris in the outer parking lot, and 22 injured. Between the explosion and ensuing collapse, our best estimate says there were likely between 70 and 85 people killed in the garage. I'm going to turn it over to Agent Bogart for some specifics on what the techs have come up with."

"Thank you, sir." Bogart stood and walked to the bulletin board where the numerous photos were attached. "From what we have been able to determine, the bomb was detonated on the ramp between the second and third levels in the southwest corner." As he spoke, he pointed to various photographs of the structure intact and destroyed. "The placement was such that the detonation was sure to bring the whole structure down, either immediately upon detonation or shortly thereafter. In all likelihood, the vehicle was a van or larger sport utility. Due to the restrictive clearance height of the garage—six feet eight inches—a larger vehicle such as a U-Haul just would not fit. Evidence suggests the bomb was a simple fertilizer/fuel-oil bomb of the type used in Oklahoma City in '95. The quantity used was less, but it would have been difficult to get much more in the garage considering the size of vehicle they were limited to using. Not to mention they didn't need as much to do what they did here. They also wouldn't have had much trouble obtaining a smaller quantity of the required materials. We have yet to isolate the source vehicle, but we should be able to soon." Bogart took his seat.

"Thanks, Charles. Okay, Bogart's given us a green light to set up a field command post in one of the large conference rooms at the convention center for our evidence guys, as well as joint ops with ATF, JSO and FDLE," Shear said, referring to the Florida Department of Law Enforcement. "ATF is tracing sales of the ammonium nitrate and fuel oil, but as Bogart said, we believe it would have been bought in small enough quantities as to not raise any red flags. Our FCI squad is running down possible leads and coordinating efforts with CIA and NSA." Foreign Counterintelligence swiftly turned into the fastest growing area within the Bureau. Since 9/11, FCI and CT squads were seeing their numbers swell while some of the comparatively mundane law enforcement squads were seeing their agent allotments dwindle. The Bureau had been in the business of FCI for years, but a number of recent failures had led to a lot of heads rolling in the Bureau. Early retirements had come by the dozens as many in the top levels of the FBI had seen the writing on the wall. "The CT squad will be out shaking the bushes. We don't know if this is an isolated event. In all likelihood, it's not. If there is a connection to ISIS or some other Islamic extremist group, we may get another hit. If you hear even the slightest hint that something may happen, you treat it like the gospel truth. Better to drop back and punt than to fumble in this game. And," Shear said, looking at Hawkins and Woodley, "I'd like to welcome Agents Hawkins and Woodley to the CT squad. These two have a bit of previous CT experience working in the New Orleans Division, and you all know from their time here they do good work. Most of you know Woodley served as a Navy SEAL and has been on HRT"—the FBI's elite Hostage Rescue Team— "for several years, so his experience will be invaluable in this investigation. Bill Jackson did a great job as Supervisory Special Agent for the CT squad for several years, but he took a training position at Quantico last month. Because

of Woodley's extensive experience in this field, he will be acting
SSA."

Hawkins turned to his partner to see him grinning ear to ear,
his brown eyes squinting. "Did you already know this?" Hawkins
asked.

"Found out about an hour ago," Woodley said. "Movin' on
up." Woodley was several years older than Hawkins and while
they were the same height the older man had him by about 50
pounds of muscle. A Texan raised on his father's cattle ranch,
Woodley looked as if he could carry a medium-sized heifer on
his broad shoulders. He had played football in high school, and
wanted to play while attending the Naval Academy, but course
work prohibited his involvement. He had sandy blond hair, a
round boyish face, and an easy-going attitude that belied a brilliant mind. He had advanced degrees in nuclear science and engineering and had served on a nuclear submarine before signing up
to be a SEAL, attending the infamous BUD/S training. Woodley
excelled in the strenuous regimen, coming out on top in every
area of the Navy's commando program and finally receiving his
Special Warfare Operator rating. He served with the SEALs for
a couple of years before he had been offered a slot on the
Bureau's Hostage Rescue Team. The pay was much better, and
his wife had gotten tired of her husband being out to sea for
months at a time. Shortly after joining the FBI, Woodley's wife
became pregnant with their first child. Two years later, their
second child came into the world. Woodley's friends joked that
maybe he should go back to sea.

"I don't know if I can deal with you being my boss," Hawkins
said.

"You're young," Woodley said with his smile firmly in place.
"You'll bounce back."

Hawkins was thrilled about his friend's promotion. He
certainly deserved it, as he had more experience and involvement with CT work than everyone else in the Division.

Shear continued the meeting. "Bogart is heading back to the

scene when we're finished here, and I'd like for Woodley and Hawkins to follow him down. The rest of you already have your assignments." He paused for a moment. "Let me make something clear. We do not know for sure who is behind this attack. We do not want to jump to conclusions or make leaps in logic. Stick with what you know or can prove. The Attorney General has made very plain we are to use the full resources available to us to prosecute this investigation, and that's what we are going to do. The 9:11 a.m. timeframe hit the media quickly, and there's a lot of tension right now in this city and around the country as a result. There is rampant speculation about who is responsible for this. The Coalition people are shook pretty bad, but most of their leaders are calling for calm. The AG is likewise staying in front of the cameras to convey the importance of cool heads. But there have already been a couple of preachers on TV who were at the Convention that lost friends in the attack that are talking trouble. Middle Eastern leaders are lining up to speak out against it—they're in panic mode. But there are a few nuts on the news thanking Allah for another strike at the Great White Satan, and the footage of people dancing in the streets in the middle of the night in Tikrit burning American flags already isn't exactly helping. The Sheriff has placed units at every Muslim center in town. The last thing we need to do is aggravate the situation with leaks and innuendo. No one, and I mean no one, says a peep to anyone about this investigation. I know there are always leaks, but the only leaks that should happen on this will come from me or Cortez. If anyone shoots off at the mouth and the press gets wind of it, I will hang your butt on my wall. This is as serious as it gets, people. Questions?" Another pause. "Alright then. Let's get to it."

CHAPTER FOUR

Most impressive, the man thought as he looked himself in the eye. In the mirror the reflection of a man with deeply tanned skin and a long black beard stared back. A sand-colored turban wrapped his head, and a dirty-looking robe hung around his thin frame. Black eyes stared out from the reflective surface, and the man smiled. His teeth were yellowed, and his gums looked in need of treatment from a dental specialist. The smile grew as he looked at the haggard Middle Eastern man in the mirror. He turned and walked to the video camera set up on a tripod. He sat on a pile of oversized pillows that appeared as old and haggard as he, stared intently into the camera, and activated the remote control.

"The suffering of the Great White Satan is a sign of Allah's blessings," the man began in heavily accented English. "The decadence of America demands punishment, and this is only the beginning. 9/11 has a new meaning for the infidels forever, and today's glorious blow against the Christian heretics will ensure that all such dogs know this: The Fist of the Apocalypse will crush all the enemies of Allah. These fools dare to speak against the Prophet and those who follow him, and now the Fist has struck them. They are not safe. They will never be safe again.

The forces of Allah will sweep all such infidels into the sea. The men will live only long enough to see their women and children die. Such is the fate of all who oppose Islam. The Fist of the Apocalypse will be the hand of Allah in swatting these insects into dust. We have only begun to bring Jihad to the decadent shores of America. The blood of the infidels will flow like water as Allah grants us victory!"

The man pressed the remote control, and the camera blinked off. He walked over and removed the disc from the camera, then strode to a nearby desk where a computer sat connected to a secure internet connection. The disc containing the video file clicked into the drive. All that remained now was to compose an email which would send the footage from an anonymous account directly to the offices of several major news outlets. The haggard looking man smiled again at the thought of the chaos he had caused already, and would yet cause when this video hit the airwaves.

"Well, I suppose congratulations are in order, Tex."

"Thanks. But like I said earlier, lousy way to get it," Woodley replied to his partner. The former SEAL had seen more than his share of buildings and other structures demolished by explosives, but almost all of them had been military targets. It wasn't as if that made the loss of life any easier, but the soldiers knew the risks when they signed up. Civilians going about their daily lives and then being ripped to shreds and crushed to death without warning was another thing altogether.

The two men were riding in Hawkins' black sedan, the Charger's exhaust grumbling softly as it climbed the bridge's incline. The clicking of the strobes on the dash matched the rhythm of the metal bridge plates under the car's tires as they followed Bogart in his dark blue Chevrolet Tahoe. All of downtown Jacksonville had been closed off—the bridges connecting the heart of the city with the areas across the river were closed to all but emergency and law enforcement personnel. I-95 remained open, but all the off-ramps leading into the heart of downtown were closed. As a result, the gridlock of what would have been rush hour never materialized. The pair of vehicles sped across the Matthews Bridge and drove past the massive stadium which housed the Jaguars NFL team. The temperature display on the massive sign overlooking the expressway declared it to be 92 degrees. A brownish haze hung over downtown, and the empty streets gave the impression of a scene from some post-apocalyptic movie. Every business in the area had closed for the day shortly after the attack that morning, and no one felt inclined to spend any time downtown. The media said there were reports that more attacks were possible. Who exactly had made such statements no one knew, but facts were not always critical to modern reporting. The result, however, *was* critical—there had been a massive lunchtime rush at every gun shop in town, with the last shotgun in stock being purchased at the Hunting Land Superstore on Lem Turner Blvd. at 2:42 p.m. Even the area chain sporting goods stores had sold almost completely out of ammunition. *Just what we need*, Hawkins had thought when he had seen those stats on his way out to the parking lot. *Everybody in town looking for a terrorist to shoot.* He couldn't blame them, he thought as he adjusted the gun on his belt wedged in by the seatbelt buckle. It reassured him to have a firearm—or two —during a time like this, but he trained extensively for years on how to use them. The last thing law enforcement, or anyone else for that matter, would need was someone shooting an innocent Middle Easterner thinking they were a terrorist.

The president of the Coalition of Christian Churches, along with other denominational leaders, had held a press conference shortly after lunch. The president of one of the largest Evangelical denominations in the country had stood stoically behind the microphones at the podium, not unlike the pulpit in his own massive church in the Bible Belt. With tears in his eyes and his voice cracking as he spoke, he called for Christians everywhere to pray for those injured and the families of those killed in the bombing. He also asked that there would be no vigilantism or violent acts in response: "Our Lord, Jesus Christ, demonstrated love towards those who took His life. He said as He hung on the cross, 'Father, forgive them, for they do not know what they are doing.' Those who committed this violent, senseless act simply demonstrate they do not know the one true God. We must pray for them as well, that perhaps the Lord might open their eyes and they would respond to the call of the God of Love. We as Christians must rise above the violence of today, allowing our great law enforcement community to do their job, just as we must do ours."

The White House had announced they were moving to condition level red, the highest level in the Homeland Security Awareness code, in light of the morning's attack. President Hathaway had held a press conference earlier in the day expressing his outrage at the violence directed toward a group of innocent people, and renewed his commitment to fight against terror. The clip continued to be played on every news program on the air throughout the day and had been shared on social media hundreds of thousands of times.

"I caution everyone against making assumptions and finger pointing and call on all Americans to pray for the families of those who have lost loved ones." POTUS paused for a moment. "We are still engaged in the War on Terror, and this serves as even more proof that the United States must be diligent in our prosecution of the fight against terrorists."

The AG had assured the nation that Federal law enforcement and intelligence agencies were hard at work in conjunction with local and state authorities to ensure the perpetrators of the vile act were brought to justice. The Director of the Homeland Security Department likewise made assurances he hoped he could keep, but an overwhelming sense of despair hung in the air like the haze over downtown Jacksonville—*it happened again. We knew it would eventually, even though we had all hoped it wouldn't. But it happened again.*

The pair of Bucars rolled past several churches and houses of faith on the way in. How many people from those congregations had lost friends or loved ones today? Were they worried they were next? Not for the first time, unwelcome thoughts crept into Hawkins' mind: how many people were in the wreckage of the parking garage that he knew? He shook his head as if to shoo away a troublesome gnat. *No time for those thoughts now. There'll be a time for grieving later. Right now, I have a job to do.* If his partner—now his supervisor—noticed Hawkins' mental struggle, he didn't show it.

As they arrived at the scene, it looked exactly as it had on TV. Seeing a tragedy on TV and seeing it firsthand always diverged at one point—the smell. The air festered with a combination of burned rubber, paint, superheated metal, and burned flesh. The sound differed greatly as well. Microphones usually muted the background noise at the scene, or at least greatly diminished it. In person a cacophony of sounds—fire trucks, ambulances, heavy machinery—almost overwhelmed a person when they first arrived. Bogart stepped out of his Tahoe and approached Hawkins' car.

"Alright, fellas. You know the rules. Don't touch anything, just mark it so we can collect it. Woodley, you know explosives—you see anything I missed, you let me know.

"Wait a minute. A Marine's not asking a Navy SEAL for help, is he?" Woodley asked, trying to get a rise out of the unflappable Bogart.

"Nope," he replied with a grin. "Just trying to make you feel good about yourself. I know you Navy boys couldn't find snot if you blew it into a Kleenex."

"That's because we don't have snot, Jarhead. We blow other people's noses."

"Right off their face. Yeah, yeah," the ET said with a laugh. "Prove me wrong, sailor," and walked toward two techs who stood waiting for their boss. Bogart and Woodley had a great relationship, a microcosm of the relationship between the Navy and the Marines. Their good-natured ribbing marked a deep respect, as well as an equally deep sense of friendly competition. Bogart was at the top of the game in the field of evidence gathering. He frequently travelled to other Field Offices and Resident Agencies—the smaller branch offices of the FBI which operated under the jurisdiction of a Field Office—and even to the FBI Academy at Quantico to share his years of experience and expertise with a new generation of ETs. Woodley had to admit that if Bogart couldn't find it, then he probably couldn't either.

Hawkins closed the trunk of his car and offered a pair of latex gloves and face masks to Woodley. Placing the tight-fitting gloves and masks on, both men walked toward the massive pile of concrete and steel. Hawkins took a deep breath as they approached, and Woodley finally spoke about the tension he had noticed in his younger friend.

"You okay there, Hawk?" He knew what troubled the younger man but thought it might be best to give him an outlet.

"Yeah, I'm alright," Hawkins replied, although his voice betrayed his true feelings. "I really don't want to find someone I know in here."

"I understand what you're going through. It's tough enough to do something like this when the dead are strangers. When they're someone you know, or possibly know, it's a lot harder." He paused for a moment. "If you didn't want to come down here tonight, I'm sure Shear would have understood."

"He asked me to come down here because he knew there was a job to do," Hawkins replied. "And he also probably thought that this was what I needed."

Woodley nodded. "Was he right?"

"I'll let you know in a few hours."

"Did you see what came in over the wire"? asked Molly Dawson, co-anchor of the 5:30 news broadcast on WJAX. She looked like most female television anchors: pretty, makeup expertly applied, hair perfectly curled and sprayed in place, expensive clothes she really couldn't afford yet—after all, she merely anchored the 5:30 broadcast. She had earned that spot, working as a field reporter on everything from light human-interest stories to traveling to Iraq to spend time reporting on the troops still stationed there, but the 5:30 news wasn't the limit of her ambition. Molly would be in the anchor chair at 11 tonight, but only as a substitute. She longed for the highly coveted co-anchor position on the 6 o'clock and 11 o'clock news. Unfortunately, the chances of that happening anytime soon were slim to none. Wendy Sears, the current female co-anchor in the time slot, had been there for almost fifteen years and didn't seem inclined to move to another area. Wendy's husband had a good job there in town—a big shot executive with an insurance company headquartered in Jacksonville—and their twin sons were the star players on the high school football team. They were both juniors, but their college choice had already pretty well locked in; changing schools now would be disastrous. Add to the fact that Wendy had won numerous Emmy awards, and the reality that she had the anchor position for as long as she wanted. This became painfully obvious to the ambitious younger anchor as time went on. As close as Molly ever got were nights like tonight, filling in for the main anchors when they were away. The two co-anchors, as well as the station manager and news director, were at an awards ceremony in Los Angeles, and couldn't get back into Jacksonville as all incoming and outgoing flights had been cancelled at Jacksonville International Airport. This had turned out to be a big day to be filling in, to be sure, but the young reporter would never be satisfied with substitute status. The only way Molly Dawson would take over the chair at 6 and 11 would be to bump Wendy out of the way, and only an event of epic proportions might cause that.

And such an event had just happened.

"Yes, I saw it," responded the producer of the 5:30 broadcast, Stephanie Boone. She too had stepped in to fill a slot tonight. Stephanie had been in broadcasting for over 15 years, working as an intern at her local TV station in Birmingham, Alabama while in high school, and had been a producer at WJAX for nearly 7 years. She had seen this look in the eye of other reporters—it usually meant they were about to do something stupid in the pursuit of a story. "I know what you're thinking, and you are out of your mind. There is absolutely no way I'm going to put my job on the line over something like this. Tyler's tight with the FBI honcho here in town," she said, referring to Biff Tyler, the station's news director. "Someone called Tyler on his cell when we got it, and he called his friend at the Bureau. The word came to hold the vid, and that's what we're going to do. You don't want to jerk around with the Feds, and you know that."

"We can't sit on a story like this," Molly said desperately. "If we hit this story now, while everyone else is sitting on it..."

"We'll be going to jail!" Stephanie blurted. "This isn't a deputy running over a kitten and the sheriff asking us to hold it. This is a major terrorist event, and the Feds are asking us not to run a video of the potential mastermind. This is a big deal, Mol, and there is absolutely no way I'm going to let you do this. I know the way these Feds work, and we could be hit with obstruction and who knows what else. The station could lose its license," Stephanie said as she turned back to her console. "No way."

"It could make our careers," Molly whispered. "Hard hitting reporter and producer, willing to risk it all to get the news to the public. Even if we get dumped here, don't you think one of the cable networks would snatch up a pair like us?"

"It could also ruin our careers," Stephanie responded softly, but Molly could tell she was making headway with her producer.

"But isn't that a chance worth taking?"

The producer said nothing for a few seconds. "What do you have in mind?" she asked cautiously.

"We're 5 minutes out from the 11:00. We can slip it in at the very beginning of the broadcast."

Stephanie shook her head. "I don't know, Mol."

"Somebody's going to break this, Steph. It might as well be us."

"We don't have time to put a package together."

"Then we run the raw footage. I'll intro it, and say this is believed to be authentic, and may be disturbing to viewers. Thirty seconds of intro should do it. That will get everyone watching."

"Thirty seconds will also give Tyler time to get us off air once he sees what we're doing," Stephanie pointed out.

"Tyler's not even here. It's his and his wife's anniversary, so he left early to take her out for dinner."

Stephanie sighed, resigned. It *was* a once-in-a-lifetime shot at breaking the big story. They would almost certainly be fired, but maybe Molly had the right idea. Small local stations, even those like their own which were owned by large media corporations, were skittish about getting the Feds angry. The big cable networks, however, might see such drive as worthy of a spot in the world of high intensity journalism.

"Let's do it."

CHAPTER FIVE

Moonlight shone through the expansive windows into the brightly lit office. A dark blue coffee mug with the seal of the FBI on one side, the words "Fidelity, Bravery, Integrity" in gold letters on the other, sailed across the wood-paneled and glass-windowed office into a tall wooden bookcase filled with mementoes of 30 years in the Bureau. The mug struck the outermost edge of the bookcase and shattered, the last few drops of coffee, spraying onto the wall like the obscenity that came from SAC Shear's mouth. The clock on the wall, almost a victim of the porcelain projectile, pointed out that it was just past 11:00 p.m. He invoked the name of Christ in a most irreverent way, and his secretary, Delores, stuck her head slowly around the corner of the door to his office.

"Sir, are you okay?" Rare had been the occasion when she had seen her boss angry enough for an explosive outburst. He generally settled down quickly, she knew, and he would never lose his cool where anyone else could see. But this was not the first broken mug Delores had seen in her tenure.

Shear turned from the television he watched and the information flickering on the screen that had caused his outburst.

"Get Cortez in here!" Again he swore, asking God to do something at the more negative end of His sovereign responsibility. He stared at the screen incredulously. "These people are the biggest idiots I have ever seen."

Cortez burst through the door out of breath. "I just saw it, boss. The networks all said they were going to hold it—"

"It's not the big networks," Shear said through gritted teeth. "It's someone at one of the local networks trying to be a big shot. We told everyone to sit on this. What in the world are they thinking?" He turned to his media rep. "We've gotta call a press conference right now, Renee. The fertilizer's gonna hit the fan over this." On screen Cortez saw a Middle Eastern man in a dimly lit room speaking in heavily accented English, claiming responsibility for the attack and invoking the names of Allah and Islam repeatedly. Behind him the SAC's secretary dabbed at the coffee dripping down the wall with paper towels. "The Director is on his way back from a meeting in Moscow and is coming straight to Jax. Delores, see if you can get the Director's plane for me."

"Yes, Mr. Shear," Delores said as she wiped the last of the coffee away and put the damp paper towels into the small plastic Tupperware bowl she had used to collect the fragments of what had been the SAC's coffee mug. Cortez never ceased to be impressed with Delores' speed and silence—she would not have even been aware of the secretary's presence if she had not heard the sound of the paper towels rubbing against the wood paneled walls. She wasn't surprised, however, that Delores remained on duty, even at this late hour. She had served the Jacksonville SACs for years, and she never went home until they did.

"This is going to be a problem," Shear said. "Tensions are too high in this town right now, and if we don't get in front of this and say something we're going to watch this town go to hell tonight, understood?"

"I'm on it, boss," Cortez shouted as she ran down the hall to her own office. A few phone calls and she would be on every network within 15 minutes.

"And Delores?" Shear shouted. "Get me Biff Tyler from over at WJAX on the phone after you get the Director. He's got a lot of explaining to do." Shear turned back to the TV and saw the local talking head expressing shock and dismay about what this video meant, her perfect hair, perfect makeup and perfect teeth appearing perfect. Anyone watching the reporter would see her barely contained excitement, and know she saw a Pulitzer in her future for breaking this story. All Shear saw was red.

Officer Steve Crabtree sat in his patrol car in front of the Muslim Center of Northeast Jacksonville sipping lukewarm coffee. A late-night prayer time had convened at the Center on behalf of the people killed that morning. *Actually, it was yesterday*, he noted as he saw the time—12:17 a.m. Three other units sat nearby in order to ensure the safety of the 100 or so men who were inside the Center. After the video of the Middle Eastern man had played on the local news, media all over the country had obtained copies and played it *ad nauseum* on TV within minutes. The result was sadly predictable: *Half of the rednecks in northeast Florida are wanting to kill themselves a Muslim*, he thought, and numerous threats were directed toward the Center in particular. Most of it would be idle threats and venting, Crabtree thought, but the Sheriff believed safe to be better than sorry. And so four deputies sat in the parking lot of the Islamic Training and Worship Center, waiting for trouble that, in Crabtree's opinion, would likely not come. He had been a deputy for 18 years with JSO, and felt he knew the people of his city pretty well. They might get torqued up and carry on a bit, but he didn't believe they would get too carried away.

At that precise moment he heard the roar of a vehicle that sounded like the mufflers had fallen off. Looking up, he saw an old 4x4 pickup swerving across the grass median and heading for the entrance. It took his mind a moment to comprehend what he saw as the truck aimed at the front of his car, parked parallel to the entrance drive to the Center. He put the gear selector into "Reverse" just as the massive brush guard bolted to the truck's frame smashed into the passenger side headlight, crushing the front bumper and fender. The force of the impact spun Crabtree's car backwards and away. His head bounced off the airbag bursting from the steering wheel, and his coffee spilled over his left side as he was thrown about inside the maimed police cruiser. With darkness creeping in, he thought: *I knew I should have kept my seatbelt buckled.*

Hawkins walked through the kitchen door, grabbed an IBC Cherry Cola out of the fridge, and plopped down into a dark brown leather chair in his living room. Out the rear of the house the St. John's River and the majestic Dames Point Bridge looked more like a special effect than an actual view, the lights on the bridge and the docks across the water shimmering in the night-time darkness. He turned the small table lamp on next to him, grabbed the remote and turned on the TV. He had purchased a new 80" widescreen TV recently, and he loved it. He almost felt as if he was sitting in the shop with the guys from Gas Monkey or on the streets with the officers featured on Live PD. The TV presently featured a broadcaster from one of the cable networks talking with several panelists about a video which had been sent to numerous media outlets from an individual claiming responsibility for the Coalition of Christian Churches bombing. Each network had notified the FBI as soon as they received it, and the Bureau had put out a bulletin to all the news agencies and networks which had received any materials related to the bombing to sit on it until the Bureau could sort through what was genuine and what was junk. Even though 20 years had passed since 9/11, people remained skittish, so speculation needed to be reined in as much as possible. A local Jacksonville station, however, had broken the story and was playing the video that had come in via email of what appeared to be a Middle Eastern man speaking in broken English. He seemed to be claiming responsibility for a group calling themselves "The Fist of the Apocalypse." Every alphabet agency within the U.S. infrastructure and all her allies were running the name—along with most of her enemies, in all likelihood—but so far no one had been able to come up with anything. It was possible this *was* a new group, but it could be a splinter off of something already in existence. A great deal of speculation swirled without the benefit of much solid information. The other news networks had shown remarkable restraint and had complied with the Bureau's wishes, but even they were starting to show a still-frame shot of the man just to keep people from changing the channel to the other networks.

Hawkins shook his head. He knew the press was just doing its job. There were some in the media whom Hawkins felt didn't know up from down, but he also knew there were a great number of conscientious people trying to do what was right. The press frequently helped as much as hindered, though incidents like this made one think more of the latter. Hawkins had muted the TV and he couldn't hear what they were saying any longer, but clearly the host and panelists remained unsettled—and angry.

Hawkins felt the crushing weight of loneliness wash over him like a sudden rush of the tide. He had grown almost used to it by now—at least, as used to it as one ever gets—but it still would sneak up on him in private moments. He tried not to think about how things used to be, refused to look at the old photographs, but the images would still spring, unwanted, into his mind. The goodbyes that were only meant to be for a few hours turned into a lifetime, the dull roar and thump which changed the course of his life in ways he never would have imagined.

This attack hit too close to home, for too many reasons.

He walked past a cabinet which housed things he didn't want to look at ever again, much for the same reason most people don't want to go to the dentist: you know it's good for you, but you know it's going to hurt. He paused for a moment before opening the door and removing a dark brown leather photo album. He walked to the kitchen counter, set the book down, and slowly opened the cover to look at the past.

The first picture was of his mother and father, standing in the middle of a town square in Spain, his mom having the time of her life and his dad somewhat less so. A picture below it showed them at the entrance to a museum, this time with a pretty young girl with tanned skin and dark hair between them.

Anna.

Hawkins closed his eyes for a moment, remembering himself taking the photo. He could once again hear the sounds of car horns and traffic, feel the cool fall breeze amplified by the narrow streets, smell Anna's perfume wafting over to where he stood several feet away. The agent opened his eyes and turned the page, where a closeup of Anna greeted him, smiling that brilliant smile, her almond eyes twinkling in the afternoon glare. Hawkins closed his eyes again, this time involuntarily, trying in vain to push away the sound of her voice. She appeared in his mind's eye, turning to him right after his mother had taken the picture, and telling him she loved him. He could feel her lips pressing against his, and he opened his eyes, wanting to get away, but wanting to remain. He glanced at the date on the bottom of the photo, thinking of how quickly time goes by. He closed the book and took a deep breath. *Why do I keep doing this to myself? They're gone. Nothing can be done about it. You couldn't have done anything then, and you couldn't have done anything now.* He placed the album back in the cabinet, and did his best to leave the memories there, too.

No sooner had he settled into his chair and turned up the volume to hear the discussion on the tv than his phone rang. He reached for the phone sitting on the table next to his soft drink and pressed "TALK".

"You in bed yet?" Woodley asked over the digitally encrypted line.

"Unwinding a bit first. Does your wife know you're calling me at this hour? She might get jealous."

"Not likely. We'd better find something to smile about while we can, because this'll turn that smile upside down."

Hawkins closed his eyes and pinched the bridge of his nose between his thumb and forefinger. "What now? We get something on this Fist of the Apocalypse bunch?"

"We should be so lucky. Just got a call as I was pulling in my driveway. Looks like some good-ole boys tried to act up at the Muslim Center about 20 minutes ago. Ran an old 4x4 into a patrol unit on security detail, then 3 drunk rednecks jumped out yelling something sweet about Muslims and ran toward the building with baseball bats and chains. One had a shotgun, but no shells. Several other JSO deputies were on scene and managed to subdue the clowns before anybody else got really hurt."

"Anybody else?" Hawkins asked, and then he caught it. "Oh yeah, the deputy in the impact car. Long day. He hurt bad?"

"They say he's got a concussion, but he'll be fine. His car's going to the heap, though."

"Just like this whole mess. I'm glad I'm just a grunt and not the boss."

"Me, too." Woodley was silent for a moment. "Ah, nuts."

"Well," Hawkins said, "you did say it was a lousy day for a promotion."

"What I *said* was that it was a lousy way to get a promotion, but both statements are true." Woodley yawned loudly into the phone. "Alright, I'm hittin' the rack. See ya in the morning."

"Yeah," Hawkins said, and set the phone on the charger.

Things could have been a lot worse for that deputy, he thought as he swallowed the last of the dark cola from the glass bottle. There had certainly been enough bad news for one day. As he placed the empty bottle in the trash can, he thought to himself: *Lord, I need you to you watch over our team during this mess, because we're going to need all the help we can get.*

CHAPTER SIX

A black BMW 750i xDrive sedan pulled into the reserved parking spot around the side of the nondescript office building. The occupant climbed out, activated the car's security system, and walked toward the secure private entrance. His stainless steel attaché case in his left hand, he punched his access code in on the keypad. A series of clicks told him the magnetic locks were disengaged, and he twisted the long handle and pulled the door open. The well-dressed executive closed the door behind him and walked into a massive office. It was not the only entrance—the main entry was through double doors guarded by a polite but firm secretary—but he preferred to come and go as he pleased without much ado.

The office was opulent, as one might expect of a man in his position. The room was 40 feet square, and completely closed off from the outside world by massive walls and ornate book-cases. The deep mahogany walls were inlaid with wrought iron details and soft lighting, and a massive desk of the same color wood awaited him. A large brown leather wingback chair called to him and he sat, placing the attaché under the desk by his feet. He had been away from the office for several days—away from *civilization*, actually—and was eager to see what had happened in the world during the week he had been camping in the Louisiana bayou. After returning home the previous night, he intentionally left the TV off and neglected the newspapers his household help had placed on the desk in his home office. He hadn't even turned on the radio—he usually listened to music on his phone while driving anyway, preferring the sounds of Khachaturian and Beethoven. He enjoyed the time with nature, away from the hustle and bustle of modern living, and he wanted the sensation to last as long as possible. Unlike many in his economic strata, he rarely stayed in extravagant hotels and resorts. No, he preferred to rough it, to commune with nature in as pure and unobtrusive way as possible. The week in the Louisiana swamp would be considered punishment by many, but he enjoyed driving his old Land Rover into the most remote spot he could find and then camping in the wild. He dreaded being back, and yet anticipation filled him in even greater measure. He felt not unlike a child finally allowed out of bed on Christmas morning who saw the presents awaiting him—excited, yet hesitant to open them, fearful of the anticlimactic revelation of the package's contents.

He pressed a button on his desk, and across the spacious office the painting which hung over the mantle of a massive marble fireplace began to transform. The tranquil Degas ballerina painting he used for a "screensaver" gave way to a cable news reporter speaking on the LED widescreen monitor. He preferred the Degas.

Until he heard what the reporter was saying.

"Earlier today what appears to be a terrorist strike took place in Jacksonville against the Coalition of Christian Churches. Hundreds have been injured, and while an official death toll has not been given many are feared dead. The law enforcement presence on site has been overwhelming, as one can imagine, and rescue crews are continuing to search the wreckage. In a shocking turn of events, footage has been released via the internet of a Middle Eastern man claiming responsibility. Leaders throughout the Middle East are trying to distance themselves from any hint of involvement. Some Christian pundits, however, are already calling for swift and strong action against whoever is responsible. But there is a question hovering in the air like this cloud of dust over the wreckage...is there another attack just around the corner?"

The man leaned back in his chair and the leather squeaked as he placed his full weight against it. He laughed, loud and full. *This was certainly worth coming back for*, he thought. *Yes. It's finally begun.*

"What a mess," said James Van Horn, Director of the Federal Bureau of Investigation. He stood in the "war room" of the Jacksonville Field Office gazing at the information laid out on several wallboards. Easels with white marker boards stood like mute sentinels around the rectangular room, each one covered with writing followed by too many question marks. "Other than the video, what have we got?"

"Good and bad, Mr. Director," SAC Shear responded in his controlled, almost comforting voice.

Van Horn interrupted the SAC. "It's just us, Bob. I may be Director now, but just a few years ago you and I were busting our humps together in Violent Crime. It was Jim then, its Jim now." James Van Horn had been appointed as Director straight from service within the Bureau to the top position. While there had been others in the Director's chair who had served as a Special Agent, none had gone directly from within the FBI's ranks to the top position until Van Horn. The President of the United States and the Attorney General had felt the Bureau needed one of its own at the helm to repair its image, with the belief that the people who know the ship best ought to be the ones to sail it. He had been Director for only a short time, but the FBI was once again resuming its rightful position as the premier law enforcement agency in the world under his guidance. This attack, however, put a great deal of pressure on the Bureau, and he knew the questions forming in people's minds would soon be lancing out in accusatory words to anyone in a position of authority in the law enforcement and intelligence communities.

"Fair enough, Jim. Our ETs were able to isolate what is believed to be the vehicle containing the explosives, a Mercedes cargo van. The techs were only able to get a partial VIN from a vehicle fragment, but they are convinced it belongs to the source vehicle. Running it for a registration now..."

"Probably rented under a false name," the Director said.

"Maybe, but there's a good chance even *that* could lead somewhere. We're not completely certain it was rented, however. Just have to make sure."

Van Horn nodded. "Anything on the Fist of the Apocalypse?"

"Nothing yet," Shear replied. "Everybody in the Intel community is turning over every rock in sight trying to find something. If it's there, we'll find it."

"Right," the Director said, sitting down in one of the executive chairs scattered throughout the room. "I have to tell you, Bob, this one is bad. I'm not in a CCC church, but I am a man of faith, and this is a terrible blow right now. Americans were just starting to feel safe again, and to see a religious gathering hit like this is really going to set us back as a country, not to mention what it's going to do to the Bureau. The talking heads are already starting to ask why we didn't see this coming."

"Let 'em talk, Jim," SAC Jacksonville replied. "This one came in under our radar. CIA said they had nothing even remotely hinting at this, and NSA struck out too. Nobody's even heard of these people. Whoever did this did it right." He pointed to a row of charts and lists. "It hasn't been officially confirmed yet, but we know they used a fuel-air bomb: ammonium nitrate and kerosene. From what Bogart says, they didn't need a lot to pull this off, so they were able to buy it in small enough amounts our monitoring programs didn't catch it. We can cross-reference all the purchases of both items for the last several months in this area, but there's no guarantee they bought it anywhere around here. Tracing them through individual material sales could take a while. As for the video sent by email, we know he recorded it on an older Sony digital camera, but whoever sent it knew how to cover their tracks. ECHELON missed it, and our own tech people are hitting dead ends on back tracking. Every time they dink around with the original file, the IP address of the original sender is randomly changed. I don't have any idea how it works, but the Geeks tell me its big time. We're working with all of our agencies as well as MI-6, MOSSAD, and a couple of others to try and match the guy in the video, but nothing yet."

Shear pointed to another page, this one with a list of names, and sighed heavily. "Here's a listing of the casualties. 72 killed, 139 injured with about half of the injured just hanging on. We've been able to ID about a third of the dead, and Rescue says we've likely found all we're going to find."

"The garage had security cameras, didn't it?"

"Yes, but there was some kind of glitch in the system that knocked out about 30 minutes' worth of video. After half an hour's worth of static, a white van is suddenly sitting there, the one we believe is the source vehicle."

"Not likely to be a coincidence," the Director said.

"That's what we thought, too. We sent the tapes off to HQ to see if they can pull anything off them, but it doesn't look good now. We're also checking out everyone who could have had access to the security cameras."

"Alright, Bob. I've got a meeting over at the Marriott with the president of the Council, the senior pastor from their big church here in Jacksonville, the Mayor and the Sheriff in 45 minutes. Anything you'd like me to pass on?"

"Yeah. Tell them we'll nail the bastards' hides to the wall eventually, but to try and keep the peace among the faithful. I'd like to keep retaliatory events like last night to a minimum if at all possible."

"Wouldn't we all." Van Horn stood to leave. "I've got to get back to Washington this afternoon to meet with POTUS, the

National Security Advisor, the DNI, and the AG, so I won't see you before I leave." He stopped and looked right at Shear. "Anything you need, Bob, you've got it."

"I need all the intel I can get. I have good agents right now, especially Woodley and Hawkins, but I still need people to do the footwork. We've got a lot of ground to cover, and the more people we can get on the front end the better. We need data, and I'd rather strike while the iron's hot."

"NSA, CIA and the rest of the IC have assured us they'll forward everything they get," Director FBI said. "They've already promised liaisons to work with our people, maybe get them stationed here on temp duty."

"I appreciate that, Mr. Director," Shear said as Van Horn's personal guards approached within earshot. "I'll keep you informed as things develop."

Van Horn nodded, smiled, said, "I'll do the same", and walked out of the war room. Shear felt badly for his old friend. Everyone wanted leadership positions in the FBI, especially the Director's job, until they got it. The pressure was almost unbearable from the outside and, to make matters worse, there were always those waiting in the wings within who wanted nothing more than to see you fail so they could have their shot. Shear had spent a couple of years in Washington as an Assistant Director, and the politics of Headquarters wore on him quickly. Things were better now since some of the good-old-boy network had moved on, but HQ would always be HQ, and Washington would always be Washington. Even though J. Edgar Hoover had died long ago, he still cast a long shadow over the building bearing his name. Van Horn was without a doubt one of the most well qualified Directors the Bureau had ever had, but there were still those who didn't like the fact that an agent sat at the top. *Heaven forbid HQ should actually understand and look out for the agents on the street,* he thought. *Things might be too efficient.* He couldn't help but laugh as he thought about his years in the FBI. Far too often he had seen good work swept under the rug because the right people weren't going to get credit for it. *Things are different now*, he thought, *thanks in great part to the 9/11 debacle, as well as several missteps that followed, and the mass "retirements" which occurred shortly thereafter.* Now the Bureau was getting back on track, but this would be yet another blotch on the FBI's already scarred face. They would survive, however; the FBI had a knack for coming back stronger and better than before after what could have been considered fatal blows. Van Horn, Shear, and others like them knew what gave the Bureau its resiliency, and it hadn't been the empty suits which had haunted the halls of the J. Edgar Hoover Building over the years. It had always been the agent on the street that made the FBI an investigative powerhouse, and when you cut your agents loose to do their job, few could match them.

Years earlier Shear had done a turn on the Fugitive Squad and he and his partner, an agent then in his fifties, had captured a multiple homicide suspect by accident. They had been driving by a pool hall the killer had been known to frequent in Chicago when the man walked out directly in front of their Bucar. Immediately recognizing the man, the older agent hit the gas and bounced the bad guy off the fender at about 15 miles per hour. The agents jumped out and cuffed the suspect, who suffered only cuts, bruises, and shattered pride. As the agents proudly brought the suspect into custody, the man turned and shouted, "The only reason you jerks caught me was because of bad luck!" Without missing a beat, the older agent spoke in his G-man voice and said: "There is no bad luck, junior. There's only the FBI." The line had stuck with Shear over the years. He had thought about having a t-shirt made with the phrase on it and selling them. *Maybe when this case is over, I'll do it. As long as the FBI isn't the one with all the bad luck.*

"Mr. President, Senator Keaton is here to see you."

"Send her in," POTUS replied. Hathaway could think of

other people he would rather be seeing first thing this morning than Valerie Keaton, a late thirty-something senator from North Carolina and Chairperson of the Senate Intelligence Committee. Keaton had not been a staunch supporter of his, and they had already had rough words in his first year in office. She *was* sharp, honest, and genuinely committed to doing what was best for the country, however. People on both sides of the aisle in Washington respected her, even if they didn't always agree with her. Such bipartisan favor had earned her a spot on the SIC, and the position as its chair. What the President wasn't looking forward to was the subject matter.

"Good morning, Mr. President,' the senator said, extending her hand. She wore a black suit with a white silk blouse, matched by her black-and-white heels. Her curly, shoulder-length hair radiated a deep red that made her fair skin appear almost china-like. She had hazel eyes and a warm smile, but she also exuded a supreme confidence in herself. Some interpreted it as arrogance, but they were mistaken. Senator Valerie Keaton was confident of her own abilities and her purpose, and she would not back down from what she knew to be right. Hathaway expected her usual firm handshake and wasn't disappointed.

"Good morning, Senator. Always a pleasure to see you. I just wish these were better circumstances." He motioned for her to have a seat in the chair across his desk.

"So do I." She sat in the chair, pulled a file from her black leather attaché and opened it in her lap. "I've spoken with DNI Price and the director of the NCTC. Both discussed their lack of advance intel on the attack in Jacksonville from any sources. The SIC will be meeting after I leave here, and there will of course be an inquiry into whether or not that was the case."

"Of course," POTUS replied. "All I ask is that no one on the Committee place any undue burdens on our Intelligence apparatus at the very time they need to be operating with a high degree of efficiency."

"I can assure you they will have room to maneuver, Mr. President. This is not a formal commission, simply a little preemptory fact-finding. It would be nice for us to be able to come out quickly with a statement from SIC independently confirming what our agencies are saying."

"Naturally. Do you have an opinion going into this, Senator?"

If Keaton had been surprised Hathaway asked so direct a question it didn't show. There was no real reason to be surprised —after all, she *was* something of an expert. A graduate of George Washington University with a degree in Political Science, Keaton had gone on to earn a Ph. D. with an emphasis on International Relations. Her dissertation had been "Shooting the Bull: The Rising Threat of New Terrorist Entities on Global Commerce" and had been picked up shortly after her graduation by a major publishing house. The book had sold half a million copies, and she had come to be a regular on several of the big cable news programs. "Actually, I do, sir. I believe this did indeed come in under the radar, so to speak. There was, in all likelihood, no way we could have prevented this."

"And what makes you think that?"

"At this point I would say it's just a gut feeling. For one thing, we have more eyes and ears on the ground in the Middle East than ever. We have ISIS and most of these groups so wrapped up in SigInt and HumInt they can't plan a trip to the restroom without someone in Langley knowing about it," she said, referring to human intelligence—field operatives—and signals intelligence—electronic surveillance.

"You think this is a splinter cell?"

"I think perhaps we are dealing with a real unknown here. They may wind up being affiliated with someone we know, but I believe that when the smoke settles we are going to find something new. I'm just not sure what."

"And the rest of the Committee?"

"I've spoken briefly to most of the others, and they are somewhat unsure. They don't want to make predictions because they don't want to be wrong."

"Insightful," the President said.

"Political would be more accurate, sir," she said with a smile. "But that's a subject for another time." She handed the file folder to the President. "Here is a transcript of my conversations from this morning. I want to make sure you have all the information you need."

"Thank you, Senator," Hathaway said as he stood. Senator Keaton likewise stood and shook his hand again. "Please keep me in the loop, and I'll do the same for you. I need your expertise. I know DNI Price certainly appreciates your knowledge." Price had quietly applauded Keaton being appointed as Chair of the SIC regardless of political affiliation, assuring the President she was the "real deal."

"Thank you, sir. I'll be in touch." The senator turned and walked out of the Oval Office. Hathaway returned to his chair and picked up the folder. He felt fortunate to have confident and trustworthy people around him —it made his job *easier*, although it was *never* easy. He had won the election by a slim majority, but the country had been experiencing good times and his approval ratings were high. Such things mattered little to him, however. He saw his position as one of tremendous responsibility to do what was right, not for this group or the other, but for the entire nation and, yes, the world. The right decisions were often not the easy ones, and he feared many hard decisions would await him in the days to come.

CHAPTER SEVEN

Hawkins walked into the area used by the Counter-Terrorism Squad, checked the message board in his cubicle, and read the pink slip of paper tacked into the cork back: "Bumped the meeting to 8:30. Sims and Walker are tied up on interviews at the hospital. See ya then. −W". Hawkins looked at his watch and saw he had just over forty-five minutes before the CT Squad would meet. Renee Cortez, the media liaison, walked up to his kiosk with two cups of coffee. She set one in front of him. "Extra cream, extra sugar."

"Thanks," Hawkins said as he took a sip. "Looks like a few of my teammates got an earlier start than I did today." Henry Sims and Sherry Walker were young agents as well, and didn't have much CT experience. They didn't have much experience at *all*, as they had only recently graduated from the FBI Academy.

"They're young and eager," Cortez said. "And they seem capable. They're a couple of years behind, but are off to a good start. I know Henry better than Sherry, but Walker seemed to be on the ball as well."

"Kurt Gordon and Steve Wilkes transferred in a couple of months before me and Woodley. They worked in Violent Crimes prior to CT."

"Making you and Woodley the CT veterans in the office." Jacksonville was a priority city because of the large airport, numerous ports, and central location at the intersection of I-95 north-to-south and I-10 east-to-west, but they had less than half of the allotment of agents they were supposed to currently possess. Only six agents working the case was far from ideal, but there had to be a balance in personnel. Robbing Peter to pay Paul was a dangerous game—it meant you would be filling one personnel hole only to rip another one open. Cortez smiled. "At least you aren't the baby in the office."

Hawkins chuckled as he nodded in agreement. "Very true." They were nonetheless well-trained Special Agents which meant what they lacked in experience they made up for in competence. Only the best and the brightest of the thousands and thousands of applicants ever made it to the coveted position of Special Agent for the FBI, and those that did were capable of doing pretty much whatever needed to be done. While new to CT the four learned fast, and Woodley and Hawkins were confident they wouldn't have to slow down for the others to catch up. "Woodley will keep all of us on the rails."

"No doubt about that," Cortez replied. "SEALs then HRT. You don't get to do either unless you're something special. Nice break getting partnered with him. I'll bet you learned a lot."

"You can say that again." Hawkins had been fortunate to get teamed with Woodley—by the nature of their partnership, he had the benefit of his friend's years of experience in the SEALs and HRT. Woodley had given Hawkins a crash-course in Special Operations almost from the first day they had been paired together. Woodley still had connections with the agents running HRT, and he had been able to get Hawkins in for a week of training with the FBI's elite strike force. "Hostage Rescue Team" was somewhat misleading, as the team's responsibility extended far beyond hostage rescue. The deception had been intentional, however. A few agents had convinced the suits in Washington they needed a law-enforcement equivalent to the U.S. Delta

Force and British SAS, among others, but with a name which would suit the politically correct elite in Washington. After the tragic events of the 1972 Olympics in Munich, everyone in the field could see the need for a trained team tasked with rescuing hostages. If HRT wound up doing more than that, well then, so much the better. Hawkins certainly did not consider himself ready to become a part of HRT as a result of his week with them —in fact, he was quite confident no amount of training would bring him to the level required of HRT operators. It took a special type of person to be an operator, just like only certain individuals could be a SEAL, a Ranger, Force Recon, a member of the mythical Delta, or any of the other lesser-known but equally effective Tier 1 operators out there. A few years ago some of the medical personnel with the Bureau wanted to do a study on HRT operators to see what effect performing at such a high level of stress had to their overall health. The results were shocking: every one of the HRT operators experienced lowered blood pressure, pulse rate, and respirations *when they breached a building and went in.*

They were anything but reckless, however. Danny Coulson, the first leader of the HRT, established their motto: "To Save Lives," meaning they should do everything possible to ensure that agents, innocents, and even criminals came out alive. Coulson went out of his way to make sure his operators knew they were not soldiers, but law-enforcement officers. This served to differentiate between HRT and groups like the SEALs, Delta, and the like: a soldier's mission usually involved the taking of life; the Law Enforcement Officer's, or LEO's, duty was to preserve it. HRT operators were more than capable of taking a life if they had to—their shooting skill was legendary—but Coulson had ingrained into his operators that taking a life, even a criminal's, meant they had failed. The same mindset still guided them today, and from Hawkins' week with HRT, he learned it was sometimes harder *not* to shoot than it was to squeeze the trigger in training.

"Well, I've got to get back to it," Cortez said as she turned.

"Yeah. Thanks again for the coffee, Renee." Hawkins turned and opened the file folder on his desk. On top of the pile of papers within was a list of confirmed dead from the Convention Center blast. There were now over 75 whose identities had been confirmed, and that was too many. He glanced down the list which contained names, sex, ages, home towns, and about a quarter of the way down came across a name he knew well: James G. Isaac, male, 67, Hazlehurst, GA. Dr. Isaac had been his family's pastor when they lived in Ormond Beach, Florida. Isaac had come to the Hawkins' home when he found out young Thomas wanted to ask Jesus to be his Savior. The pastor had patiently explained it to the boy, just as Hawkins' parents had: "The Bible tells us everyone has sinned, Tommy, and that we can't get to God and heaven on our own. This is why Jesus came to earth. He said, 'I am the way, the truth, and the life'. He died on the cross to pay for our sins and to purchase our place in heaven, and He rose from the dead on the third day to prove it all to be true. All we have to do is place our trust in Jesus as our Savior, and ask Him to change us from the inside out, and He will." Hawkins told the preacher he had already done that, and Dr. Isaac smiled. "Just making sure, Tommy." Two weeks later Dr. Isaac baptized Hawkins on a Sunday night at the church. Isaac stayed as pastor for several years before leaving to go to another church. Hawkins still loved the man and had kept in contact with him over the years. Isaac had not been thrilled when Hawkins told him he had decided to be an FBI agent— none of his friends in ministry were—but Isaac had told him: "Hawk, if God wants you to be an FBI agent, you'll know. If He doesn't, then that's all right; you love being a pastor. If He does want you in the FBI, then it's because He has a reason for you being there."

Those words rang hollow in Hawkins' ears. He closed his eyes and pinched the bridge of his nose. He knew this was coming, that there was a good chance someone he knew had been killed or injured in this tragedy, but he didn't expect someone so close to him to be one of the victims. Once again, terror had struck those close to him...

He reached for the phone, knowing he needed to call Isaac's widow, Carolyn. He held the phone in his hand for a moment, paused, and set it back down. He closed his eyes once again. *God, you know I don't even know what to say right now. I'm so angry I can't even see straight. But Lord, I'm asking you to give me the right words to say to Carolyn Isaac. I also pray you'd help me to do what you put me in the Bureau for: to catch whoever is responsible for this and see that they pay for it.* He opened his eyes, picked up the receiver, and pressed one of the buttons for an outside line. He dialed the number from memory and waited for the woman's voice to pick up. With each ring his heart sank further into his chest, and found itself going deeper and deeper into the pit of rage growing larger in his belly.

E. J. Niels sat in front of his computer workstation at CIA Headquarters in MacLean, Virginia. Everyone still called the region "Langley", although the name had been officially changed to MacLean almost 100 years ago. Some traditions died hard, and referring to the area where the Central Intelligence Agency sprawled across the Virginia landscape as Langley served as a prime example. The interior of those heavily guarded buildings, however, contained something altogether different from the serene exterior. Although it had suffered much bad publicity in recent years, the CIA had once again begun staking its claim as the premier intelligence gathering organization in the world. Their contribution to the work of the NCTC was substantial, and they were continually expanding their capabilities. Working hand in hand with the National Security Agency through their joint F6 Special Collection Service, the CIA had its fingers in nearly every political pot across the globe. Their SigInt, or Signals Intelligence, was better than ever thanks to the strong working relationships between most agencies within the IC, and HumInt, Human Intelligence through field operatives, similarly improved each day. Despite their progress, however, a sense of shock and determination flowed in equal parts throughout the Agency: shock that they had no outside warning about a terrorist strike on U.S. soil, and a determination to help find those responsible and ensure it did not happen again. While federal law enforcement and intelligence agencies had made mistakes in the past, they were committed to learning from them and working harder than ever before to be the best.

Niels sat in a large room filled with stations exactly like his, with dozens of desks separated by small dividers rising only inches above the surface of the desktops. The 3 linked 27-inch monitors in front of Niels had multiple windows open, the largest containing a frozen image of the Middle Eastern man from the video claiming responsibility for the attack on the Coalition of Christian Churches meeting. His trained eye stared at a high-resolution enlargement of the man's face. A background window popped up in front of the face, with a message contained within: "SEARCH COMPLETED! NO RECORDS FOUND MATCHING REQUEST." He moved his cordless mouse and clicked on the window containing the face. He sat back in his chair and reached absent-mindedly for the villainous 12-inch Cobra Commander action figure sitting on the file cabinet in his cubicle, neglecting the heroic G.I. Joe standing next to the villain's spot. Whenever he tried to identify an "unsub"—an unknown subject—he would grab one of his toys and fidget with it. Niels had grown up playing with the military toys, and as he grew older his affection for them remained. He had an extensive collection—regarded by many as the finest around—but he also had his personal favorites and rotated them in and out of his cubicle. His supervisors had wondered a bit at first about a CIA analyst that kept toys at work, but they soon realized his skills were good enough that any eccentricities would be overlooked. At 27 years of age, Niels had already risen to be one of the top image analysis officers in the intelligence community. He had received offers from the NSA to come on board with them—they were, after all, the largest single employer of mathematicians and computer experts in the country, and his skills were highly desired by the super-secret cryptology organization. But CIA was good to him, and he enjoyed a bit of seniority and independence here at Langley, so he planned on staying for a long time.

The modern post-9/11 era demanded that he work extensively with other domestic intelligence and law enforcement agencies, like FBI, giving them any information they might need. Many mistakenly believed CIA had no jurisdiction to operate within the States. In reality the Agency had the authority to pursue any leads regarding threats to national security regarding foreign powers and their agents, regardless of where it led and who it involved. The Agency had been involved in a number of domestic incidents, albeit with a high level of discretion. POTUS had clarified and expanded the jurisdiction of the CIA, and they were enjoying successes lately unlike any they had seen in years. Some previous Administrations had severely diminished the operational capability of the CIA—and virtually every other federal law enforcement, intelligence, and military agency in the U.S.—and it was finally being allowed to do what only CIA could do: gather intelligence and work covert ops everyone needed done but no one wanted to do.

Niels leaned forward, noticing something he hadn't before. He bent the action figure in his hands into a pose worthy of such villainy and placed it back in its spot on the file cabinet. He clicked his mouse over a button marked "MAGNIFY", and the picture enlarged again slightly. He clicked another button, and the computer program compensated and adjusted the picture for greatest clarity. He grimaced, at the result. He no longer saw what he had, so he clicked "UNDO". The picture returned to its

previous state, and so did the irregularity he had noticed. He mumbled something to himself, grabbed a pen, and made several notes on the legal pad he kept beside his keyboard. The program running on his screen wouldn't let him magnify the image to the extent—and with the clarity—he needed, so he'd have to use another. He had friends who could write any program he needed —that is, if he couldn't do it himself, which was a rare occasion. A few modifications to the program he had been using might give him what he needed, but he wouldn't know until he tried. Niels opened another window allowing him access to the program's code and began working. He had a suspicion about the video, or at least the man in it, but he wasn't ready just yet to share his ideas. He preferred to have his ducks in a row before he spouted off, and this trait helped establish Niels as a reliable expert in his field. The analyst smiled as he typed away on the keyboard, rising to the challenge set before him. Niels lived for this sort of thing, and it rarely got better than this.

CHAPTER EIGHT

"Thomas, are you there?"

Hawkins snapped out of his momentary trance and responded to the woman's voice on the other end of the line.

"I'm sorry, Mrs. Isaac. I'm still here."

"Well, you need to stop it."

"Excuse me?"

"You need to stop blaming yourself for what happened to Jim. You're thinking if you had stayed in the ministry this might have turned out different somehow."

"That's not exactly true," Hawkins replied sheepishly.

"I remember when you called Jim, when your friend in the FBI began recruiting you. You wondered why God would lead you to seminary, allow you to pastor a church, then suddenly open a whole new door for you. You wondered if you had disregarded God's call on your life by even considering the Bureau. Do you remember what Jim said?"

"How could I forget? He said, 'God called you to be a *minister*, and such a calling is not accomplished exclusively by being a pastor. You may be able to make a difference in people's lives as a Special Agent in ways you never could from behind a pulpit.'"

"He also said everything in your life up to that point—seminary, pastoring—all prepared you for what you would need to do in the FBI."

"They still haven't included 'Seminary Graduate' in their list of priority skills," Hawkins quipped.

"Well, maybe they should," Jim Isaac's widow replied. "You're very tenderhearted, Thomas. God can use that in what you're doing now."

"I'm not sure I have much tenderness right now."

"You've suffered enough loss in your own life without taking on the losses of others," she said. "There's a difference between sympathizing with others and taking on their burdens. Until you separate the two, you'll never be completely free. How are *you* doing, anyhow?"

"Wait a minute," Hawkins said incredulously. "I'm supposed to be talking to you about how *you* are."

"Thomas, I know where Jim is right now, and so do you. Your parents...and Anna..."

"Let's not talk about that right now."

A moment of silence hung over the phone line. "Very well. Don't you worry about me, Thomas. I'm fine. Of course I'm shaken over the loss of my Jim, but I'll be fine. I have a few people nearby who'll laugh and cry with me over the next few days. Do you have anyone who can laugh and cry with you?"

Hawkins sat in silence. "Not at the moment."

"Well, I'll keep praying the Lord brings somebody into your life you *can* laugh and cry with. Everyone needs that. Especially you."

"Thanks." Another pause. "Mrs. Isaac..."

"I know, dear," she said in a motherly voice. "You just catch those responsible for this so they can't do it again. Make Jim proud."

"Count on that," Hawkins said. "If you need anything..."

"I'll call you. Stay in touch, Thomas." The line clicked off, and Hawkins found himself reluctant to set the phone down. He felt more alone than ever, and didn't know why. He had several good friends, Mark Woodley in particular, but he still felt trapped behind walls of glass, keeping him isolated from those around him. He leaned back in his desk chair and rubbed his temples, closing his eyes. Maybe he *had* made a mistake leaving the ministry and becoming an Agent. Maybe that was why he couldn't seem to find any peace. He never blamed God for his loss--or anyone else's—but he often wondered why he had been spared, what purpose God had for him in becoming an FBI Special Agent. Maybe solving this case and bringing these murderers to justice would help.

Or maybe he *was* just lonely.

Whoever said patience was a virtue was a mindless fool with no plans of his own, the man thought. He sat in a Spartan office, filled with a couple of file cabinets and basic office furniture. The walls were bare, and nothing sat on his desk which didn't serve a purpose—desk calendar, LED desk lamp, three pens, and a laptop. In his opinion, ornamentation served no purpose other than to create needless clutter. It also let others know things about you—your likes, interests, loved ones—all things to be exploited by one's enemies. Far better to remain as anonymous as possible, he thought, even to those who knew you. He opened his laptop and powered it up. His calendar program opened, reminding him of an appointment from earlier in the afternoon. He clicked on "Dismiss", and the reminder window vanished. He still had several days before the completion of his present project, and, as far as he was concerned, it couldn't get here soon enough. The FBI hadn't found anything of substance as of yet, but it was only a matter of time before his covers started to be pulled back. The next project would take them in a different direction, giving them other trails to sniff. But that was several weeks away, and much could happen in a short time. He reached into his desk drawer and pulled out a bottle of whiskey and poured some into a small glass. He longed for one of his Cuban cigars, but he never allowed himself to smoke in his office. He reserved the luxury of smoking exclusively for his home, and he couldn't leave just yet. There was work to be done which could only be accomplished with the equipment he had in his office.

He tapped a few keys on his laptop, and a secure Internet link opened. Through this link he could send messages over the Internet untraceable by even the best computer experts in the intelligence community. He was completely anonymous, allowing him to send messages to his cell groups in the United States with impunity. His operatives had been in place for months now, preparing themselves for the mission before them. He knew they would succeed: they were as motivated in their endeavor as he was, albeit for very different ends. He composed a message, and then sent it to their respective email accounts, set up with the same encryption and randomization as his own. Even so, the messages contained no words which might trigger the American intelligence community's ECHELON email searching program. ECHELON did much more than scan emails, of course; it served as a global communications interception system. Trillions of intercepts were made each day: telephone conversations, internet downloads, satellite and cellular communications, every means of modern communication was susceptible to eavesdropping by the United States, Canada, the United Kingdom, Australia and New Zealand, ECHELON'S "parents". Of course, it was impossible for the NSA and other intelligence agencies to even begin to thoroughly scan the vast amounts data that would be pulled in, so they devised certain key words and phrases which would trigger a program that flagged the recorded transmission and processed it for further investigation. Even though he remained confident the wording of his emails were innocuous enough to avoid scrutiny, he knew the intelligence gatherers—particularly the Americans' National Security Agency were always on the lookout for even the slightest hint of something. He had been careful, he knew, but taking reckless chances like sending unencoded messages from registered email accounts would be foolish. The programs which served to mask his identity, as well as those of his operatives, were relatively easy to obtain—a few dollars thrown at a young man in an internet café were all that was required to obtain most anything a person could want—and it was reassuring to know they could communicate when they needed without fear of interception. If the NSA or some of the other intelligence agencies figured out how to crack these programs—and sooner or later, they would—then they could wreak all kinds of havoc. But for the moment, it all worked just fine.

He clicked the button marked "SEND", and the message flashed to individuals hidden around the globe, waiting for their next orders. It would be a month before the next event would take place, but his operatives needed time to get into their places. Such operations were becoming increasingly delicate as the FBI and other federal agencies were more cautious than ever before, and they would be on edge after Jacksonville. But that suited him just fine. He enjoyed the challenge, the thrill of staying one step ahead of the authorities. He had successfully navigated these waters before, thwarting the authorities when they should have had him dead to rights. Each successive narrow escape had further emboldened him to the point where he was quite confident he wouldn't—no, he *couldn't* be caught. He was charmed. He certainly wouldn't say he was blessed. The thought of God giving him anything repulsed him. He needed nothing God could offer him—in fact, he longed to see what he could take from God. He thought of the violence and death in Jacksonville, and thought of what was yet to come, and it made him smile. *So far, so good.*

"Bring her in," SAC Shear said from inside the interrogation room. Without hesitation a female agent brought in Molly Dawson. Her appearance was much different from what Shear had seen on the television earlier. Her hair looked somewhat mussed, her makeup was faded, and she definitely wasn't smiling.

"This is harassment!" she screamed, her voice shrill with nervous tension. "You are violating the First Amendment!"

"And you have violated several federal laws," Shear said, "now shut up and sit down." She stood frozen for a moment. "NOW!" Shear shouted, and the young TV reporter nearly jumped out of her shoes. She sat carefully in the chair and tried to regain her composure and her defiance.

Shear saw this and struck fast. "You have violated a direct request from the FBI to withhold a piece of unconfirmed video footage that is evidence in an ongoing federal investigation. Not only have you demonstrated poor judgment and bad reporting, it is a federal offense as you have now interfered in the investigation of a felony, tampered with evidence, and put federal agents investigating the case at risk, just to name a few things. The FCC could yank the license from the station, and make sure no radio or TV station would let you be more than the janitor, not to mention what kind of charges we could recommend to the U.S. Attorney."

"I..."

Shear cut her off. "What you did was stupid, irresponsible, and dangerous. You have put unverified, undocumented evidence before people that could cause major problems for not only the local area but internationally. What do you think this is going to do for relations with the Middle East? We've already had several people injured as a direct result of your poor judgment!"

Dawson cried without holding back now, her mascara making dark trails down her cheeks. "I'm sorry," she sobbed. "I just wanted..."

"Frankly, missy, I don't care what you wanted. What matters is you have royally screwed up."

"What...what's going to happen to me?"

"That hasn't been decided yet, at least on our end. But there is someone else who wants to talk to you." Shear pressed the button on the intercom. "Come in."

Ed Tyler walked through the door of the interrogation room. Shear thought the look on his face was comparable to a father who had just found out his daughter had driven the getaway car for an armed robbery, part anger and part disappointment. He wasn't sure which was winning out right now. He stood and walked past Tyler to the door, and turned before he walked out.

"Ed wants to talk with you and let you know how much he appreciates the situation you've put him and everyone else in at the station. And by the way," Shear said as he walked out the door, "I hear Wal-Mart is hiring."

CHAPTER NINE

Two black Suburbans, running with no lights, rolled to a stop on a secluded dirt road on the Northside of Jacksonville. Located across the Dames Point Bridge, which had once been called "The Bridge to Nowhere" by those opposed to its construction in the 1980's, the Northside had become a hotspot for new growth in the area. In addition to shipping and maritime construction facilities along the St. John's River, new homes had popped up at a rate which threw environmentalists into a tizzy. It was on a dirt road along the backside of one of these developments that the ebony vehicles coughed into silence as their modified V-8 engines were switched off. In order to maintain adequate performance levels for various conditions and situations, the heavily armored vehicles' engines had been equipped with superchargers which boosted power and enabled them, even fully loaded with gear and six men, to keep up with most sports sedans.

On cue both vehicles spewed forth six shadows each. Each shadow was an HRT "operator", an FBI Special Agent trained and equipped on par with the finest Special Forces teams in the world. Each of the 12 men was dressed identically: black fatigues, tactical boots, and balaclavas—facemasks with only an opening

for the eyes. Underneath their fatigues each wore next generation temperature-regulated body suits, composed of a
Kevlar/Nomex weave providing both ballistic and flame protection. Kevlar helmets sat atop their heads, while ballistic goggles
afforded them eye protection. Tactical vests contained almost
everything an operator could need in an insertion: flashbangs,
extra ammunition, knives, and various specialty items. Each
operator had a Springfield Armory 1911 .45 caliber pistol slung
low on their thigh, 7 rounds in the magazine and one in the
chamber, plus 3 extra mags on the opposite leg, but several
carried different primary weapons. The breachers carried
Remington 870 12-gauge shotguns, loaded with double-ought
buckshot, as well as breaching charges—small explosive packets
designed to open doors the bad guys didn't want opened. As the
name suggests, the breacher bore the responsibility of getting
the door open and allowing the rest of the team to go in.
Primary operators carried the Heckler and Koch MP5SD6 9mm
submachine gun. With an integrated suppressor built onto the
end of the barrel and subsonic rounds, the loudest sound the gun
made was the clicking of the shells being ejected and new rounds
being ratcheted into the firing chamber. Each team also had a
sniper, in this case armed with a Remington M40a1 sniper rifle.

Johnny Obermeyer served as breacher for Alpha Team, also
known as a "door-kicker", and the job that suited him well. At
6'3" and 270 pounds, he had the intimidation factor down pat.
When he first went through HRT training, his instructors
steered him away from breaching. "You're too freaking big, Johnny," one had said. "Taking a shot at you and missing would be like
missing the side of a barn."

"My teammates and I'll just have to make sure they don't get
that shot off, sir," was his reply. Despite his massive size, and the
fact he could bench press 570 pounds, Obermeyer came across as
polite and gentle as could be. When it came time for HRT to
spring into action, however, it was a different story.

Alpha and Bravo teams knelt on the ground behind the side

by side 'Burbs. Their leader was a Marine-turned-FBI agent named Bill Hall, whose short stature and medium build belied the corded steel under his skin. Hall was known far and wide for his outspoken ways and frequent reprimands for saying things that others thought but would dare not speak. He was equally regarded for his expertise and professionalism in the field. There were few operators in the world with Hall's ability, and he knew it, but it didn't hamper his leadership in the slightest. His men would follow him off a cliff, but his goal was to make sure they would never have to.

"Okay, girls, you know the play," Hall whispered, his voice echoing in the teams' earpieces. He looked at the snipers. "Warren, Stanley, you guys get into position. Our eye in the sky will give us any heads up we might need on the way in. You copy, Blackbird?"

"Roger that, Teacher, we copy." Nearly a mile above their heads hovered a modified Bell Boeing V-22 Osprey tilt rotor aircraft, equipped with the latest cutting-edge surveillance and reconnaissance capabilities. Only a handful of these modified aircraft were operational, and several had been assigned to use in counter-terror ops by FBI, CIA, and NSA. Manufactured using the latest stealth technology and equipped with electronic sound-canceling devices—high-tech "mufflers"—which rendered it all but inaudible, the modified Osprey had proved itself to be worth the exorbitant amounts of money spent in researching the technology required for the stealthy eye in the sky. "All clear from up here. AFLIR is active, and we are a go." AFLIR stood for Advanced Forward-Looking Infrared, a next generation of the proven FLIR technology used by the military and most police departments in their own helos. The new high-definition version allowed them to look through structures and identify the occupants of a multi-level building. Hall was certain that some civil rights groups would go nuts when they found out about it, even though its use required approval by a Federal secret-warrants judge, but it was a powerful tool to keep operators safe when going into a potentially deadly situation.

Without a word, the two snipers went to take up positions giving them total coverage of the target house, a modest two-story a quarter-mile away through the underbrush separating the subdivision from the dirt road. One of the snipers would be responsible for the front and east side, the other would cover the rear and west sides.

Hall went on. "While we're waiting for them, remember we want these guys alive. Doesn't matter what they've done. Standard ROE applies here," referring to the Rules of Engagement which dictated HRT operations. "If they die, we lose. Also remember these zero-lot-line houses are really close together, so watch your fire. We don't want Joe Innocent gettin' capped 'cause we were sloppy. And watch your flashbangs. Don't toss them into the computer desk or file cabinets or I'll let you explain why you torched perfectly good evidence. AFLIR recon confirms their locations, so be careful. Questions?"

There were none, which pleased Hall greatly. He was proud of his men—they knew their jobs well, at least as well as the best in the world. "All right then. Buck, man the com-net." Jay Buck, the communications expert for Alpha and Bravo teams, immediately hopped up and took his place in the back of one of the Suburbans. The rear area of this particular vehicle had been setup with the communications network, comprised of satellite uplinks to the Jacksonville FO, FBI HQ in Washington, and real-time pictures from Blackbird and other surveillance imagery, courtesy of the Integrated Overhead Signals Architecture, or IOSA, which coordinated all of the United States' satellite imagery capabilities. Buck was the only one on the team with direct communication to those observing the operation from the Field Office. Alpha and Bravo teams' commsets were short-range and digitally encrypted, and they relied on Buck for their contact to the rest of the world. He activated the line connecting him to the observers at the FO and HQ. "Schoolboy to Principal."

"Go ahead, Schoolboy," Woodley's voice came through the small speaker.

"Waiting on spitballs for a go."

"Roger, Schoolboy. We're standing by."

After a few moments of silence, a voice came over the secure line used by the operators. "Spitball Alpha on the playground." A second voice came shortly after. "Spitball Bravo on the playground." The snipers for Alpha and Bravo were in place.

Hall looked around at his teams and nodded. "Roger that. Alpha and Bravo on their way." The remaining men split into two groups and headed for their target.

Buck radioed in. "Schoolboy to Principal. Class is headed to the playground."

"Roger that, Schoolboy," Woodley replied. He almost ached with a desire to be out there with HRT. Hall was a good man, one of the best, but Woodley was a hands-on person and would have preferred to be there for this delicate operation. There was a good chance the three men in this house had evidence linking them not only to the bombing at the Coalition of Christian Churches convention 2 weeks prior, but also to other cells operating in this country. It would be very easy for that evidence to get destroyed by either the operators or the suspects. Being assigned as Supervisory Special Agent, however, meant Woodley had to stay at the FO so he could better manage the situation, at least according to Bureau protocol. *I could manage it better if I was there!*

There were so many variables in this one. The three men inside were all students at an area university, all from the Middle East, and all here legally. One of them, however, had worked in security at the Convention Center and was the only person who had access to the recordings of what transpired on the day of the explosion. Another had been positively identified by several eyewitnesses as renting the van discovered to have contained the explosive materials. Although he had used a false ID and credit card, security cameras had captured his image clearly. Woodley loved the irony of that one—they had eliminated one incriminating video, but never thought about the rental place having surveillance cameras. *Typical sloppy kids*, he thought. *Lucky for us, bad for them.* The third student remained the unknown factor: he could be an innocent student, simply picking lousy roommates, or he could be something more. None of them had prior criminal records, nor were they on any State Department watch lists, all of which meant nothing, of course —terrorists didn't usually sign up to be placed on such things. They lay low as long as possible, and the fact was most terrorists weren't identified as such until they had already killed someone.

A voice sounded through the speaker in front of him. "Schoolboy to Principal. Alpha and Bravo are on the playground. Awaiting permission to play ball."

Woodley looked at SAC Shear, standing across the table from him. Next to Shear stood Hawkins, who looked like he wanted to be there as bad as Woodley. As if he read Woodley's mind, Hawkins nodded and winked at his partner. Shear also nodded, and said "Go."

Woodley spoke into the mic. "Play ball."

Miles away, Buck switched over to the secure channel used by his teammates. "Schoolboy to Teacher, ball is in your court. Repeat, ball is in your court."

Hall nodded to himself. He and Alpha Team were poised by the front door, and Bravo Team had already signaled they were in position on the back porch. Both snipers checked again and gave a green light. "Blackbird, we ready to play?"

"All three are downstairs. Two still in the living room in front of the TV playing with their VR headsets, and one in the kitchen rummaging through the refrigerator."

"Thank you, Blackbird. Stand by." He took a deep breath through his nose, and felt his heart rate slowing. Everything seemed to go into slow motion as he spoke: "Play ball on 3.

1...2...3."

Exactly as Hall said "3", the charge Obermeyer had set on the front door exploded, blowing the solid wood door into pieces, just as the rear patio door likewise exploded into a hailstorm of glass and wood fragments. Another operator tossed a high-powered flashbang toward where the center of the room, aiming at the seated men wearing the VR headsets. The new generation flashbangs were upgraded to overcome noise-cancelling headsets which had become commonplace. An instant later a blinding flash turned the inside of the darkened house to daylight, with a parallel flash occurring in the rear of the home, matched by multiple synchronized "bangs" that rattled Hall's teeth. Obermeyer threw his considerable mass through the door, shotgun in front of him in firing position, screaming, "FBI! ON THE GROUND, NOW! NOW!" One of the men lay on the ground, holding his head and screaming in pain or fear or both, the other still sitting in a large overstuffed chair. He had lost his VR helmet, dropped his game controllers and had one of his hands between the cushions of the chair, and was looking directly at Obermeyer. Hall and the others were piling into the room, with Obermeyer still thundering in a booming voice, "DON'T EVEN THINK ABOUT IT! LET ME SEE THAT HAND SLOWLY! SLOWLY!" The young man froze, seemingly torn between what he should do. Hall aimed his MP-5S directly at the spot between his eyes. "Don't do it, kid. You'll never make the shot."

The young man twitched, preparing himself for action. Obermeyer stood even taller, trying to use his size to intimidate the young man. "You heard the man, kid. Don't try it."

The young man seemed to relax for a moment, and smiled. "For Allah", laughing as he said it, and snatched a pistol from the chair cushion with startling speed. At the same moment Obermeyer shouted "No!" and jumped for him, swinging his own shotgun like a baseball bat to swat the gun away. As he did, he threw his body in and elbowed the man in the jaw. The young student folded like a house of cards and fell on the floor next to his companion, who still clutched at his head but now only moaned. Hall walked up to Obermeyer and saw the "gun" was attached to a cable.

"VR gun for their video games," the big man said. "My kid and I have the same thing."

"You rotten punk kids are all the same," Hall said. "Who in the blazes has time for video games?" A team member behind him shouted, "Clear!" A shout came from the kitchen. "Clear!" Another voice came from upstairs, also confirming the area had been cleared of threats.

Hall keyed his mic. "Schoolboy, this is Teacher. Game is over, 12 to 3. Field is secure."

"Roger that, Teacher. Will forward to Principal."

Hall turned to see Obermeyer looking at the TV screen and chuckling. "What is so funny?"

"They were playing a military shooter, and they were playing as terrorists. They had just lost, I guess, when we came in."

"Wrong, big guy," Hall said, cocking his fingers like a pistol at Obermeyer, "they lost before we came in."

"Maybe," Obermeyer shrugged. "But why would this dumb mutt whip out a gun-shaped controller, knowing we'd blow him away when he did?"

"Dunno. But he has you to thank that we didn't. By the way, if you're going to jump in the line of fire, a little more notice than a shout of 'No!' would be greatly appreciated, ya big oaf."

Obermeyer smiled behind his balaclava, and his slight Southern drawl thickened. "Yessir. Wouldn't want ya to go shootin' me, sir."

Hall turned as the man from the kitchen was brought in, and at first Hall thought he had been badly injured. The man's face was covered in a chunky red substance, and his eyes were squeezed shut and watering profusely.

"When the breaching charge went off, our boy here put his face into a bowl of salsa," a member of Bravo Team reported, holding the handcuffed man by the arm. "Extra spicy, I presume."

"Nice. Put him over there with Dumb and Dumber. How's the screamer?"

An operator hovered over the man who had been lying on the floor screaming when Alpha Team had come in.

"He was in front of his buddy in the chair when the flashbang went off. He has some minor burns to his face, nothing major, but a lot of bleeding to his ears. He won't be hearing anything for a while."

"Too bad," Hall said.

"You don't know the half of it," the operator said. "Screaming Mimi had this in the back of his pants," and held up a Glock 9mm pistol.

"And it looks like our other buddy just grabbed the wrong gun," Obermeyer said from across the room. "There's a Beretta 9mm tucked in the cushion here."

"Took their video gaming seriously," Hall said. "Okay, girls. We secure here till the other units arrive. Good job."

CHAPTER TEN

Case Officer Samantha Land sat in a plush chair in the office of
the Director of National Intelligence while he spoke softly on
the phone. Headquartered at the Liberty Crossing Intelligence
Campus 15 minutes from CIA Headquarters, the DNI was
responsible for overseeing and ensuring the effectiveness of the
entire intelligence apparatus of the United States. The National
Counterterrorism Center was housed there as well, collating and
processing staggering amounts of data that poured in from what
seemed like countless sources. The DNI reported directly to the
President of the United States, and was responsible, along with
the National Security Advisor and Secretary of Defense, for
keeping POTUS informed of goings-on in the intel community.
The present DNI was a man who knew the world of intelligence
backwards and forwards, one John "Jack" Price. Price was a tall,
lean man with a hint of a paunch beginning to show in the pull
of his tailored suit jacket. He was almost bald, with just a
shadowy halo of white hair, and a carefully manicured goatee of
pure white. Looking much younger than his age, most were
surprised to learn of his involvement in intelligence operations
dating back to the heart of the Cold War. Price had seen and
done it all and lived to tell about it, although he never did. Even

his wife of over 40 years, Fay, had no idea all her Jack had done. Although he hated hiding things from his beloved wife, he had to admit it best she never knew. Their marriage had been an exception: most individuals in the Clandestine Service suffered from a divorce rate that was far too high.

After many decades as both a member of the Clandestine Service and filling various executive-level positions at CIA, Price had been asked by the previous Administration to come in and try to turn the wayward ship U.S. intelligence had become, and he agreed. One of his covers over the years had been a turn with the State Department, which gave him a public face for the process of nomination and approval, keeping his past as a case officer unknown but to a small handful. Price had quickly earned respect from both sides of the table in Washington, and his knowledge of the Intelligence Community and its intricacies won over those on the inside. Price had served a year as interim Director of Central Intelligence Agency prior to being tasked as the Director of National Intelligence, but his track record and decades of experience were unmatched. Everyone in the circles of power knew the job of DNI was his until he decided he was tired of it, and that wasn't likely to happen any time soon.

Despite his credentials and position, Director Price came across as easy-going and friendly, his South Carolina drawl lulling people into a false sense of security that he was nothing more than a dumb redneck who fell into his position more by luck than by skill. He had used this many times to his benefit over the years, but those who knew him never mistook his gentility for naïveté.

Land sat almost unmoving while Price finished his telephone conversation. She looked down at her lap and brushed lint from her black skirt. Her matching black jacket hung on the coat rack just inside the Director's door. She couldn't help but wonder why Price had called her in again after hearing her report yesterday afternoon. The 29-year old Case Officer had briefed him on all the possibles behind the attack in Jacksonville, based on her

research of terrorist operatives with Middle Eastern ties operating out of Western Europe and the United States. She had told
Price this seemed to match the modus operandi of ISIS and
others of their brand of extremism, but they couldn't be certain
just yet—analysts were reviewing the video sent in and were
dissecting every aspect of it. If it *was* ISIS, they would want to
claim it for themselves, which made it seem unlikely Fist of the
Apocalypse had any connection to them. No one knew anything
about FOA, including Land, and she had at least a cursory
knowledge of most of the groups operating out of the Middle
East. But it was also true there were new groups popping up
each week. Some formed because someone in the group wasn't
satisfied with the current level of violence and decided to go out
on their own, while some were totally new. Although it wasn't
surprising this could be a neoteric entity, she found it frustrating
because they had to start from scratch, and this case was too big
to have nothing to go on for long. Her attention was drawn back
to her boss at the sound of the handset being placed in the
receiver.

"Thanks for coming by, Sam", Price said. "Sorry to keep you
waiting. I know you have work you want to get to."

"No problem, sir," she replied. "I'm afraid I don't have
anything new for you this morning..."

"I didn't expect you would." He leaned forward over his desk,
folding his hands in front of him on the polished cherry wood
surface. "That's not why I called you in."

Land's face gave away the concern which flashed through her
mind. CIA had a relatively new director, a brilliant Marine
General named Dorothy Sullivan, and DNI Price had been
calling the ball on most of the sensitive operations until she
could be brought fully up to speed. She wondered if she was
going to be put under the direct command of General Sullivan.
The thought didn't cause any particular concern for Land, as she
had a great deal of respect for the general. She had gotten used
to a certain degree of leeway under Price's supervision, however,

and that would require some adjustment. "Now, don't panic," DNI said, smiling as if he read her thoughts. "I need to reassign you from London for a little while. Have you ever been to Jacksonville?"

"Once or twice," Land replied. "Busy place to be right now."

"Exactly why I'd like you to go there. FBI needs a liaison with the Agency, and you're the one I'd like to go and represent us. You're as knowledgeable a person as I have that either isn't in deep cover, in the field, or...well, let's face it. Some of our people don't interface well with other agencies. A few of the people in Analysis are a little protective about their knowledge"

Land smiled—she knew what Price was talking about. She had served in the military and had learned the importance of working with just about anyone, whereas some in the Agency still believed if they worked for the knowledge then they shouldn't have to share it with anyone outside of CIA. Although today's atmosphere of "share and share alike" was mandated by the National Counterterrorism Center, there were still some old school Case Officers who played ball by the old rules.

"If that's where you need me, sir, that's where I'll go."

"Don't sound so resigned to it, Sam," Price said. "You'll have free reign to operate as you see fit. Whatever resources you need, you'll have. Your main contact will be a Special Agent by the name of Woodley, a former SEAL. His right hand is a man by the name of Hawkins. Preacher in his previous life, from what I understand, but turning out to be a heck of an agent. Should be right up your alley."

"Not likely, sir, but we'll see. When do I leave?"

"There's a plane waiting to take you to Jacksonville now." Price stood, signaling the end of the meeting. "Any resources you need, you let me know. Our spot in Jacksonville is sending somebody to pick you up at the airport," he said, referring to the nondescript shipping company not far from downtown which served as a clandestine CIA base of operations. CIA had many such fronts around the country, as well as the rest of the globe, for "coordination" purposes. "Good luck, Sam. Call if you need anything."

"Will do, sir." Price took Land's jacket from its place on the coat rack, handed it to her, and walked her to the door past his receptionist. "Oh, and Sam?"

"Yes, sir?"

"Try not to punch any of these guys through a plate glass window this time, all right?" Price asked with a smile. "Our discretionary budget's tight enough as it is."

Land smiled back. "No promises sir," and she pivoted out into the hallway. She walked down the hall and turned the corner, heading towards the elevator which led to the secure parking area underneath the campus. From the elevator it was a short distance to the squat metallic turnstiles that granted entry and exit into the Underground. They were similar to the ones upstairs in the main lobby, with a spot to place one's ID card and a keypad to enter the matching PIN number. If the code didn't match the card, the turnstiles would not open, and an electronic voice would loudly scold the person. This, of course, would garner the attention of the CIA's uniformed Special Police Officers, or SPOs. Far more than just security, the uniformed men and women were Federal law enforcement officers with a surprising amount of authority and jurisdictional reign even beyond the CIA compound, expanded due to the fatal shootings of two employees in front of the compound entrance in 1994. They maintained a watchful eye whether the turnstile allowed someone through or not. It was bad enough to get scolded by a turnstile, but the SPOs—well, they took their jobs seriously. Security was especially tight on the lower levels, but Land had no difficulties as she passed her ID over the scanner pad and typed in her code.

"Code accepted. Please walk through," the turnstile said in a serious metallic voice. She walked into one of the garage areas located on the first sub-level where a black Suburban waited to whisk her to the Gulfstream G650 jet waiting a few miles away at Edwards Air Force Base.

Hawkins read over the sheet in front of him for the tenth time. Khalil Rafa Malawi looked up at him from a black and white student ID photo taken a year or so earlier when the young man entered North Florida University. Another black and white photo was paper-clipped next to the one taken from the student ID, this one a still from the surveillance camera in the shop where the van that would become a bomb was rented. It didn't take a photo expert to confirm the man in the two pictures was the same, although three such professionals already had. File folders on the other two men arrested earlier that morning—Ali al' Xuffash and Zari Muhammed, both 20 years old—lay on the desk, the information contained within already locked in Hawkins' memory. Malawi wasn't the renter—Xuffash had obtained the van—but Malawi had been there all the same. Muhammed wasn't in the video—he had been the tech consultant for the Convention Center that had tampered with the garage camera recordings. It would be a while before he could hear any questions anyhow, as both of his eardrums had been damaged by the exploding flashbang grenade. He could talk, however, so they'd get to him soon enough. Xuffash, the one who actually rented the van under a false name, was still nursing a concussion from when Johnny Obermeyer from HRT had nailed him. *Xuffash should be grateful he still has a head*, Hawkins thought. *Stupid punk kid. Trying to get himself killed so he could be a martyr. Stupid.*

Hawkins had to take a deep breath. He found it more and more difficult to contain the rage he felt. How could anyone who claims to know God kill people whose only crime was not being like them? He knew, of course, many who claimed to be Christian had committed atrocities in His name, but Hawkins firmly believed anyone who did such things could not be a true follower of God. "You will know them by their fruit", the Bible said. *The fruit hanging from the trees of this kind of scum is poisonous.* Death was never pleasant, but the senseless murder of innocents enraged him. He knew he needed to talk to God about his inner turmoil, but right now he just didn't feel like it.

Hawkins heard footsteps approaching his cubicle, and he knew who it was before he heard the voice. "Go time. Ready for some small talk?" Woodley asked, tapping the file folder in his own hand against the edge of one of the padded cubicle walls.

"You know it," Hawkins said as he stood. They walked down the hallway and around the corner, past the Command Center, and headed upstairs to the interrogation room where Malawi was being held. "How you want to play this, Hawk? You the good cop or me this time?"

"You'd better be the good cop," Hawkins said. Something in the younger man's voice made Woodley stop in the middle of the stairwell.

"You sure you want to do this, Hawk? I know you're riding some rough waters on this, but you've gotta stay at the helm. You can't let your..."

"I know, Mark, I can't let my feelings about this get in the way. I'll do the job," Hawkins replied, trying to sound more certain of what he was saying than he was. "I just figure it'll be easier for me to play unsympathetic right now."

Woodley nodded, said "Fair enough," and started back up the stairs. They approached the secure area where agents sat guarding the entrance to the room in which Malawi sat. Another door to the left of the one leading to Malawi opened into a space which allowed observation of the interrogation room from behind a mirrored window. An agent sat behind a console, running video and audio recordings of everything transpiring in the space where Malawi sat whether he was alone or not. Woodley tapped on the door frame.

"Hawk and I are goin' in, Suze."

"Already rolling, Mark. We're good to go." Susan Hicks, FBI

Special Agent and head of the Surveillance Squad, smiled at the two agents. Hicks was in her late thirties and looked more like a television news reporter than an FBI agent. An attractive woman with long brown hair and a winning smile, she would have been as much at home in front of a camera as behind one. She smiled at Hawkins as she saw him, and he returned the smile. "How ya doin', Suze?"

"Not bad, Hawk. You okay?" Hawkins and Hicks had worked together on a few occasions, and had even had dinner twice. Hawkins liked her—there wasn't much not to like—but there hadn't been any real sparks, although the two had become good friends. Hicks noticed no one seemed to be able to spark Hawkins' interest much beyond friendship. She knew he had been a pastor, and he remained very committed to his faith, and that made it more difficult for him in some ways. She had heard about his loss, and knew he kept it buried as deep as possible. But she knew there was something—more specifically, some*one* —he was looking for he just hadn't found. Or maybe she *had* been found, then lost, on that street in Spain.

She also knew Hawkins was having a difficult time dealing with *this* case. The pastor-turned-special agent learned the names of several other friends who had died or been severely injured the day of the explosion, and his mood seemed to grow darker with each day which passed without an arrest. She hoped now that these creeps were in custody Hawk's spirits might brighten, but she knew these three were probably just the tip of the iceberg in this deal. These kids didn't have the gumption to pull something off like this without someone guiding them.

"It can always be worse, Susan," Hawk replied as he and Woodley stepped into the room where Malawi sat waiting.

The young man looked up at the two federal agents as they walked into the room. Hawkins noticed the expression on Malawi's face to be quite different than the one pictured on the student ID. While the college picture reflected the face of a pleasant 18-year old with his whole life before him, the face looking at him in the 12-foot by 14-foot room was a declaration of arrogance and hate. Hawkins realized he had curled his own fingers into fists before he was able to relax.

"Mr. Malawi," Woodley said, "I am Special Agent Woodley, and this is Special Agent Hawkins. We'd like to talk to you about your involvement in the bombing of the Coalition of Christian Churches meeting on June 7 here in Jacksonville."

"I'll tell you nothing!" Malawi spat. He looked like he had been through a rough night. His black, curly hair looked like a rat had taken up residence in it after fighting for possession, and his eyes were bloodshot—either from lack of sleep or extra spicy salsa. He was dressed in a black short sleeved t-shirt with tight blue jeans cuffed at the ankles and leather sandals, all of which looked like he had put them on after they had been run over by a convoy of 18 wheelers. "Where's my lawyer? I don't have to say anything 'til he gets here."

"No, you don't," Hawkins said, walking around behind the long wooden table at which the young man sat. "But you could. And that would make life much easier for you." Hawkins leaned over the table, placing his palms flat on the surface inches from Malawi's own intertwined fingers.

"I'm not interested in doing you any favors," Malawi said. "You people came barging into our house in the middle of the night..."

"Look, sunshine," Woodley said, sitting on the corner of the rectangular table farthest from Hawkins and Malawi, "We have video footage placing you with one of your friends at the location you rented the van from. We know this vehicle was the same one used to contain the explosives that were detonated in the parking garage at the convention center. We know your other friend erased the security camera tapes showing the two of you driving the van into the garage and leaving it. If you help us now, it might go easier on you later."

Malawi chuckled as he shook his head slowly. "So what if a bunch of Christians died? The world's a better place without them. They were nothing but a bunch of narrow-minded bigots anyw..."

Malawi was cut off in mid-sentence as Hawkins suddenly slammed his fist down next to the young man's intertwined fingers. Woodley fully expected Hawkins to grab the front of the young man's t-shirt, snatch him up from his chair, and jerk him across the table. He leapt up from where he sat prepared to intercept any further action, saying something Hawkins couldn't hear over the blood pounding in his ears. Malawi made a sound somewhere between a grunt and a squeal as Hawkins drew in close.

"You listen to me, you little punk," Hawkins snarled through gritted teeth. "I'm not gonna sit here and listen to you spit this puke at me. You're going to tell us everything you know RIGHT NOW, or so help me there won't be enough of you left for your sorry lawyer to find!"

"Hawk, ease up!" Woodley shouted, pulling at Hawkins arm. "This isn't the way to do it!"

Hawkins shrugged his arm roughly, breaking Woodley's grip. "Back off, Mark! "I've had enough of this little tough guy." He faced Malawi again. "How do you think your evening is going to go when the people in lockup find out you're responsible for the death of dozens of innocent Americans? You'd be surprised at how patriotic criminals can be. And how much they love doing terrible things to people who have done worse things than they have." Hawkins eyes narrowed. "This little dirt bag is going to tell me everything he knows, and he's going to do it *now*, or he's going to experience some fine southern hospitality in the county jail." Hawkins drew his face as close as he could to the terrified Malawi's without touching. The smell of salsa and sweat almost overpowered him, but Hawkins didn't flinch.

"All right, all right! Get him off me!" the young man screamed. Hawkins pivoted and slowly stepped out of reach. The young man looked up at the agent. "What's wrong with you, man?"

Hawkins moved toward Malawi again, but Woodley stepped in between. "Your best bet, kid, is to shut up about him and put up about whoever's steering you and your buddies. If you want, you can keep sitting around waiting for an attorney, but I'm real tempted to walk out of this room and let the chips fall where they may for you."

Malawi seemed to sink lower in his chair. "I don't need an attorney. I'll tell you what you need to know."

"We're listening."

"We were a part of a club on campus comprised of students from Middle Eastern nations. Our club sponsor was Xuffash's father, Ra's. He helped us all out financially—paying for food, gas, even our rent. Then Xuffash told a couple of us his father would pay us even more money if we would do something for him."

"And that was?" Woodley asked.

"He wanted to pay the Christians back for their insults against Islam and the Muslim world, particularly the Coalition. Their Convention was well known, and would make a powerful symbolic strike against the Christian infidels, he told us. All we had to do was rent a truck. He would have people load it with what was necessary, and then we were to drive it to the parking garage. We already had access to the security camera tapes, and would have no problem disabling them. So we rented the truck and drove it to a warehouse across the river and left it overnight. The next morning we went back and drove the truck to the parking garage. That was it."

"That was it?" Hawkins asked. "Dozens of people dead or wounded, and all you can say is, 'That was it'?"

"Don't get pious with me," the young man spat, his defiance rising again from within. "How many Muslim and Palestinian deaths are you Americans responsible for? As your President says, you are at war. You should expect casualties."

Woodley saw Hawkins tense up and intercepted him before he could lay his hands on the student, who leapt backwards out of the chair trying to get away from the agent struggling to get to him.

Hawkins pulled back and paced several steps away. "I'm all right," he said, turning back to stare daggers at Malawi.

Woodley banged on the door, and immediately two other agents came in. "Get this piece of garbage out of here and into a cell." The two agents came in and carried Malawi out, the young man refusing to meet Hawkins' withering gaze.

Woodley turned to Hawkins. "That's a pretty good start. The younger they are, the dumber. If he'd have held out for an attorney, we'd have been days behind. Good act, by the way. Really over the top. I thought you were gonna kill him yourself."

Hawkins sensed the sarcasm in Woodley's voice, but knew he was saying it for the benefit of the audio and video recording equipment monitoring the interrogation room in which they still stood.

"As long as it gets the job done, I'll put on the show," Hawkins said, and walked out of the room. Woodley caught the double meaning in his friend's words but said nothing as Hawkins walked down the hall. Hicks leaned her head around the corner. "Nice job on the info. You two make a better team than Batman and Robin." She lowered her voice and motioned for Woodley to come out of the interrogation room and into her recording studio. "That wasn't an act. Nice job covering at the end, but we both know Hawk was about to take that guy apart."

"I understand why."

"So do I, Mark, but I've never seen Hawk like this. I'm afraid he's too close on this case."

"I'll keep an eye on him Suze, but it's my call to make. He's too good, and I need him. He'll be fine. Hey, we got the info, didn't we?" he said, walking away.

"Just watch him, Mark. Don't let him do anything stupid."

"He'll be fine," Woodley repeated as he rounded the corner. But he knew Hawk had to get the load off his chest, and soon. The last thing Woodley needed was one of the best agents around to get bagged for beating the tar out of a suspect in an interrogation room. He passed by the break room and saw Hawkins sitting at one of the tables there, staring out the windows overlooking the parking lot and the nearby twin buildings. Woodley fed a dollar bill into the machine and got a can of Country Time lemonade. Two quarters dropped into the change holder, and he deposited them for another can. He sat down next to his younger partner, opened both cans, and slid one towards Hawkins.

"This'll cool you down," Woodley said. "Good job in there. Just make sure you don't ram into me so hard next time, huh? You know I bruise easily."

Hawkins cracked a smile. "Yeah, you're a real daisy." He picked up the can and sipped from it. "Mark, I'm..."

"Don't do it," Woodley interrupted. "Not necessary. I know what's going on, and you didn't go too far. A little more intense than usual, but it got the job done without breaking any regs or legs. And we've got a name and a money trail."

"*Raysh* al' Xuffash," Hawkins pronounced the name phonetically. "Wonder how he spells that."

"We'll find out," Woodley said. "That, and much more." The men sat silently for a few moments, both drinking from their cans of lemonade.

"I want these bastards, Mark. I want them to pay for what they've done."

"They will Hawk. They will."

CHAPTER ELEVEN

Thomas Hawkins sat staring at two faces on his computer screen. One was the man who had sent the video claiming responsibility for the bombing in Jacksonville; the other was Ra's al Xuffash, a Saudi shipping magnate living large in France on the Riviera. He had a wife, Melina, a pretty woman originally from Greece, and two children—Talia, 17, and Ali, whom the FBI now had in custody. Xuffash owned his own shipping company, Xuffash Transport Systems, and had gone from having two rusty trawlers 25 years ago to owning a fleet of cargo ships that crossed the seas with millions of dollars in cargo every day. He had attended New Orleans University and earned a degree there in Marketing and Finance. It was also in New Orleans he met his wife and started his business. Now the 48-year old multimillionaire lived it up in Monaco in a sizable estate overlooking the Mediterranean Sea. Nothing showed up in intel reports about him being a devout Muslim, but there were a number of entries detailing donations to questionable organizations. That he had no love for Americans was well known. *He should fit right in with the French*, Hawkins thought. Nothing seemed to indicate he would be motivated to pay a bunch of college students, including his own son, to blow up a bunch of Christians, however, and it didn't take a facial analysis expert to see the two men on the screen before him were not one and the same.

Hawkins closed his eyes and took a deep breath. He had to get his anger under control, or it would seriously damage this case. That was something he just could not allow. But he wasn't having any luck laying the anger down, either. Woodley meant well, and was as good a friend as he had, but Hawkins just couldn't seem to voice what was on his heart to him. *Lord, I know You're there for me, and I am so grateful for that. I know Your grace is sufficient for me, and Your strength is made perfect in weakness, but I am really in need of some help. Mark is a great friend, but I need somebody I can vent with, someone who'll understand. I can't even let go of something that happened years ago, much less stay clear on this. I don't want to get in the way of this investigation. Forgive me for not handling things the way I should. But please, send me some help.*

Hawkins heard someone clear their throat, and he looked up to see Mark Woodley standing at the edge of his cubicle. "I hate to interrupt you, but there's somebody I want you to meet."

"Who?"

"CIA liaison by the name of Sam Land. The Director of National Intelligence specifically called this one back from the field to work this with you."

"Wait a minute. Did you just say with *me?*"

"Yeah," Woodley replied, looking a bit sheepish. "I hate to tell you this, but you and I are gonna have to part ways for a bit. I want you in the field, but I have to supervise, and that means Shear wants me around here more. The CIA Spook will be your new best friend."

Hawkins threw his hands up in mock disgust. "Great. I'm probably gonna be stuck riding around with some psycho spy who'll try to whack me first chance he gets if I get out of line."

"Maybe," Woodley said with a smile, "But I think you should meet the Case Officer before you pass judgment."

"Fair enough." Hawkins stood from his desk and followed

Woodley down the hall toward SAC Shear's office. As he entered the large office all he saw was Shear standing behind his desk.

"Hawk, I'd like for you to meet Case Officer Sam Land," SAC Jacksonville said, gesturing to Hawkins' left. In the far corner, rising from a chair, was Case Officer Sam Land. Not at all what Hawkins was expecting, Land rose and walked to where he and Woodley stood.

Land reached out to shake hands. "Pleasure to meet you." Hawkins noticed her perfect fingernails, cut short of course. Her hand was soft when he took it, and yet he could feel the surprising strength it contained. She had light-colored hair, platinum highlights streaking through like veins of silver, cut just above her shoulders. Her makeup was understated, tasteful, with dark eyeliner highlighting green eyes that seemed to have a light burning behind them. The black jacket she wore covered a light blue shirt, the collar of which lay perfectly over the lapels of her jacket. Her skirt was long enough to be professional but short enough he couldn't help but notice she had the legs of a sprinter. She wore black heels with a strap that buckled around the ankles, and walked like she could run in them without a problem. He caught the scent of her perfume, understated, but there.

Hawkins found her breathtaking.

"The pleasure is mine, Officer Land."

"Don't speak too soon, Agent Hawkins," she replied with a smile. "You haven't had to work with me yet."

"Likewise."

"I assume Woodley told you that you and Land will be working together on this case, Hawk, Shear said. "You two will be the lead agents on this thing, and our Director and the DNI have given you free reign to carry it however and wherever you need."

"Looks like we may need to go to France, sir," Hawkins said. "I was just reviewing Ra's al Xuffash's file and he presently resides in Monte Carlo."

The SAC nodded. "We've got a Legat in the region I can get

involved," referring to the Legal Attaché the Bureau had at the U.S. Embassy in the French capital. A Legat was a Special Agent, but had no enforcement powers in the foreign locale where they were stationed. The Legat's main job was to make friends in the region, and use those contacts to gain intelligence, as well as pass it on. "I'm sure the Agency has resources in the area?" Shear asked.

"We should through the Consul General in Marseille, and State always has resources available." It had almost become a joke over the years; saying someone "worked for the State Department" often meant that person may or may not work for one of the more covert agencies within the United States' governmental infrastructure. "I can run a quick check on our way to the airport. We have a jet Director Price put at our disposal."

"All right then. I'll have our Legat snoop around and find out how connected our boy Xuffash is before we nail him. The last thing we want is any crooked cops screwing this up for us."

"And I'll have our resources get surveillance up on him ASAP."

"Good luck, both of you." Shear sat down, and the three left his office.

"I've got to grab a couple of things," Hawkins said. "Meet you downstairs at my car. It's..."

"The black Charger?"

"I would ask you how you know, but you'd probably just give me some smart CIA answer, right?"

She smiled, a beautiful thing to behold. "You're pretty sharp for a preacher boy. See you downstairs." She turned and walked toward the secure entrance leading to the parking lot.

Woodley chuckled. "Man, you got a tough assignment. Having to go to the French Riviera with a beautiful spy. I'm sorry I had to do this to you, Hawk."

Hawkins closed his satchel, picked it up off his desk, and walked for the exit. "Is she beautiful? I hadn't noticed," he said, smiling his way down the steps to the waiting Case Officer.

"I need to stop by my house and pick up a few things for the trip," Hawkins said as he pressed the ignition button. The car growled softly to life.

"No problem." Land reached into her briefcase and pulled out an electronic tablet. She removed the stylus from the attached cover and began tapping on the device. He turned onto the Arlington Expressway, made a U-turn, and headed onto Mill Creek Drive toward the river and his home. "Have you ever been to the Principality of Monaco?"

"I've been to France. I went on a tour with my parents when I was 14. Started out in London, took the Chunnel from Folkestone to Coquelles, and then on to Paris. A great trip, but I was too young to really appreciate everything I saw."

"It's a beautiful country," Land said as she continued to enter data. "The French government may be a pain to deal with right now, but many of the people are great. Some Parisians can be snobby, but the rest of the country is a joy. Many of the troublemakers in France come from other countries for protests and the like. The French people are down to earth and friendly, contrary to what many say. You just have to watch for the pickpockets in Nice."

Hawkins nodded his head. "So, have you been to Monte Carlo?"

"Actually I have, once. I was still in the Army, but was working a joint mission with CIA in Nice, and we tailed a guy over into Monaco. Beautiful place, but we got into some ugly stuff on that one." Hawkins could tell by the way Land had spoken it had indeed been ugly, so he left it lying. He knew how painful memories could be.

"So when did you find out I used to pastor a church, before or after you got here?" Hawkins asked.

Land chuckled. "I like to know who I'm working with. Besides, your friend Woodley told me to watch out because you were also an ordained minister and you weren't to be trusted."

"He's right," Hawk said with a smile.

"We'll see."

They drove in silence as he turned onto Fort Caroline Road. Land closed her tablet as they approached Hawkins' driveway. "You live on the river?"

"Yeah. The house was built about 10 years ago. It came on the market right after I transferred here. Got a great deal on it. What really sold me was the garage." As they rolled down the concrete driveway, the house came into view. Land noted the house seemed modest for its location. Most of the homes visible from Hawkins' lot were borderline mansions, but his was a simple colonial brick two-story with a charcoal gray roof and white trim, no more than perhaps 2800 square feet. The size of the garage attached to the home made the biggest statement. At least as big as the rest of the house, the 4 single-bay doors opened into bays three cars deep. Another door large enough to hold a motor coach loomed at the end of the structure. The garage was constructed of the same materials and design as the house, and she could see the whole thing was climate controlled.

The car's horn honked, and Land turned to see Hawkins waving at his neighbor, a salt-and pepper haired man with a bamboo walking cane, cleaning a black coupe in his own drive-way. The man raised his hand, waving back. Hawkins pulled up in front of his garage and stopped. He opened the door and stepped out of the Charger and spoke to the other man.

"You want to come over and do mine next, Harry?" Hawkins shouted. They were neighbors, but a distance of about 50 feet separated their driveways.

"I don't think so," Harry Allen replied. "I don't have *that* much time." Both men laughed as Hawkins walked over toward the older man. Allen was in his mid-sixties, and stood about 6'5" with a lean build. Allen stopped wiping on his black Pontiac GTO as Hawkins approached. "You doing okay, Tom?"

"Doing fine, Harry. I just wanted to let you and Jane know I might be out of town for a little while. If you'd keep an eye on things, I'd appreciate it."

"Sure thing, Tom," Allen replied. "Hope you have a safe trip."

"Thanks," Hawkins said, turning back to his own yard. "See you soon." Allen knew what Hawkins' did for a living, but he never asked too many questions. He respected Hawkins and what he did, and that meant a lot. It was nice having good neighbors, and he only had the Allens. Their house was to the right as you looked at them, and to his left stood nothing but woods. Hawkins had a state-of-the-art security system and didn't need anybody to keep an eye on his house, but he and Harry had gotten into a pattern of watching out for each other's places. Good neighbors did those things, after all.

As he walked back to his house, he saw Land standing in the open doorway of the first single garage door. As she heard him approaching, she turned to him. "Okay, I'm impressed."

Inside the garage was a collection of vehicles she expected more from a movie star than an FBI agent. An eclectic lineup filled the space: a gleaming black Buick Grand National, an older silver T-top Camaro SS parked next to it; a black Dodge Challenger Hellcat Widebody, and a gray Ram Rebel pickup behind it; an orange 1972 Corvette convertible; and a pewter Chevy Avalanche with "LINGENFELTER" written in vinyl letters across the windshield. A light green 1968 Shelby GT500 sat on a lift rack and, sitting in the back of the garage, was a white 1966 Pontiac GTO with a black vinyl top and a yellow 1971 Plymouth Hemi 'Cuda convertible. The walls were lined with shelves filled with automotive supplies and adorned with banners advertising various automotive products. It looked more like the service facility at a car dealership than an individual's garage.

Hawkins grinned proudly. "My hobby. I love automobiles. Grew up around them. Just in my blood, I guess."

"And here I thought you'd be just another boring FBI agent," Land said with a smirk. "Turns out you're a Jay Leno wanna-be."

"Something like that," Hawkins replied. "I'm going to run upstairs and grab my stuff. You're welcome to come in, if you'd like."

"I think I'd like to stay out here and admire your vehicles, if that's ok."

"Knock yourself out," he said. "I'll be down shortly," and headed into the house. Samantha Land walked to each vehicle and noticed they all looked like museum pieces. Barely a speck of dust could be found on any of them, even the Shelby that sat on the lift with two wheels off and no exhaust system. The 'Cuda convertible and the GTO, however, appeared even cleaner than the rest. While all the vehicles seemed to be parked in spots specifically laid out for them, something about those two set them apart. Hawkins obviously didn't drive them much, if at all, as they were parked in the far corner. Land knew enough about cars to know the 'Cuda was extremely rare—only 11 like this were built, if she remembered right—and it would be worth as much as every other vehicle in the garage combined. Plus the house. And probably the neighbor's house. Her father enjoyed cars as well, hence much of her knowledge.

The closing of a door interrupted her inspection. She turned to see Hawkins with a suitcase and a hanging bag in his hands.

"You like my collection?" he asked.

"As I said, I'm impressed." She pointed to the yellow Plymouth. "Is this a real Hemi 'Cuda convertible?"

"Sort of. Long story behind that car, and most of the others." A strange look came across Hawkins' face. "Maybe I'll tell you about it sometime. Right now, I believe we have a plane to catch."

Land could tell there was indeed something special about that particular car, and it involved more than money. No need to push the issue now, however. "Right you are," she said and climbed into the Charger. Hawkins stowed his luggage in the trunk, fired up the car, headed back down the driveway, and aimed for the airport.

CHAPTER TWELVE

Donald Molson sat outside the little café just off the Champs Elysees sipping a cup of *café au lait* and reading the French language edition of *Fortune* magazine. He stole a glance at his watch and found his friend to be a fashionable 7 minutes late. In all the years he had known Philippe Dupain he had never seen the Frenchman arrive on time. Molson had been in the FBI for over 30 years, the last 5 of which had been spent as the Bureau's Legal Attaché in Paris, and he clung to the clock. Molson could be counted on to always be punctual, and he expected the same of others. When he had been SAC in Miami, and later Assistant Director over Criminal Investigations, those under Molson knew to be late was to incur his wrath. Many an agent had been thrown out of a meeting no sooner than they had walked in because of their tardiness. Molson knew such outbursts would only serve to satisfy the French Intelligence Officer's desire to rile his American friend, so he continued sipping the cup of hot, potent liquid. It was a beautiful day to be in Paris, the temperature hovering at 71 degrees—he still didn't care for metrics, particularly regarding temperature—and there was barely a cloud in the sky. As he looked back down from the blue heaven above him, he saw the familiar form of his associate approaching.

"Good afternoon, *mon ami*," Dupain said. "Sorry to keep you waiting."

"It's not a very good sign the first words out of your mouth to me are a lie," Molson quipped, standing as the other man arrived at the small table. "Glad to see you."

"Now we are even in our lies," Dupain replied as he sat. Almost immediately a waiter appeared at the table. Dupain ordered a glass of burgundy, and the waiter strutted off. "How have you been, my friend?"

"Very well, thank you. Ann and I just returned from a Rhine Cruise. Lovely scenery through Germany."

"If Germany is so lovely, they would never have desired Paris, *non?*" The waiter arrived with Dupain's glass, accepted several Euros from him, and departed again. "I'm glad you enjoyed yourself. Me, I have no time for vacations as of late."

"Sorry to hear that," Molson said, taking a sip from his coffee cup. "Anything you'd like to tell me about?"

Dupain smiled and swirled the burgundy in his glass. Molson had met the Frenchman years ago at a State dinner in Washington, several years before his posting as Legat in Paris. Dupain had worked in the French Foreign Ministry, seeming to be nothing more than a mid-level flunky. Molson had been something of a mid-level flunky himself at the time, and so the two struck up a conversation, ridiculing the pomposity of their superiors as they postured over the Veal Piccata. Having that in common seemed enough, and the two became, if not outright friends, kindred spirits on opposite sides of the ocean. When Molson transferred to Paris as Legat for the Bureau, his first action was to invite Dupain and his wife to dinner. While Dupain's wife shared the locations of the best shops and cafes in Paris with Molson's , the two men spoke in the verbal shorthand so often used between two government employees whose job involved information. Dupain had worked his way up to become a senior official within the French Ministry of State, and the two once again found themselves on a relatively equal footing. Such a friendship could be mutually beneficial, even more than before, Molson had suggested, and Dupain had agreed. For several years now the couples had dined together at least once a month, and Molson and Dupain had met at this, or one of a dozen other outdoor cafes, at least that often. Even when they had no real business to speak of, the two men enjoyed the repartee integral to each of their meetings.

"I can't make it that easy for you, now can I? Think how bored you would be if I told you everything you and your friends across the sea wanted to know. Then you would have to do no work of your own."

"That's all right. I'm sure CIA knows anyway." Molson saw his friend stiffen at the remark. Dupain didn't like it, but he knew the American was almost certainly correct. French intelligence might as well send briefings to Langley as well as CIA had them covered. It was just the way things were, however, and Dupain settled back down almost immediately.

"So, what do you want to know that you don't already?"

Molson lowered his voice slightly and held his coffee cup to his mouth to conceal the movements of his lips from any who might be watching. The digital scrambler in his coat pocket created a field of white noise around him so anyone trying to eavesdrop electronically would hear nothing but static, even if someone tried using a laser mic to listen in. People sitting too close would wonder why their cell phones weren't getting a good signal. "We're about to move on someone in the country who is tied to the event in Florida. I need to know we won't have any local problems."

"Here in Paris?" Dupain said from behind his glass. Molson acknowledged Dupain knew his tradecraft well—no one would be hearing anything he had to say, either. Neither man worried the other would be taping this conversation, as there was an unspoken understanding between them. They never asked if the other wore a wire—they knew such a thing would be unseemly among men with their unique relationship. But both nonetheless took precautions.

"No. South of here. Think about what a royal mess it could be if the wrong people get involved."

The Frenchman lifted an eyebrow. "I see. Will you allow me to get the check this time?"

"Kind of you to offer." Molson slid the bill to Dupain, who picked up the ticket and imperceptibly moved the small slip of paper out from underneath that contained a name. Dupain smiled.

"You are a cheap date," the Frenchman said. "I can assure you I have you covered this time. I will even get the tip."

Molson smiled back. "You're a good man, Frenchie."

"Hmmph," Dupain replied. "If word of that gets out, we are both in trouble."

"Thank you, sir" Thomas Hawkins spoke into the secure phone line mounted on the wall next to his leather-covered seat. The Gulfstream jet in which he was currently a passenger cruised at 37,000 feet over the Atlantic Ocean. He replaced the handset into the receiver, stood and walked across the aircraft to where his new partner from the Central Intelligence Agency sat. Information scrolled across multiple displays in front of her at an alarming rate.

"And I thought I had all the good toys", Hawkins said.

Case Officer Samantha Land sat behind a console covered with computer screens, various input devices, and multiple secure communication systems. "Actually, I'll give credit where credit is due. Most of these systems originate with NSA. This new secure satellite internet connection is Fiber optic-level fast around the globe, regardless of altitude and weather conditions. I can access our databases—and, as long as I've got clearance, yours, NSA, DoD. It's a whole new world with all this cooperation."

"Cooperation is the new buzzword, in spite of the some of the bureaucratic 'improvements.'" Some of the elements of restructuring federal agencies to improve response and protective elements following 9/11 were all well and good, but he had long-serving friends in other federal agencies who told him all it did was add more bureaucracy and personalities that often had to be stroked. The Law Enforcement and Intelligence Communities seemed to be working together smoothly on their own now, but how it all fit together wasn't up to him one way or the other.

"Not only that, but the fact we are considered to be at war means all kinds of info exchange. Theoretically, anyway. But that's old news to you, working CT."

"I haven't been in for a while, until CHURCHBOM. The Bureau hasn't always enjoyed very good interagency communication, even in the months following 9/11. Even then they could barely get Field Offices to cooperate with each other, much less other agencies. Guys who were around back then said they got more out of their buddies in the military than anything else. I guess it's all in who you know."

"As I said, it's a whole new world, Agent Hawkins."

"Call me Hawk. 'Agent Hawkins' takes too long to say."

Another smile. Land's eyes squinted when she smiled, and Hawkins would swear her face really glowed. Corny as it sounded, he nonetheless thought it to be true.

"'Case Officer Land' is even worse," she said. "Just 'Sam' is fine."

"All right, Sam. What have you got?"

"CIA does have a couple assets in the region, but they're tied up on other stuff, so it doesn't look like we're going to have any on-the-ground surveillance. Monaco is real funny about any spying going on in their square mile, but they're usually very friendly with us. We actually have better diplomatic relations with them than France does most of the time. In the meantime, I've been researching our boy and his father. Pulled their phone records—home, work and cell. Right now I'm running their Internet accounts, and checking the servers where their emails are archived. The phone records are being cross-referenced with the master databases at NSA containing all the known phone numbers of terrorists and otherwise nasty people. Same with emails. If either of these goons has talked to a known baddie in the last few months, we'll know it. We'll also keep our own archive of what we find, file it under their names, and keep it for future use."

"Once it's digital, it's always out there somewhere," Hawkins said. "I know a good bit about the cell phone and data tracking. People tend to be surprised when they find out we're able to retrieve emails off the main servers even after they've been deleted. Been very handy in White Collar."

"Not only that, but with ECHELON we're tapped into every digital comm system in the world. We even have access to most of the fiber optics wrapping around the globe. We've greatly expanded even in the short time you've been out of CT."

"Wait a minute. How do you know how long I've been out of CT? A minute ago you acted like you knew nothing about it."

"Don't forget—I *am* CIA."

"Great. Stuck in a jet over the Atlantic with a sneaky Spook. Anything else you know I should be aware of?"

"I believe 'Investigation' is still in FBI, isn't it? You tell me."

"Give me a few minutes on your computer."

She laughed, a wonderful sound. "Get your own."

The chiming of two secure phones ringing at the same time confused the two, causing each of them to look at their respective phones and back at each other. Land reached for her phone, resting on the table in front of her. Hawkins likewise reached for his phone and answered it. "Hawkins."

"Where are you?" Mark Woodley asked.

"Winging my way to parts unknown with a sneaky Spook. What's up?"

"Your job may have just gotten harder. A nursing student at

the hospital Xuffash Junior was taken to recognized him. When she saw a bunch of guys guarding him she got curious. Some rookie cop was in talking about a major bust on the Northside where, he heard, they had busted three college students for possible involvement in terrorist activities. The nursing student put two and two together, and the news spread from there. She went for her 15 minutes of fame and called CNN. They're sitting on it for now, but it won't be long before Xuffash's name and college ID picture are all over the airwaves."

"Fantastic. That ought to make Daddy Xuffash good and nervous."

"Shear got in touch with the Legat in Paris. The French are being weenies, but they won't interfere. The police in Monaco have been given a heads up. State Department has talked with the Prince, and we're good to go as long as we don't break too much. Xuffash is known in the area as a wealthy shipping magnate, but he's not connected to any muckity-mucks anywhere as far as we can see, or that they say. CIA is putting an eye in the sky on him ASAP, so they'll be able to follow Xuffash if he gets spooked and tries to run. But I suppose you know that much already."

Hawkins looked at Land, who had turned to look at him at the same time. They both smiled at each other and turned away. "I'm learning a lot. Anything else?"

"Yeah. I got the info you wanted about your 'sneaky Spook', but I had to go through my DIA connections to get it. She was recruited into the Agency out of the Army. She was—are you ready for this? —a door gunner on a Blackhawk helo. Good soldier, too. She flew a number of missions for CIA, not only behind a Mini-gun, but also on the ground doing both recon and communications. She's certified in every small arm our Armed Forces have in their armory, and she's not bad with a rifle, either. She kicked the backside of everyone in her personal defense class, including the instructor. They put her through school while she was in, and she wound up getting a degree in Political Science. She's also fluent or functional in several languages—French, Farsi, German, Russian, just to name a few. She's been in the Agency now for about 3 years, and has become quite the darling of the DNI. He's given her a prime post in London. She's not just an analyst, Hawk. She's a door kicker."

Hawkins glanced over to the Case Officer seated at her console. Land was talking intently to the person on the other end, and he couldn't help but notice the well-toned legs crossed under the console deck. "She's got the legs for it." Hawkins squinted his eyes and shook his head. "I don't believe I said that."

Woodley's laugh crackled over the digitally encrypted line. "Now you're starting to pay attention. I was beginning to wonder if you were going blind. She may be a 'sneaky Spook', but she's an attractive one."

"Have to be careful about saying such things nowadays, you Neanderthal. If you tell me to ask for her sign and get her phone number, I'll never speak to you again. Anything else before I hang up on you?"

"One more thing, Casanova. She's a PK."

"A preacher's kid? You're kidding."

"Would I kid you? Methodist preacher from Florida. Nice family."

"Good to know. Thanks, Mark." He lowered his voice even further, turning towards the back of the aircraft's cabin. "I know everybody's into sharing info, but make sure I'm up on what's going on with our people back there, all right?"

Woodley chuckled again. "Now *you're* talking like a sneaky Spook. Talk to you soon."

"Right," Hawkins said, and tapped the screen on his phone. He looked over to where Land sat, still engrossed in her conversation. He wondered what she was learning. Or to whom she was talking. Maybe she had a significant other already. Maybe she was married. Surely Woodley would have told him if she was married, wouldn't he? It would be harder to know if she had a boyfriend.

Hawkins chuckled at the fact he struggled with jealousy over a woman he had met only hours earlier.

He shook his head and moved to a seat in the rear of the cabin, reclining the seatback as far as it would go. Setting his watch for local time in Monte Carlo—which would now be just after 8:00 p.m.—he crossed his arms on his chest, stretched his legs out in front of him, and closed his eyes. He figured the long flight would be as good a time as any to get some shut-eye. Besides, he knew all too well sleep was something a field agent needed to get when the opportunity presented itself, because one never knew how long it might be before the opportunity presented itself again. He closed his eyes and sleep escorted him into its warm embrace with the swiftness of a jet streaking over the Atlantic.

CHAPTER THIRTEEN

"Wake up, sleepyhead."

Hawkins opened his eyes and saw Samantha Land standing in front of him. She had changed out of her stylish black suit into more practical field attire. A charcoal gray windbreaker covered a black t-shirt; the jacket came several inches past her waist—useful for covering the gun that no doubt rested in a holster on her hip or under her arm—and fell over black jeans. Black UnderArmour shoes covered her feet. *Good choice in shoes.* Hawkins favored the brand not only for their comfort but for their durability and performance. He preferred the Magnum Stealth boots with their steel-reinforced toe for operational field use, but the UnderArmours were a close second and, if you had to do much walking, were lighter and more comfortable over the long haul. He looked down at his own clothes—navy blue suit, white dress shirt, blue-and-silver-patterned tie, and black dress shoes—and realized he needed a change as well. "Are we there yet?"

"On final approach now. Thought you might want to change into something more comfortable before we hit the road to Monte Carlo."

"Just thinking the same thing myself. Be right back." Hawkins stood and, gathering his overnight bag, headed to the lavatory in the back of the aircraft. It was cramped, but he had enough room to change clothes. He pulled on a black t-shirt and blue jeans, and then laced up his own black UnderArmour shoes. He replaced the ankle holster, then put his Sig 9mm in place. The big .45 Glock took its position in the holster on his belt, along with two extra magazines in pouches on his back. He put on a black windbreaker that had at least fifteen pockets and a rain hood in the collar. It was a size larger than he needed, but the added room was useful for concealing gear. The bottom of the jacket fell a good three inches lower than the holster that held the .45. He pulled out a toothbrush and brushed his teeth, then washed his face. He needed a shave—his five-o'clock shadow usually presented itself by lunch—but that would have to wait. His black hair still held its shape, thanks in part to the short cut and to the paste keeping it in place hours after it had been applied. Hawkins didn't think of himself as vain, but he had always prided himself on being neat. Ladies seemed to make a big deal of how good-looking he was, but it always made him uncomfortable. He was never quite sure how to take compliments on his appearance, so he generally dismissed the praise. He thought of all the playful arguments he'd had with Anna over a certain male celebrity who she thought was "hot", and Hawkins thought just looked like he needed a bath and a shave. She would then point out that guy was a movie star and Hawk wasn't, but the actor didn't have her, either. Hawkins had felt he definitely got the better end of the deal.

Anna had often told him he was the most handsome man she had ever seen, his dark hair and blue eyes sweeping her away every time she looked at him. She had thought he was good looking, and it had been enough for him. She had steered his fashion sense somewhat, and it hadn't changed all that much since...suddenly he felt guilt over how he was feeling toward the beautiful CIA case officer. He knew it was foolish, and he knew

Anna would scold him for it, but he felt it nonetheless. He hung his shirt, suit and tie on a hanger, dropped his dress shoes into the bag, and walked back out.

Land gathered her own things and put them in order in the main cabin, and she looked up as he approached. "Now you look like a field operative," she said. "Nice shoes."

"Thanks. Great minds think alike."

Land smiled, and Hawkins was pleased. "Of course. I trust you know United States agents operating in a foreign country are not permitted to carry unauthorized weapons."

"So I've heard," he replied. "I'll take my chances, though. I'd rather have something other than my fingernail clippers to throw at someone if they start shooting at me."

"Fingernail clippers are unauthorized weapons, too."

"They can have my clippers when they pry them from my cold, clean, neatly manicured hands."

"What do you know?" Land said as she placed her own firearm in a holster on her hip. "Great minds *do* think alike."

The Gulfstream jet touched down at the Nice International Airport with a chirp of its tires on the tarmac. Hawkins and Land gathered their bags and stepped out into the cool French night.

"So how do we get to Monaco from here?" Hawkins asked. As if on cue, a black Mercedes E-class sedan hummed into view and pulled up in front of them. A man who looked to be about Hawkins' age emerged from the driver's seat.

"Good evening, *mademoiselle, monsieur*. The car is yours. Be safe." A Range Rover pulled up alongside, and the man climbed into the back of the dark gray sport utility. Without another word, he closed the door and the Range Rover sped off into the night.

"Forget I asked."

"I'll drive," Land said as she tossed her bags into the trunk and entered the driver's side. Hawkins followed suit, taking his place in the passenger seat. Hawkins was tempted to ask if he

could drive, but decided it best if he remained the passenger—
not only because he had no idea where they were going, but also
because he wanted to see how well this CIA Case Officer could
drive. Land clicked the gear selector into "D+", and the car
purred away, aiming towards the road to Monte Carlo.

Ra's al Xuffash sat on the terrace of his Monte Carlo home
sipping a glass of burgundy wine and thumbing through a French
language edition of *USA Today*. He rarely had the opportunity to
read a newspaper anymore. After all, they were out of date by
the time they went on sale. Instead, he relied on the Internet for
information on the world around him. A busy man, he preferred
to have the most-up-to-the-minute information he could gather.
Occasionally, however, he still liked the feel of newsprint on his
fingers as he sipped on a fine French wine. The Americans were
still pouting over France's belligerence in recent military
conflicts, and although French leaders had bent over backwards
trying to ingratiate themselves to the obnoxious Americans,
French wine still wasn't back to enjoying the export levels it had
previously. This all suited Ra's al Xuffash just fine—it meant
there was more for him to drink.

The TV played in the background, tuned to one of the
international cable news channels. He had the volume subdued
so as not to disturb his leisurely reading. His wife and daughter
were inside the house asleep and leaving him alone, which also
suited him. Xuffash had no real use for either of them, or any
woman for that matter. The daughter wanted nothing more than
to spend all her money on clothing and finery. He could not
imagine how clothes with so little cloth could be so expensive.
He had told her she looked like a whore, but it only seemed to
inspire her to further insolence. His wife was no better, always
defending the daughter's behavior and railing at him for lavishing
gifts upon Ali. The one good thing his wife had done was give
him a son. Yes, Ali had turned into a fine boy, one that made his

father proud. He was getting a good education in the United States, and would use the very education he was getting against the imperialist Zion-lovers who instructed him. Xuffash smiled at the sweet irony. His own wealth, generated by the shipping company he had built from the ground up, would surely be overshadowed by the success of his son.

Xuffash snapped from his reverie at the mention of his son's name. At first, he thought his wife had invoked their—*his*—son's name, but then he realized it came from the direction of the TV. On the screen next to the female news anchor a picture of his son appeared, seemingly taken from a student ID. He started to reach for the remote to increase the volume when he heard a crash from inside the house. He turned to look inside and saw nothing out of the ordinary. *Probably my wife breaking something valuable with her clumsiness*, he thought. *Can't she even figure out how to turn a lamp on?* Unable to find the remote, he leaned closer to the television, only to hear a female voice scream briefly. This time, he stepped away from the TV and started into the house, still turning back to look at the TV to try and discern what was being said. He grew angry these two females he was forced to contend with were once again pulling him away from something important, something having to do with his precious son. As he approached the staircase leading to the home's first level, a figure dressed in black from head to toe stepped into view. Xuffash paused, his brain trying to assimilate what was happening. Suddenly he saw what he thought to be a flame from a cigarette lighter and felt three stinging blows to his chest, as though someone had jabbed him hard with a hot poker. He looked down to see three holes in his upper chest, from which deep red blood was beginning to pour. He looked up in time to see another flash, and this time the invisible poker struck him in the forehead, throwing his head back so the last thing he saw was a brief glimpse of his own reflection in the skylight above him, a red dot on his forehead. *How did that get there?* was the last thing he thought before he fell into eternity.

. . .

Nearly half a world away, E. J. Niels sat at his desk. He had worked well into the evening, but he didn't mind. This never seemed like work to him, more like a game, a puzzle to be solved. He still couldn't believe he got paid to do this. He had already solved one puzzle—the man in the video claiming responsibility for the Jacksonville bombing was not Middle Eastern, but turned out to be Northern European, possibly from the British Isles. Niels had forwarded the info directly to DNI Price, as he had been ordered to do, then dove into his next task.

Land had asked him to pull satellite images of Xuffash's home and surrounding areas to enable them to get a better sense of the area. Niels had put in to task an IntelSat to the area, and within a few minutes the affirmative order had come down from DNI himself: Price had made it plain that any resources needed by Land were to be allocated. There would be other Case Officers working other aspects of this case under D/CIA Sullivan, but Land answered directly to DNI Price and had been given a long chain on this mission. Many knew Price seemed to show great favor to the lovely young Case Officer, but no one really complained. Those who knew Price had seen him take special interest in many Officers over the years, always those with talent and promise, and nearly all of them had gone on to spectacular careers in the Intelligence Community and beyond. Land wouldn't advance because of Price's favor alone, any more than had the others: she had more than proven her mettle as a field operative.

Images opened across Niels' monitors. One window displayed high-resolution real-time images, another a text block indicating the past hour's worth of imagery was being down-loaded into OILSTOCK, a high-resolution interactive geographic-based software system that could store, track, and display near real-time and historical SIG-INT related data over a map background. It took a little time to receive due to the super-high resolution, even with the huge amounts of bandwidth available to him, as huge amounts of digital information poured through space to land-based receivers through fiber-optic cable into the lines feeding into the CIA's secure network. Niels surveyed the live feed and saw a quiet scene. It was after 2:00 a.m. in Monaco, and the house and surrounding area had become quiet. He noticed a few lights remained on at the home and saw what must have been Xuffash sitting on his deck reading a paper. With a few clicks Niels was able to read the by-lines on the French-language *USA TODAY* in Xuffash's hand. He also noticed the man needed to clean his fingernails badly. Niels looked at his own nails self-consciously and turned to fetch a paper clip. He bent one end of it outward, and began cleaning the black gunk out from under his own nails when he noticed Xuffash had moved. He tapped on his keyboard and the image suddenly leapt back to a view that seemed to come from about 50 feet overhead. Xuffash had gone inside and seemed to be going to bed— the lights winked off in the room adjoining the patio. He switched to infra-red to get a better picture of where Xuffash and other occupants of the house might be, when he caught a glimpse of a hot glow on the street just down from where Xuffash's patio overlooked. The hood glowed orange and yellow, meaning the car had been running recently. He expanded the feed again, and saw something that drew an expletive from his lips unbidden: a body lying on the floor in the room Xuffash had just entered, rapidly fading from red to orange to yellow, with a spray of orange around the body glowing against the cool blue floor. He scanned the immediate area, but saw only the cooling glow of the room lights. There was no trace of anyone else nearby, so he made a few adjustments, and the image faded to show the first floor, where two other bodies lay in similar fashion in separate bedrooms. These bodies were fading into the blue spectrum several steps ahead of the body upstairs. He still could find no sign of the intruder who had shot Xuffash and the other occupants of the house, which meant the gunman/gunmen knew they were likely being watched from above, and had equipped themselves with insulated body-gloves which would render them invisible to IR scans. Niels spun and grabbed the phone on the adjoining "L" of his desk.

"Call the DNI, and get me Case Officer Land now!"

CHAPTER FOURTEEN

Everything looks the same in the dark, Hawkins thought. *Even the French Riviera.* The road they curved on was a nondescript highway that looked much like any other divided four-lane he had been on. Land steered the car onto an exit, and soon he saw the dark torn asunder by light. Monaco shone like a garish jewel, even at this hour. People walked the streets as if it were mid-afternoon, police officers mixed in at regular intervals.

They turned onto the street leading to Xuffash's residence, a grand avenue housing some of the wealthiest people in Europe. Large homes were built with no expense spared by people whose only financial concerns involved how much more their neighbor had spent and what it would take to one-up them. Monaco had no income tax, and so the wealthy had even more to lavish on their extravagant dwellings. Many of these massive structures sat empty—Land had checked on ownership of nearby properties and found over half of them were vacation homes, not used more than two or three months out of the year. Such "residences" often allowed individuals to claim citizenship in Monaco, thereby allowing them to pay no income taxes whatsoever.

As Land turned the ignition off, her cell phone quietly vibrated in her pocket. She reached in, pulled it out, and activated it. Before she could say a word, a harried voice came through.

"Sam, don't go in that house!"

"What? E. J., what are you...?"

"Listen to me. I've been monitoring the imagery on OILSTOCK and we've got a problem at your location. It looks like somebody just whacked Xuffash and whoever else was in the house."

"*What?* Who? Is the shooter still inside?"

"Don't know. I can't get a clear image of the shooter. They must be suited up in some insulated gear, and atmospheric conditions are making other amplifications a no-go."

"Any sign of their POE?"

"Point of entry is negative. No indication of entrance or exit. They could still be in there, Sam. This just happened less than 2 minutes ago."

"And you're just now getting to me?"

"Took a second for Operations to lock onto your Sat phone signal."

"All right, E. J. Where's our backup?"

"About half an hour out. They were tied up in Marseilles..."

"That won't do us any good," Land spat with disgust. "Watch our backs, E. J."

"You're not going in..."

"We are, and I'm switching to earpieces. Bring Hawkins' online, also."

"Sam, shouldn't you..."

"Just do it!" Land whisper-shouted as she placed a small clear ring around her right ear, a small tube extending slightly into her ear canal. She handed an identical device to Hawkins. "Put this in your ear. We'll be hooked together with our eye in the sky back home."

"Somebody already got to Xuffash?"

Land nodded as she drew her firearm, a Sig Sauer P226 9mm pistol, and pulled back on the slide. A bullet ratcheted into the firing chamber, and fourteen other bullets moved upward in the magazine like angry hornets waiting to fly. "Dead, along with his wife and daughter. Shooter's using a thermal bodysuit, which can't be detected by our IR, and long-range night vision is out. We're going to have to be very careful."

"Right," Hawkins said, chambering a round in his own .45. "I'm assuming your friend E. J. was going to tell you we should wait for backup."

Land turned in her seat to look at Hawkins in the eyes. "I know FBI agents prefer to use overwhelming force when dealing with suspects, but we don't have that option right now. A gunman just popped our main lead in this case, which tells me the shooter is tied in at a high level. We need to get him, alive if possible, and that means we have to go in. I've gone in on many occasions without backup and done just fine." She smiled at him. "Besides, I've got you backing me up."

"Nice. Let's hope we're not walking into a trap here. We don't even know how many shooters are inside."

"Be a little flexible, Hawk," Land said. "You're in the foreign field now. It's different."

"This whole case is turning out to be different." Hawkins took a deep breath. "Alright. Let's hit it."

The Federal Agent and Case Officer disembarked from the black sedan two houses down from their target, a distance of about 500 feet. Although large stucco walls fronted each of the large homes in the area, the driveways were open and available for all to enter. Hawkins thought to himself the people in these homes assumed they were safe, and they weren't uninformed in thinking so—Monaco had the highest per capita of police officers in the world, with nearly 700 uniformed officers covering not much more than a square mile. Not one was in sight, however, and he wondered if that was an accident.

Land took the lead, crouching at the entrance to the gated driveway. Hawkins pointed to a car parked across the street.

"BMW M3. That'd make a good getaway car." He automatically looked at the car's license plate and memorized it, just in case.

"It may be what it is," Niels said in his ear. "The hood's giving off an IR glow. It couldn't have been shut off for very long, but there's been no motion in or around the car since the shooting. I'm reviewing images from the last hour to see if it..."

"Worry about that when we need to, E. J.," Land whispered. "You ready, Hawk?"

"Let's do it."

Land eased her head around the corner, looking for a hint of anything that might erupt into a hail of gunfire. Seeing nothing, she crouch-sprinted to the garage area no more than 20 feet from the entrance. The house loomed above her, a graceful sidewalk curving away from her up towards the front door. Hawkins followed suit and came up beside her.

Land pointed up the sidewalk to the ornately carved mahogany door, and shook her head. *Don't want to go that way. No cover.*

Hawkins nodded, and pointed around to the side of the garage. He eased his way around the corner, and saw a door which led into the garage. He gingerly touched the doorknob, and the door moved—unlatched. Whoever had come through here hadn't closed the door all the way.

"You don't have one of those fiber optic cable cameras on you by any chance?" Hawkins whispered.

"Left it in London."

"We'll swing by and pick it up later." He touched the bottom of the door with his foot, and edged it open, careful to remain behind the block wall surrounding the doorway. When bullets failed to come sailing through the opening, he crouched down and peeked inside. He was able to make out a Porsche Cayenne Sport Utility and a BMW 750i in the darkened garage, lit only by a small LED light glowing over a workbench near another door. He stepped inside, and Land came in behind him. She worked her way along the wall toward the closed garage doors, gun at a low ready, Hawkins walking slowly along the front wall. They reached the opposite wall from where they had come in at the same time, and approached the door. Hawkins had to turn the knob to open this one, and he did so slowly and deliberately. The door whispered open—thank heavens for good hinges—and the two stepped into the semi-dark hallway.

They were able to see three doors on the right length of polished mahogany wall, and two on the left, with a staircase at the hall's far end that went up a few steps and then curved in an upward spiral to the left. Hawkins and Land edged along opposite walls, 10 feet apart but exactly across from one another, looking into the rooms on the opposing side. They took turns crouching and peeking into the rooms on their own side—a study, an entertainment room, a full bath—then they came to the bedrooms. Hawkins looked inside and saw a room lit by a bedside table lamp. A book lay on the floor next to the bed, and a figure lay motionless next to it. A woman lay in a pool of blood on the floor, her peaceful face in stark contrast to the horrible scene of death. Hawkins counted 3 bullet wounds to her chest, centered in the sternum. He turned to go back into the hall, when Land's voice came through his earpiece. "I'm coming in behind you." She walked in and looked around, seeing what Hawkins had.

"I've got one, too. Young girl, maybe 16 or 17. Blunt trauma to the head, three bullets in the chest. Looks like her top was ripped open first."

"We interrupted him," he whispered, and wondered what kind of sick monster they were dealing with. He looked past Land at the open doorway behind her. "Our shooter is still here."

Land nodded, and immediately crouched into a tactical squat, ready to move in any direction at a moment's notice, her gun at the ready. Hawkins noted the ease with which she operated in potential combat situations. He felt the tightness in his chest he always did when dealing with armed confrontation, in spite of his rigorous training, but Land looked as relaxed as if she were sneaking through the house playing hide and seek with a toddler. He could only hope that he looked more professional than he felt. He closed his eyes for a moment, giving them a moment to adjust to the dim light in the hallway, peeked around the edge of the doorframe, and moved gingerly into the hallway. The spiral staircase loomed in front of him, Land moving once again on the opposite side of the hall and slightly behind.

"Those stairs are a deathtrap. E. J., do you see anything at all?" Hawkins breathed.

"The two of you," the voice in Hawkins' ear replied. "I'm working on rescaling the imaging program so I can pick up condensation points in the house."

Hawkins understood immediately. "The shooter's breath. Can you do that?"

"If this guy fogs a mirror, I should be able to find him," Niels said.

"Unless he's using a rebreather," Land interjected.

"Got him! He's..."

Niels continued talking but neither Land nor Hawkins paid him any heed, as bullets sprayed from the top of the spiral stairs, the only sound being of metal slugs tearing into the wood-paneled walls around them. Hawkins and Land both fired in the direction they thought the fire was coming from and sprinted back into the bedroom doorways they had just recently emerged from.

"I said he's at the top of the stairs!" Niels shouted through their earpieces.

"We've definitely got to work on your timing, E. J.," Hawkins whispered, then looked at Land. "Full auto with a suppressor."

"MP-5SD, probably. Sub-sonic rounds." Hawkins realized she wasn't talking to him, but rather verbally categorizing her opponent's weapon. "Good choice," Land said. "At least we know we rank wasting bullets on full auto."

"He's not going for accuracy. He just wants us to keep our head down. You keep shooting."

"What are you going to do?"

"Catch him when he tries to slip out the front." Hawkins crouch-ran back down the hall towards the garage, using the sounds of Land's gunfire—deafening in the confined quarters of the house—to cover him bursting through the door into the garage. He was glad to get outside into a larger area. People were always firing guns at each other indoors in the movies and TV, and acted like it was no big deal. Like many other things, entertainment had little to do with reality. He had only fired four shots from his powerful .45, with Land firing five from her smaller but potent 9mm, but his ears rang and his temples ached. He burst through the side door into the cool evening air.

"Hawkins! He's heading out the front door, and he's fast," Niels reported, catching the blur of motion from the non-radiant IR shadow.

"Are we sure he's the only shooter?" Land said.

"Yeah, he's the only other one breathing besides the two of you. You guys keep it that way, okay?"

"Workin' on it," Hawkins growled through gritted teeth, and spun around the corner. He saw a black-clad figure sprinting across the lawn. The figure saw him at the same time, and sprayed 9mm slugs towards Hawkins at a rate of 900 rounds per minute. The MP-5 held 32 rounds, and could discharge the entire magazine in just over 2 seconds of continuous fire. While nowhere near accurate at that rate of fire, is was more than enough to keep a target's head down. Hawkins' dove for the ground toward the shooter, however, and returned fire of his own. While the MP-5 was nearly silent, Hawkins' big .45 boomed as it spat fire and hollow-point slugs at the assassin. This obviously threw the figure off, causing him/her to misstep in preparation for jumping the short wall in front of the house. The shooter hit the edifice with a grunt, them clambered over. Hawkins ejected the empty magazine and stuffed it in his pocket, then slapped a new one in place. He heard Niels say something about the shooter heading for the parked car across the street. Hawkins rounded the driveway opening in time to hear the M3 he had seen earlier start, and a door close. He fired several shots into the back window as the tires howled, desperately trying to gain traction as full throttle was applied. The driver banged it off the rev limiter as the car rolled forward through a haze of burnt rubber, hit second gear and took off. Land ran past him towards their own waiting sedan, firing as she did. Hawkins ran to catch up. He had just gotten inside the car when Land gunned it, throwing him back in his seat and slamming his door shut. The Mercedes roared as its V-8 sent power to the rear wheels. The car hesitated for a moment as the traction-control system asserted itself, then accelerated hard as the wide Michelin tires found grip.

"We're really going to have to push this thing to keep up," Hawkins said. "That M3's got us by about a bunch of horsepower and probably 500 pounds less weight."

"You're not saying I'm fat, are you?" Land quipped as she threw the black sedan around a corner. Hawkins could feel the Mercedes' seat bolsters inflating in an effort to keep him in place.

"Not a chance," Hawkins replied, placing both hands on the dash in an effort to steady himself. He suddenly remembered what a lousy passenger he made. He would have preferred to be behind the wheel. It wasn't that he didn't approve of Land's driving—quite the opposite, the woman could *drive*—but he just preferred to be behind the wheel, especially under the conditions in which he now found himself. Sooner than he would have expected, Land had closed the gap and they were gaining on the speeding BMW.

"There's someone else in the car with our shooter," Hawkins said. "The car started before he got in."

Land pitched the big Mercedes through a turn, tires squealing their displeasure at holding the road surface at their current velocity. "It almost certainly has remote start." "He could be alone," and as if in response, gunfire erupted from the passenger side window. The staccato chatter of semi-automatic gunfire combined with the roar of engines echoing off the buildings blurring past. "Or not."

"I don't think he has arms that long," Hawkins said. "Different gun, too, AR-15, I think. No silencer." He stuck his arm out the window and returned fire, shattering the passenger side mirror on the BMW and forcing the second gunman to momentarily cease fire. The M3 swerved onto a street littered with stragglers who had closed the casino down. The people looked at them as they roared past as if they were watching a movie being filmed. *No stunt doubles here,* Hawkins thought. They looped past a large hotel with a fountain in the courtyard, and shot onto a more secluded thoroughfare that whisked them out of the Principality of Monaco and into France.

"Get close to the back bumper and PIT them," Hawkins said, referring to the maneuver used by police to tap the rear bumper of a fleeing suspect's vehicle and send it into a spin. Land attempted to get the nose of the Mercedes just past the rear of the BMW, but the other driver recognized what she was attempting and swerved to the right and accelerated.

"That thing *is* fast," Land said. "Hold on!" she shouted, and hit the brakes. Hawkins had seen it at the same time: the passenger had gotten into the back seat to get a better firing position, and opened up. Hawkins and Land both ducked down behind the dashboard as bullets peppered the windshield, hood, and grill of the Mercedes. Before Hawkins could recover, Land threw the shift lever into reverse, nailed the gas, and flung the Mercedes backwards just as a giant fiery hand lifted the front of the car like a child's plaything. He knew what had caused the explosion: a round from an M-203 grenade launcher, mounted under the AR-15, had been fired at them. *Well-equipped hitmen* was Hawkins' last thought before white airbags turned to darkness that clouded in around his vision.

CHAPTER FIFTEEN

I must be alive, because my head wouldn't hurt in heaven, Hawkins thought. He assumed the throbbing pain was a good sign he remained among the living on the earth, but he wasn't sure that was the best thing right now. He gingerly opened his eyes and saw tiled ceilings and dim recessed lights of what could only be a hospital room. Without looking any further down, he did a self-check: he wiggled his fingers, his toes, rotated his hands and feet, then moved his legs and arms. No major pain, and everything seemed to be there. He felt his chest, and there were no tubes protruding from him, no neck brace. He felt his forehead, and grimaced in pain. *Oh, yeah! That's where it hurts.* He looked down and saw he lay under the standard linen sheet and knit blanket he had seen in every hospital he had ever been in, and likewise recognized the snap-on gown he wore. He heard the door to his room open, and Hawkins tensed as two men walked in. He realized he might not be in a friendly place, and his mind cleared. He reached his left hand onto the side of the bed and found the hard metal bedpan hanging there. He was thankful they didn't use the lightweight, inexpensive plastic ones most stateside hospitals had gone to—those didn't leave as big of a dent in someone's head if it had to be used as a weapon. If he had to, he'd clock one with the bedpan to stun him, then use him as a shield until he could reach the other. One was obviously a doctor, in his white coat and stethoscope hanging from his neck, while the other wore a suit and tie. The more he looked at the suit, the more his confidence rose the man was some kind of government rep.

"How's that head, Agent Hawkins?" the doctor asked. Hawkins saw the man's white coat had "Dr. Robert Grove, M.D." embroidered above the left breast. Grove appeared to be a few years older than Hawkins, of medium height and weight, with glasses and short, spiky hair that was already graying at the edges. Hawkins was somewhat relieved the doctor spoke English, and seemed to know who he was. The man in the suit smiled a friendly enough smile, but Hawkins kept his hand on the bedpan.

"It's still there," Hawkins replied.

"Good," the physician chuckled, "because you're going to need it a little longer. I'm Dr. Grove. I checked you and Case Officer Land out when you were brought in last night. It's fortunate both of you weren't hurt much worse than a bump on the noggin."

The other man finally spoke up. "Agent Hawkins, I'm Richard Cone, Special U. S. Liaison Officer in southern France." Hawkins knew a SUSLO was an NSA foreign field officer, but this man looked as though he could have been a medical equipment salesman. Cone wore a dark suit with a white shirt and red striped tie, his black wingtips gleaming despite the low light in the room. Cone looked to be in his mid-fifties and wore half-rimmed metal glasses. His girth, while far from considerable, seemed to indicate he spent more time seated behind a desk in recent days than running ops in the field. Nonetheless, Hawkins had no doubt this Cone was still more than capable of taking care of himself.

"How's Sam—Case Officer Land?"

"She's fine," Cone answered. "Dr. Grove here says the two of you have a few bruises, but nothing major. You actually were banged up worse than Case Officer Land."

"So where is she?"

"She was here in your room until just before we came in. She went to get a cup of coffee and call in to Langley. She said not to let you go anywhere until she got back."

"Okay, so where am I?"

"This is a small medical facility we operate in Marseilles under the cover of being an urgent care and trauma center. We are open to the public, but we obviously have other reasons for being here."

"Handy," Hawkins said. "So am I cleared to get back in the game?"

The doctor shone a light into Hawkins' eyes, squeezed the bridge of his nose, and felt the base of his neck. "Looks good to me," the doctor replied. "Just take it a little easy for the next couple of days. No car wrecks or blows to the head."

"I'll do my best."

"You don't have a concussion, but you still need to go light for the next two or three days. If you need something for pain, take these," and he handed Hawkins a bottle with "Stout" written on it in red ink. "Just don't operate heavy machinery or firearms after taking them."

"I'd better stick with Advil then."

"Right," Grove chuckled. "Well, I hope I don't see you again very soon," and he walked out of the room.

"Your gear is in the closet over there, Agent Hawkins," Cone said. "If you want to get cleaned up, the bathroom is behind that door in the corner. I'll have a briefing ready for you and Case Officer Land shortly. And by the way," he added, "you can let go of the bedpan now. I don't think you'll be needing it." He stepped into the hallway and closed the door behind him.

.   .   .

"You cut that awfully close, didn't you?"

The man could hear the irritation in his employer's controlled voice, even through the phone. "Unfortunately, there wasn't much choice in the matter," he explained. "The FBI had taken Xuffash's son into custody, and they had obviously discovered the connection. Had I not been there at that time, the senior Xuffash would now be in United States custody. My assistant and I were more than able to deal with the situation."

"All you have done is succeed in drawing undue attention to yourself too early in the game," the voice on the other end of the line said. "We have only just begun, and it would be easy for this whole thing to be disrupted. We must be cautious."

"And we are, sir," the man replied in as soothing a tone as possible. "I am prepared to initiate phase two to further distract the Americans, as well as further tying up our loose ends. The incident in Monaco will soon be placed at the rear of their concerns."

There was a moment of silence as the employer considered this. "We can't afford to be reckless, and what you did in Monaco bordered on just that. I don't want to lose my best operative, particularly when we have much yet to accomplish."

"I understand, sir, but you needn't worry. I plan on being more—circumspect in the future."

"Keep me posted," the employer said, and the line went silent.

The man leaned back in the chair in his office. He reached into the lower left desk drawer and removed a flask containing a potent vodka. He felt his nasal passages clear and his throat burn as he swallowed the clear liquid. Yes, it had been a close call last night, but he had accomplished his task, as always. He had escaped the American agents, although the one had certainly gotten his attention with several well-placed shots from what sounded like a .45. He had escaped them both, however, his accomplice doing quite a number on their car. The driver had done a good job of job of avoiding the full brunt of the high explosive grenade's blast, but the car had to have been armored to be as relatively undamaged as it was. The particular shell that struck the pursuing sedan should have blown it to bits instead of rendering it merely undriveable. This confirmed for him the involvement of CIA— in the State Department cover they often used, the Agency had access to Diplomatic Security Service armored sedans and SUVs on the Continent for use in their operations. Besides, they were doubtless looking in on him with some of their surveillance satellites. He wondered if the thermal regulated bodysuits had accomplished their task of hiding him from infra-red scans. As much as it had cost him to procure them, he certainly hoped so. Well, it wasn't entirely true he was concerned about cost, as it was his employer who had the deep pockets paying for all of the operational equipment required. Nonetheless, he did hope the suit served its purpose, as it would undoubtedly be needed later.

He replaced the flask in the drawer and activated the secure email program. He then typed the message containing the go-code for the operatives waiting to carry out phase two, as well as a confirmation for dealing with some loose ends. *This will give them something else to think about.*

Ali al' Xuffash lay in his hospital bed under constant guard. His head ached from where the big FBI agent had struck him, and the room periodically swam around him. Ali could close his eyes for a moment, take a few deep breaths, and the waves of nausea seemed to pass for a time. His hate gave him the greatest clarity and comfort, however. Oh, how he hated these smug Americans. He was captured now, but his father would soon have him free, of that he was certain. Then he would recover, regroup, and he would be able to continue the fight against the infidels.

He was no longer sure he could trust his two partners in the destruction of the parking garage, however. They were *soft*, and had feared capture. He had only been holding a video game controller in his chair that night, but if the FBI hadn't come crashing in when they did, they would have found two dead bodies a short time later. The two had been his friends for a couple of years, but if they couldn't rise to the call, then they were a liability, encumbrances which needed to be cut away before they hindered him.

His father had made it very plain to him their mission would not be easy, but their reward would be great. He smiled at the thought of pleasing his beloved father, but the smile caused his head to throb once more. He was just about to call for a nurse to give him more medication for the pain—at least the American infidels would permit him that—when the door creaked open and a tall woman wearing surgical scrubs walked in, the light from the outer hall stabbing into the darkened room. Her silhouette was different from most of the other nurses who had been caring for him. This one had the look of a supermodel, tall and curvy, even in her scrubs. *It was a good looking woman indeed*, he thought, *who could be attractive in scrubs*. Shutting the door behind her, the room fell into near darkness again.

"How are you feeling?" she asked, her voice breathy and suggestive. Much friendlier than my other nurses, too, he thought. She must not know who I am. Or perhaps she does, and she is sympathetic. He had heard of women who were attracted to serial killers, writing them love letters while they rotted away in their prison cells. Perhaps he was about to get lucky.

"My head is killing me."

She touched his head gingerly, almost provocatively. "I have something for your head," she said, her French-accented voice soft and soothing. "This will make the pain go away." She took a needle from her pocket and injected the contents into the port on the IV running to his arm. He thought of saying something to her about how attractive she was, but decided to wait until she had injected the meds. He wanted to make sure she didn't with-hold pain medication in case she was offended by his overture. He felt the coolness of the liquid as it went into the vein, and then just as suddenly it turned to fire. He started to scream in pain, but the nurse stuffed a washcloth in his mouth and pinched his nose. Fire was coursing throughout his body now, and if his arms and legs had not been strapped to the bed he would have clawed his flesh away in an attempt to remove the source of his agony. His eyes bulged as he struggled for breath that would not come. Capillaries in his eyes ruptured and burst, and it felt as though his insides were being melted away by an unseen inferno.

"You have failed in your mission," the woman whispered as she leaned in close to his face. "You deserve nothing less than the fate of the infidels." Through the agony, the young Xuffash's mind raced. *No! I have not failed! I was just beginning!* He felt sharp pains in his chest, as though someone were ramming flaming metal spikes through his torso. He was dying, ripped to shreds on the inside by something he could not see, something he could do nothing about. All he could do was die in horrible agony, with no one to help him.

The pain was so bad coherent mental processing became swiftly impossible, and the final thought he was able to piece together before his mind was reduced to broken shards was: *Is this what my victims felt?*

"I'm just glad you two are alright," Director of National Intelligence Jack Price said over the secure line. "And Bob Shear would never forgive me if we let one of his favorites get killed."

"I'm thankful for quality armored Mercedes," Samantha Land replied. "Considering the hit we took, the car held up surprisingly well. It wasn't a direct hit, fortunately, which is no doubt a factor. The Merc won't be going anywhere anytime soon, though."

"You ought to have other transportation there by the time

the two of you are released," he said. "We have our people scouring the house, and the Monaco police have graciously agreed to stay out of the way for the moment. SecState made a call to his Highness the Prince and was assured of nothing but cooperation."

"Something a little quicker would be nice if we have to chase M-series BMWs."

DNI chuckled on the other end of the line. "I'll see what we've got available. The SUSLO out of the local U. S. consulate —Richard Cone, whom you've already met— will take care of your local arrangements. Niels is running the video from the satellite as well as ATM and security cameras along your chase route to see if he can get a clear shot of the car's tag or occupants. Monaco is covered with security cams, so hopefully they'll turn up something. NSA is collating data on Xuffash's communications for the last couple of days to see what numbers and emails show up, so we should have some actionable intel shortly."

"Yes, sir. We'll be ready to go when we need to."

"You be careful, Sam," Price said, his voice taking on a fatherly tone. "I don't relish the idea of losing you, either."

"Thank you, sir. I'll do my best to make sure you don't." Land replaced the phone on the receiver and stood from the nurse's station desk where she had been seated. She walked around the counter and walked back down to the room where Hawkins had been sleeping. It was a contest which part of her body hurt the worst—her head, struck by the inflating front and side airbags, or her chest, where the seatbelt had asserted its protective restraint against her shoulder and sternum. The pain she felt was minimal considering what could have been, she thought. The Mercedes they had been driving was prepped for special service use by the DSS—usually reserved for high-level government officials traveling abroad. The car had underbody protection comprised of a super-strong lightweight reactive armor that was revolutionizing military armor applications. Reactive armor, in essence, exploded back at an explosive shell, driving the majority of the blast away from the intended target and towards the source of the explosion itself. The resultant reactive detonation wave served to nullify much of the damaging effects of the explosion upon the intended target. A heavy-duty composite was used in other areas of the vehicle—hood, doors, roof, trunk, fenders—and although not as sophisticated as the reactive armor, it was still of sufficient thickness to make a grenade attack survivable. The clear composite that replaced the conventional windows was enough to stop a Remington 700 round or two, although such a hit would weaken the material enough that a third shot would likely penetrate. The tires were filled with a self-sealing gel which enabled full protection from bullets, but there were ways around that, too. It wasn't ideal, but the real world didn't afford the kind of invincibility James Bond's fictional world did. Still, the idea was the shooter would only get one shot at that window. It wasn't equal to the pinnacle of four-wheeled protection designated Cadillac One, POTUS' motorcade vehicle lovingly referred to as "The Beast", but neither was anything else on four wheels. The Mercedes Land and Hawkins had been driving was as attack proof as one could make a road-going civilian type vehicle, but far from invincible as Hawkins and Land could attest to.

She walked into Hawkins' room and heard the water running in the bathroom. She walked over and sat in the chair next to the empty bed and pulled the tablet from her satchel. She tapped at the screen and activated the secure satellite uplink, allowing the CIA operative to check her email. The latest updates from various IC sources were waiting, including special updates on information relating to the Jacksonville bombing. She opened the email update from Jane's Information Group, an open-source intelligence powerhouse with over a century's experience. She found Jane's was accurate up until the last few hours, including a statement indicating there were possible connections to European groups and/or individuals. She shook her head in amazement: the access the Jane's group had to intel sources was frequently excellent, often amazing, and occasionally shocking. Several of their publications—Jane's Fighting Ships, Jane's Aircraft of the World, as well as several others detailing every known weapons system in use or development around the world —were considered standard equipment on nearly every U.S. warship, intel office, and resource room. Jane's was excellent at walking the line between revealing too much and being relevant for research. While strictly dealing in non-classified information, Jane's services nonetheless made-up-to-the-minute information accessible. Land finished reading the article, then closed the program and switched off the tablet. As she placed the device back into her briefcase, the bathroom door opened and Hawkins stepped out. He had scruff on his face had been shaved away, and his hair was neatly swept forward and spiked slightly in front. He was wearing blue jeans and a white compression t-shirt, but his feet were bare as he walked from the bathroom. Land noticed he was more muscular than she originally thought. He tossed a small toiletry bag into the nylon travel bag resting on the bed.

"You look better than you did a little while ago," Land said with a teasing smile.

Hawkins wanted to say *You look pretty good yourself*, but he stopped himself. Barely. Land had the front of her hair pulled up into a braid and pinned across the top of her forehead. She had just enough makeup to know it was there but also to be subtle, with heavier makeup around her eyes which made them all the more piercing. She wore a tank top which showed off the musculature in her shoulders and arms. She wasn't bulky, but she had the look of a gymnast—or a mixed martial arts fighter. "I wish I felt better than I did a little while ago," he replied. "Although I suppose I should be feeling worse. That was some armor that car had."

"We've been in cooperation with some research for Secret Service and DSS. They have seriously upgraded the Presidential motorcade over the years, using all sorts of ultra high-tech materials."

"Well, if we're going to be chasing any more M3s, I want to be in front of it, not behind it. Can you request something with a little more thrust than that E550? Maybe an M5?"

"I don't know if we have any of those sitting around the motor pool," Land replied. "We just blew up a $100,000 car, so they might not be so eager to give us another one."

"Your boss said he'd get you anything you need, right?" Hawkins asked with a wolfish grin. "Tell him you really need a faster car."

"Actually, I already did. I also specified it needs to be as well armored as the last one."

"Better to avoid the hit than take it," Hawkins said, placing his weapon into the holster on his belt. "Maybe we need a Lamborghini. You okay?"

"Bumped around a little, but nothing major. You gave me a good scare, though. I couldn't get you to wake up, and I had to drag you out of the car. One of our associates with a flatbed came and carried the car off, and we put you in a cargo van to bring you in. I was afraid you had internal head injuries."

"I may have, but who could tell?" Land smiled at him, and took a step closer.

"Just don't scare me like that again, all right?" she said, her voice not much above a whisper. Hawkins felt as though there were electricity arcing between the two of them. He hadn't felt like this in years, wasn't sure he could ever feel that way about a woman again, and yet, here they were. Both of them were almost breathless, drawing nearer to one another with each passing second. He closed his eyes, millimeters away from her lips.

And he froze.

"I'm sorry, Sam. I...I can't."

"Can't what?" she said, her frustration evident. "Can't kiss me? It's not that hard, is it?"

"It's not that, Sam". He tried to turn away, but Sam grabbed him by the arms and looked up into his eyes.

"Then what? What are you running from?"

"I'm not running from anything, I just..." Hawkins paused, never looking away from her. "I really don't want to talk about this right now, Sam."

"I'm not asking you to talk," she said, and pulled him into a kiss he had been waiting years for. He wasn't sure if it was from the car wreck, but he swore there were fireworks going off. He was caught up in her, the feel of her lips against his, the smell of her perfume. It was intoxicating. They kissed until they had to breathe.

"Now. That wasn't so bad, was it?" Sam asked.

"Didn't think it would be." He returned her smile. "Sam, I need to tell you about some things."

"Not now," she said. "You don't owe me any explanations."

"I think I do."

"Then you can tell me when you're ready, not when I've kissed it out of you." They both laughed.

The opening of the door to Hawkins' room interrupted their conversation. A woman dressed like a nurse stuck her head through the opening.

"Mr. Cone wanted to let you know he was holding off on the briefing until morning, as he was called away." She turned and closed the door behind her as she went back to her duties.

"Wonder where he went," Land said. "Well, at least we get a chance to catch our breath." She turned to look at Hawkins, and he noticed something deep in her eyes when she spoke. "I'm really sorry about what happened out there on the road. I could have killed us both..."

"Are you kidding?" Hawkins asked. "How could we have known they'd be packing a grenade launcher? We're not dead—not even badly hurt—so don't worry about it. We'll be more careful in the future. Besides," he added, "God isn't going to let us get blasted until he's done with us. I know you're a preacher's

kid, and I'm not preaching, but you know when it's your time..."
Hawkins paused for a moment, and it was Land's turn to see
something boiling in his eyes. "When it's your time, all the
armor in the world can't protect you." He shook his head almost
imperceptibly, and then went on. "Come on. Cone's holding off
our briefing until morning. Let's hit the commissary and get a
bite to eat."

Land nodded, and followed Hawkins out the door and down
the hall. She didn't know what that reaction was about, but she
intended to find out. Despite what she had been able to learn
about him from his government dossier, Hawkins' file was not
entirely open. No agent in his position—or hers, for that matter
—had files which were readily accessible. Most agents and officers had their personal information wiped from the Internet
entirely. The nature of their work assumed opponents would
attempt to hack into personnel files from the outside in an
attempt to gain leverage, and the only way to secure the data was
to isolate and compartmentalize each one. Any attempt to access
them remotely would result in tripped system alarms all over
Virginia, Maryland, and Washington. Rather than jump through
all those hoops, she decided it was easier to find out more in
person once she got to know him. What she knew was public
record: he had been a pastor and seminary student, and had been
recruited by an SAC into the Bureau. But there was no mention
of much beyond those details. He clearly had a great deal of
wealth, but he spoke only in passing about an inheritance.
Where did it come from? He was obviously remembering something when he hesitated before they kissed, and when he made
the statement about how nothing could protect a person when it
was their time to go, but what? Something had happened at
some point in Hawkins' life which had left deep marks upon
him, but when, and what? He had likely lost friends in the attack
on the Coalition of Christian Churches, but this seemed like an
older wound than that. It was as if he were trying to be something he wasn't and found it difficult keeping up the front. She

wanted to know what it was—not just because it could determine how he reacted in different situations, but because she was falling for this man she had nearly died with, and she knew he was feeling the same way. What makes a man leave the ministry and become a Special Agent with the FBI? Something was driving him, and she wanted to know what it was.

She just wasn't sure what it would take to find out.

CHAPTER SIXTEEN

"So, are the Braves goin' all the way this year?" Officer Jeff Hilton, Atlanta Police Department, asked his partner.

"I've got $100 bucks on the line they do," Officer Lisa Henderson replied. "I think they've got a good shot, if they make the plays they're capable of." The two officers were stationed outside of the Peach Tree Grand Hotel, where a semi-annual meeting of the Catholic-Jewish Alliance of Georgia had gathered. The unlikely group had been meeting for several years, and had been able to see past their differences to have a cultural and moral impact on their community. Because of the events several weeks prior in Jacksonville, several uniformed officers were placed around the immediate vicinity of the hotel. The meeting was nowhere near the size of the Coalition of Christian Churches—no more than 100 people were to be in attendance this evening—so half a dozen officers had seemed to be plenty. In addition, the group had hired several security guards to preside discreetly over the dinner and meeting. They had received no intel suggesting anything out of the ordinary, and they felt confident the situation was covered.

"How'd you do in the pool?" Hilton asked, lighting a cigarette.

"What, about how long Joey could stick with just one girl-friend? I was spot on—twelve days."

"So you're the one who got all my money," Hilton joked, taking a hit from the cigarette nestled between his fingers.

"Yours and a bunch of other saps. What were you guys think-ing? You knew Joey couldn't have just one girl at a time."

"Hope springs eternal," the man replied. "Just call me an optimist."

"I'll call you over to see the new monster TV I bought with my winnings," Henderson replied with a grin. Henderson was in her mid-twenties, a surfer girl from California who moved to Georgia while still in high school. Graduating from the Univer-sity of Georgia with a degree in Criminal Justice, she turned down a position with the Georgia Bureau of Investigation to be a street cop in Atlanta. The blonde-haired, well-tanned young woman had settled nicely into the role of police officer, much to her parents' chagrin. They had wanted her to be a lawyer, but her athletic, adventuresome nature could think of nothing worse than being trapped inside an office all day. Instead, she found great joy in putting her blond hair in a ponytail and fighting crime on the streets of Atlanta. Her partner, Jeff Hilton, was a 15-year veteran of the force. He stood a bit taller than her 5 foot five inch frame, but he didn't share her athleticism. Hilton had developed quite a bulge over his gun belt, and he could no longer blame it on the bulletproof vest he wore. Henderson bristled about being made to wear her vest because she didn't want to look "pudgy" like Hilton.

"You won't let me in." He took on a mocking tone. "'*No smoking in my house!*'"

"That's right," Henderson replied. "You need to quit smoking those things anyway. They're going to kill you."

"Yeah, yeah. I already have a mother, Henderson. Besides, you don't wear a vest half the time, and that could kill you."

"I'll bet you die from smoking before I die of a gunshot wound."

"Tempting wager," Hilton replied, blowing smoke at the younger woman. "But the way your luck's been running, my wife would be signing over my insurance policy to you."

Henderson laughed as a truck backfired somewhere nearby. It backfired again, several times in a row, as if someone had just pulled a couple of plug wires off the engine. She looked at Hilton as he threw his cigarette down and cursed. "That's coming from inside the hotel!" he shouted, and ran from where he stood at the curb into the lobby of the Peach Tree Grand Hotel. Henderson followed hot on his heels, drawing her firearm as she ran. Inside, they were greeted with pandemonium. People were screaming and stampeding out of the lobby and away from the hallway containing the banquet rooms where the Catholic-Jewish Alliance of Georgia was meeting. Hilton snatched the radio handset from his left shoulder and keyed the mike.

"Delta 321 to Central. We have shots fired, repeat, shots fired at our 10-20. Copy?"

"Central to Delta 321, we copy. We are dispatching additional units to your 20."

Shots rang out from down the hallway. "Tell them to hurry it up, or it's not going to do us any good!" he shouted. The gunfire died down, and there were no other people running at them from the banquet room down the corridor. He looked at Henderson. "We've got to know what's going on in there."

"How did the shooters get in?" she asked.

"Right now, that's the least of our worries." Moans echoed from the room, but no more shots were fired. "There were rent-a-cops in there. What happened to them?"

"Let's take a look," Henderson said, and moved closer to the banquet room. Hilton started to call her back, but he wanted to go in, too. He moved behind her as they "sliced the pie"—a term used to describe a method of angle-walking around a doorway as to get a maximum view through the opening with a minimum of exposure to fire from the other side. She shuddered at what she saw: bodies strewn across the room, lying on the floor, hunched over the dinner tables where they had been eating a fine dinner before death beckoned them. What she didn't see were any shooters. She turned back to Hilton, who nodded agreement. They gingerly eased their way into the room and saw the full extent of the carnage. There must have been at least 50 people shot, including wait staff and two security guards whose guns lay on the ground next to them. There were moans from the few who were still alive, but there were far too many who made no sound at all.

"Central, Delta 321. We need multiple paramedic teams here ASAP. We have at least 50 victims with GSWs", referring to the gunshot wounds. He wondered why he bothered using the acronym. Anyone listening in would know what GSWs were, and it didn't save much time in saying it. The truth was it was simple habit; the law enforcement community, like the military, loved their lingo.

"Delta 321, repeat. Did you say 50?"

"10-4, Central. 50."

Hilton heard a sound from the head table on the far side of the room, and he and Henderson simultaneously aimed their weapons at the source of the sound.

"Don't shoot!" a security guard shouted as he raised his hands above the table. "Please don't shoot me! I'm one of the security guards here. Did you get them?"

"Come out from around the table, sir, with your hands where we can see them," Henderson shouted.

"No problem," the guard replied, his arms extending over his head. His hair was disheveled, and he was white as a sheet, but he seemed to be unharmed. "Did you get the shooters?"

"Did they come this way?" Hilton asked. "What did they look like?"

"They were Middle Easterners," the guard replied. His name badge said "Peterson". "Four of them. They were dressed like caterers and wait-staff. They pulled automatic weapons out from under their serving carts. They killed the other two guards first, then opened up on everyone else. I came from the back," pointing to a door which led to the kitchen area. "I got a couple of shots off at them, then they opened up on me. All I could do was stay down."

"Don't blame you for that," Hilton replied. Henderson had moved to check on the two guards lying several feet away. She turned back to Hilton and the other guard after examining their bodies.

"You said they killed these guys first?"

"Yes," the guard said. "They were close by to where the first shooter was."

"Did you notice what kind of automatic weapons they were using?"

"No," Peterson replied. "It all happened so fast."

"Interesting," Henderson replied as she stood from where the corpses rested.

"Because both guards appear to have been shot at close range in the head by a single shot, not automatic gunfire."

"I don't know how to explain it," the guard said, and with astonishing speed pulled his gun from the holster on his belt and aimed it at Henderson. Hilton fired his pistol several times into Peterson's chest in what seemed like slow motion, and the guard slumped to the ground. Hilton's hand shook with adrenaline as he fumbled to put his pistol back into its holster. He looked down at the guard, then turned to see Henderson, who had stumbled several feet backwards as Hilton fired. He was about to ask the younger woman if she was all right when she stumbled backwards against the wall and slid to the ground. It was then he noticed a dark, wet circle forming on her uniform shirt.

"Henderson!" he shouted, as he eased her to the ground. He grabbed the mike on his shoulder again. "Officer down! Repeat, Officer down! Delta 322 is down with a GSW!" He lay the officer down and looked at her wound. She was losing a lot of blood, but he couldn't figure out from where.

"Hang on now, Henderson, you hear me?" Hilton insisted.

"Rescue's going to be here in just a second." Blood spread across the front of her uniform. "Where are you hit?"

"Shoulder," Henderson gasped. She had two bullet holes in her chest, one center and one just below her badge. The blood came from a third hole, one that had found a path behind the leading edge of her protective vest and penetrated into her left shoulder. The amount of bleeding indicated the brachial artery had likely been hit.

Hilton knew he had to get the bleeding stopped. He tore the red pouch from the back of his duty belt and ripped it open. Everyone on the detail had been given a small kit containing basic first aid materials in case of just such an emergency. He cut the sleeve off Henderson's left arm to better access her would, and blood poured forth. He opened a QuikClot dressing and applied it to the wound. Henderson grunted in pain, but the bleeding slowed immediately. "You hang on now, Henderson. You've gotta show me that big TV, remember?"

"Looks like you win," Henderson said, and coughed painfully, finally able to catch her breath enough to speak.

"What?" Hilton stammered.

"The bet," Henderson coughed. "The vest or the cigarettes. Maybe I should have taken up smoking."

Hilton shook his head "Not a chance. You ain't going anywhere," he said, his vision blurring with tears. "You've got to stick around to see me quit smoking."

Henderson chuckled, then grimaced. "Yeah, I don't want to miss that." She relaxed a little, even as continued pressing against the wound. Hilton looked down to see how much of her blood had already poured out onto the floor, mixing onto the banquet room floor along with the dozens of others she had sworn to protect.

"If your people can't do better than this, then maybe you need to put different agents in play," the Attorney General huffed towards the screen. On the display were several faces: SAC Jacksonville Robert Shear, FBI Director James Van Horn, SAC Atlanta, and the Directors of the ATF and the Georgia Bureau of Investigation.

'That's neither fair nor helpful, sir," SAC Atlanta snapped, sounding angrier than he would have liked. "This was pulled off by a splinter cell operating with a high degree of independence. We had no precursors to this attack, and have no indicators of any clear connection with the group involved with the incident in Jacksonville."

Director Van Horn interjected. "Our agents aren't miracle workers or mind readers. They can only follow as far as the facts go. We clearly have a number of unsubs who are operating outside of known parameters, and our agents are doing the best they can with what they have."

"Then they'd better get more," the AG replied. "Along with the DNI, the SecDef, and the Director of Homeland Security I just had my butt chewed off by the President. Our necks are on the line here, and I need you all to get ahead of this."

"Our agents are doing everything in their power, sir," Van Horn said calmly. They've got some hot leads they're pursuing now that we believe are going to help give us some actionable intel."

"Well it better happen quick. I don't want to have to sit in the Oval Office again and explain how we let more American citizens die on our watch." The AG ended the call and the screen went dark.

The Director of the Federal Bureau of Investigation sat back in his chair. How in the world had this happened? It was all but certain that this attack was connected to Jacksonville. It was equally certain that it wouldn't be the last such incident. When and where would the next attack occur? What was it going to take to prevent future attacks, if they could be prevented? POTUS made it clear to the various Directors such failures were unacceptable. President Hathaway was a reasonable man, and therefore he knew there was no way to provide 100% guarantees against such tragedies any more than one could guarantee the weather, but he nonetheless wanted his deputies to know they needed to crank up their efforts. The AG was known for being hot-headed under the best of circumstances, so incurring POTUS' wrath was a surefire way to light his fuse. James Van Horn stared at his phone for a moment, then dialed the number for SAC Jacksonville. After a series of clicks and two rings, Special Agent in Charge Robert Shear answered.

"Be glad you aren't SAC Atlanta," Van Horn started.

"I'm not sure I want to be an SAC at all right now," Shear replied.

"Want to trade?"

"I won't even dignify that with a response. Jim, I'm sorry we didn't catch this."

"Bob, I'm certainly not calling to reprimand you. This couldn't be helped. But we know they're likely going to try this again somewhere. We've got to ramp things up a bit."

"So what do we do, put the National Guard at every religious gathering in the country?"

"We may be closer to that than you think," Director FBI replied. "We need leads, Bob, and we need them yesterday."

"One of those leads just got capped in Monaco. Nearly lost one of mine and one of Price's. But they think they're on to something there." An Agent stood at Shear's office door, looking as if she had just run a marathon to get there. "Can you hold on a second?" Van Horn gave an affirmative, and Shear covered the phone's mouthpiece. "What is it?"

"Sorry to interrupt, sir, but we have a major problem."

Hawkins sat listening to the briefing given by the SUSLO out of Marseilles, Richard Cone. Cone had multiple high-resolution display screens mounted on a wall behind him, displaying images of Xuffash's file, the satellite images of his home, photos of his shipping offices, crime scene photos of Xuffash and his family, and surveillance camera footage taken from various cameras along Hawkins and Land's chase route. He looked at Land and saw her absorbed in the videos taken of their pursuit.

"Initial results show 9mm as the caliber of the assassin's weapon, which would match your assessment of the usage of an MP-5SD," Cone said. "There are a lot of those out there, so it doesn't tell us much."

"That tag does, though," Land offered, rising and pointing to the tag on the back of the M3, a barely visible blur in one section of footage. "If we could get it cleaned up a bit…"

Cone nodded. "Already have, but Hawkins also had the presence of mind to get the tag number when he spotted the car. We were able to confirm the number without clear camera shots." He pressed a button which called up a French automobile registration certificate. "The car belongs to one Seth Warrick, resident of Paris."

"It can't be that easy," Land said.

"It's not. The car had been reported stolen the day of the shooting."

"Doesn't mean anything," Hawkins interjected. "He could have reported the car stolen knowing he was going to have to use it."

"That wouldn't be particularly smart," Land quipped.

"Nobody said our shooter was smart. It also could have been an ego thing. 'I'm going to do this using my own car and still outsmart them'. He might have thought he could do the deed and get out before anyone got there. I don't think he was waiting around for someone to arrive. He had torn the shirt off the girl. He was getting ready to…" Hawkins paused, leaving it unsaid. "He got caught up, like an impulse he couldn't control. It slowed him down and messed up his plan. He had been going for subtlety until that point. Getting another vehicle might attract attention, so use your own high dollar car in a neighborhood full of high dollar cars and no one notices. Wouldn't be the first time someone tried it." Hawkins rose and walked toward the screen showing the vehicle registration. "What do we know about this Warrick?"

Cone typed on the keyboard below the multiple displays, and the satellite image of Xuffash's house was replaced by what looked to be a driver's license photo with the man's information compiled in a dossier format. Hawkins knew the programs now in use by FBI and other agencies could pull any known photo of a person, gather all their pertinent information and compile it into a neat file in only a few seconds. All the people taking selfies on their vacation and at restaurants not only updated their own profiles but also provided information on everyone in the background as well. This particular photo showed a man who looked to be in his mid-thirties, bald, with long, lean features which made his face seem as if it had been pulled taut by invisible hooks. "He's originally from England, 35, 6'1 and 185 pounds according to his file. He's currently employed by a company called Biomedical Engineering and Research, or BEAR, an American-owned company headquartered about 60 miles south of Paris. He was Director of Foreign Operations for two years and then promoted to CEO a year and a half ago. Graduated from Oxford with Honors and worked as a youth director at a nearby church while attending. You two may have something in common."

"Or maybe not," Hawkins said. "I've heard of BEAR before. They're a medical research company responsible for the discovery of cures and treatments for certain forms of cancer and infectious diseases. Making huge headway against cancer in Europe, but the FDA has been slow to approve their treatments for use in the U.S. They're also on the cutting edge of genetics and cloning research. Questionable sponsors and possibly unethical research practices made them seek a base outside of the U.S. They seem to fit in nicely in France, although I think they still have an office somewhere back in the states."

Land smiled. "I'll bet you don't even eat French fries, do you?"

"Not if I can help it," Hawkins replied. "I think we need to pay a visit to Mr. Warrick."

"I can have a helicopter carry you both there," Cone said. "I agree this would be worth looking into."

"Let's go ahead and find out everything we can about BEAR while we're at it," Hawkins said. "I know generally about their 'questionable sponsors', but I want specifics. Where does their money come from? And, I want to know more about the owner —something Matheson, if I remember—than his mother does. If the CEO is dirty, the one holding his leash probably stinks, too." The chirping of Hawkins' secure phone interrupted him. "Excuse me for one sec," he said, and activated the device. "Hawkins."

"This is Shear. Are you sitting down?"

"I don't like the sound of that."

"Xuffash is dead."

"I know. I was there."

"Not him," Shear declared. "The son."

Hawkins felt his heart drop into his stomach. "What? He was in custody! How'd that happen?"

"We don't know yet, but the other two students are dead also. Someone apparently poisoned all three with something nasty. They haven't done the autopsies yet because there isn't much left, and because they have to properly quarantine the bodies and everyone who came into contact with them within the last 24 hours. FEMA is running the show on the quarantine, but at least they're trying to be low-key about it."

"No small task."

"You know it," SAC Jacksonville replied. "Anyway, it may take a while to find out exactly what killed them."

"Someone was starting to sweat a little, it seems."

"Maybe a lot. But it's worse than losing our boys here, as if that wasn't bad enough. We had an incident in Atlanta last night.

We've got over 50 dead in a shooting at a Catholic-Jewish community meeting. One Atlanta police officer was shot, but it looks like she's going to pull through. We're trying to keep it out of the media, but we all know what that's like."

Hawkins felt his heart sink further into his chest. *Again,* he thought. *More senseless deaths because of someone's misplaced rage.* "It's really going to hit the fan when word of this gets out. We're assuming it was connected to Jacksonville?"

"We're pretty sure. One of the few survivors was actually one of the gunmen, posing as a security guard. He shot the Atlanta officer, but her partner lit him up. The shooter was also wearing a vest, so he's sore but alive. He's at a hospital in the area now, to make sure he doesn't have any internal hemorrhaging or anything, but we're moving him to a secure facility further south as soon as he gets cleared. I'm sending ASAC Williams and Woodley up to escort him. The Marshals are going to help with security and transport." The United States Marshals Service were experts in the apprehension and transport of dangerous fugitives and felons, often in a subtle manner. Such subtlety would be important right about now, Hawkins thought.

"We have a name yet?"

"Working on it," Shear replied. "We're running him through all our systems to see if we get a match, but he's not what we expected."

A thought hit Hawkins like a bolt of electricity. "What nationality is the shooter?"

"American," Shear answered. "Caucasian. We always watch for foreign extremists recruiting within our borders, but..."

"This may be something else, sir," Hawkins interrupted. "We have a possible lead on our shooter here in France. We may be looking at something totally different than what we first thought."

"Interesting you say that," Shear said. "I'm just reading an email from the DNI saying our boy in the video isn't Middle-

Eastern at all. It seems he's a fair-skinned Caucasian under a lot of makeup."

Hawkins spoke what both men were thinking. "FOA may be something totally different than what we were looking for."

"Let me know what you find," Shear said. "I'm sure you'll be hearing from Woodley soon."

"Yes, sir," Hawkins replied, and the line clicked off. "Can we access JWICS on one of these screens?" he asked, referring to the Joint Worldwide Intelligence Communications System, the government's top-secret-only intranet.

"Sure can," Cone replied, and switched one of the displays over. Another display showed information from the Department of Defense's INTELINK, the highly classified internet service used by the IC, and the Defense Intelligence Network, a classified news network, both operated by the Defense Intelligence Agency within the Pentagon.

"What's going on, Hawk?" Land asked.

"Take a look for yourself, Sam," he replied as he pointed to the monitor. On the screen a government reporter detailed the grim events in Atlanta, as well as the deaths of the three suspects in Jacksonville. The regular media was reporting the shooting in Atlanta as the work of a disgruntled employee, and the deaths of the suspects in Florida was completely off the media radar.

"This case is shutting down faster than we can open it," she said.

"Not if I can do anything about it."

"So, what now?"

"Let's get loaded for BEAR."

CHAPTER SEVENTEEN

The MD Enhanced Explorer helicopter cruised at 150 miles per hour over the French countryside, its sleek white hull gleaming in the morning sun. The green fields swept underneath, and Hawkins marveled at the beauty of the small, ancient towns dotting the landscape.

"It really is beautiful, isn't it?" Samantha Land said. She sat with her tablet attached to a portable keyboard that rested in her lap. She downloaded more information on Seth Warrick, the CEO of Biological Engineering and Research, a man who seemed to have some blank spots in his life story. She and Hawkins had learned he apparently had some run-ins with law enforcement, but those records were either sealed or destroyed. Even more mysterious was the owner of BEAR, a man by the name of William Matheson.

"Too bad we don't have time to really sightsee," Hawkins said. He turned in his seat towards the Case Officer. "I can't stop thinking about Xuffash and his family. He and his wife had gunshot wounds, with no sign of a struggle. The daughter had a bruise on her head, blunt trauma, in addition to the GSWs, and a possible sexual attack. There's something about that detail which isn't sitting right. What kind of hitman would take the time for a sexual assault? Pretty strong compulsive behavior. And there's something weird going on here with our boy Warrick. Sealed police files, missing years, and his car is stolen and used in the assassination of a key player in a terrorist event on U.S. soil."

"Matheson's an odd duck, too," Land added. "A billionaire many times over, he's been something of a recluse for the last number of years. Most people attributed his lack of public appearances to throwing his entire life into the company and supporting cancer research, but there were several years where it seemed as though he, like Warrick, had simply dropped off the face of the earth: no address, no phone number, no credit card usage or bank withdrawals—none of the things which mark a modern existence. And yet, here they are at the top of one of the most successful and aggressive medical research companies in the world. Neither one seems to have any background them- selves in biochemical research, but that hasn't affected the success of BEAR. In fact, as you mentioned, the company has recently gained notoriety and acclaim for its successful treat- ment of several forms of cancer, including brain tumors and melanoma which are ordinarily very difficult to overcome."

"My father had a melanoma years ago," Hawkins said. "He underwent a radical new treatment at a university in the Carolinas which, along with a lot of prayer, saved his life. When I read about BEAR's research and success with melanoma, it struck a chord with me. That's the only reason I know anything about them."

"That's the only reason *anyone* knows about them, but it's enough. The company's successes have brought worldwide atten- tion to the company, and the money has poured in. The United States Food and Drug Administration had begun to dig into the company when they were based in the States, and had found some things they didn't like. Before they could really drill down, Matheson packed up shop and moved to France. Certain leaders within the French government had been elated to steal the successful company away from the U.S., and BEAR has flourished in the friendly environs created by France."

"Where were they based in the States?" Hawkins asked. Land tapped on her tablet, and looked up at him.

"New Orleans."

"The French Connection," Hawkins replied. "Must've really been crazy about *café au lait* and *beignets*," he said, referring to the coffee and powdered sugar-coated square doughnuts made famous by the Big Easy's Café du Monde stores. The helicopter suddenly slowed, banked, and descended towards a large industrial complex.

"Behold the BEAR," Land said. Hawkins marveled at the scale of the Biological Engineering and Research facility. Building after concrete building stretched over an area of land no less than 45 acres, with a myriad of transport trucks and employee parking scattered about between the structures. There were two helicopter landing pads he could see, each at opposing corners of the property. Their bird dipped towards the pad on the eastern most part of the facility, closest to what looked to be the administrative building. As they approached, two women stepped out of the large glass doors leading out of the building and walked towards the helipad. Hawkins and Land exited the helicopter and walked towards the women who waited just at the pad's edge.

"*Bon jour*. My name is Elle, and this is Manon. We hope you had a comfortable trip."

"It was pleasant," Land said. "We appreciate Mr. Warrick squeezing us in on such short notice. We know he is very busy."

"He was more than happy to accommodate you," Elle replied. "Please, come inside." The two women turned and led Hawkins and Land into the building, the words "ADMINISTRATIVE OFFICES" etched into the stone façade in English and French. The lobby was non-descript, not unlike what one would expect to see in a large doctor's office. Elle led them down the hall, while Manon stopped at the reception/security desk. Elle was short, bespectacled, and showed she spent a good deal of time at her desk. Her dark hair was pulled back in a long ponytail which hung down the back of her suit jacket and ended just above her waist. Manon was much taller, almost as tall as Hawkins in her high heeled shoes, and her short-cropped black hair, chiseled features, and muscular form informed both Hawkins and Land she was likely more than just a receptionist. Land in particular took notice of her, and had the aching feeling she should know the woman called Manon, but she just couldn't figure out from where. It continued to plague her as Elle led them into an office at the end of the hallway.

"Mr. Warrick is waiting. You may enter," she said, and stepped aside. Seated behind a desk smaller than one might expect for the CEO of a successful company was Seth Warrick. He looked up as the two Americans entered, and stood from his leather wingback chair. The tailored wool suit, pressed dress shirt, and silk tie seemed incongruous with the head rising above it. Warrick's smooth scalp hovered over eyes that looked as if they were bulging from their sockets, the pale skin of his face offset by dark circles encompassing the bulging orbs. His eyes were pale blue, yet such a strong shade both Land and Hawkins wondered to themselves if they were colored contact lenses. He smiled—an expression that seemed unusual for his face, as though the muscles required to do so were flaccid from lack of use—and extended a hand.

"Welcome to you both," Warrick said with a strong British accent. "I hope you had a pleasant ride in."

"I've had worse. My name is Samantha Land, Mr. Warrick, and this is Thomas Hawkins. We appreciate you fitting us in to your busy schedule on such short notice."

"More than happy to, Ms. Land," Warrick replied. "Please, have a seat, both of you," he said as he motioned to a pair of oxblood leather wingbacks in front of his smallish mahogany desk. The two Americans took their seats.

"Getting right to the point, Mr. Warrick, we'd like to talk with you about your car," Hawkins said. "As you know, it was involved in an incident down in Monaco."

"Bugger of a thing," he intoned smoothly. "I only took delivery of that M3 a little over three months ago. I had some special work done locally by a Dinan affiliate to give it a little more steam, you know," Warrick said, referring to the tuning house that specialized in making BMWs even more potent than they already were. "You spend all that money on something that some riff raff runs away with."

"Being something of a car person myself, I can appreciate your frustration," Hawkins said. "When did you notice the car was gone?"

"As I was leaving for the evening," he said. "I came outside to trek home, and it was gone."

"Not an easy car to steal, is it Mr. Warrick?" Hawkins continued. "These new cars have pretty sophisticated security systems and are harder to steal every year."

"Absolutely, Mr. Hawkins. But, as I just told the inspectors a short while ago, I have a man who has detailed my autos for the last year or so, and I allow him a key and remote for the car. He picks it up after lunch, takes it off to clean it, then returns it before I leave for the day. At first I thought perhaps one of us had gotten our days confused, but when I couldn't reach him on his cell phone, I decided it best if I notified the authorities."

"What is his name?"

"The detailer? Claude Shelley, lives about five miles or so up the road. I gave his address to the *Gendarmerie*."

"Has this Shelley ever been in any trouble that you know of, Mr. Warrick?" Land asked.

"I wouldn't be letting him drive my M3 if I knew of any such thing, Ms. Land, I assure you," Warrick said with a chuckle. "In fact, Claude came very highly recommended by some established clients he has in Paris. A fine, upstanding young man, by all accounts."

"People are not always what they seem, Mr. Warrick."

"I suppose you're quite right, Mr. Hawkins. Is there anything else I can do for either of you?"

"No, sir, you've been very helpful," Land said as she stood. "We'll see what comes up with Mr. Shelley."

"Thank you very much for your time, Mr. Warrick," Hawkins added as he also stood. "I hope you recover your car soon."

"I don't," Warrick laughed. "I wouldn't want it back after it's been all shot up and such!"

"Right," Hawkins laughed. He turned to see Elle waiting for them in the doorway. "Thanks again," and the two Americans followed the receptionist back down the hallway. As they walked past the receptionist/security desk, Manon was conspicuously absent. Land saw another face that looked familiar, however: a man wearing a security guard uniform entered a solid looking door with a keypad mounted on the wall next to it, and Land swore he looked as familiar as Manon had. He glanced at Land, then quickly walked through the door, closing it just as swiftly behind him.

Elle dutifully marched them out to the helipad, where the Enhanced Explorer sat waiting. As soon as they approached the pad edge, Elle stopped and, as if on cue, the whine of the helicopter's dual Pratt & Whitney Canada PW206E turboshafts rose in pitch.

"I hope you are successful in finding the perpetrator of this crime. *Bon chance*," she declared, turned on her heels, and marched back inside.

Land looked toward the helicopter awaiting their entry. "Friendly woman," she said sarcastically. "Quite a contrast to the charming Mr. Warrick."

"*Overly* charming," Hawkins added. "A little *too* slick, especially for a man whose car was just used in the murder of three people."

"So do we go check out the detailer? He seems like a plant to me."

"That'll be a waste of time. I think we've found our skunk."

"So we don't even talk to the scapegoat, check out his story?"

"We won't have the chance. If I'm right," Hawkins said as he opened the helo door for Land, "he's already dead."

CHAPTER EIGHTEEN

Supervisory Special Agent Mark Woodley sat in the passenger seat of the black Suburban outside the Peachtree Regional Medical Center in Atlanta. The SUV was parked in the pouring rain on the back side of the facility, half a block away from the Maintenance entrance, which would be used to bring Matthew William Everett to the unmarked white Dodge Sprinter van parked in a spot marked "Deliveries Only". Woodley and ASAC Walter Simmons had learned the shooter's name on the flight out of Jacksonville, his identity revealed by comparing his mug shot with the Georgia driver's license database. Everett was sore but otherwise unharmed, and he had been released from medical care. The FBI had managed to keep Everett's name and where-abouts from the press thus far, and they wanted to keep it that way for a little longer. Suspects in this case were turning up dead at an alarming rate, and Woodley needed this one alive. He shifted in his seat slightly and looked at the clock on the radio display: 5:45. Atlanta was already waking up, and the Perimeter would soon be choked with morning rush hour traffic. Many of Atlanta's residents would try to hit the roads a little early because of the heavy downpour, knowing it didn't take much to snarl the roadways around the south's largest city. The hospital was located at one of the main roads on the I-285 loop, and Woodley didn't want to get into a heavy traffic situation transporting this guy. He keyed the mic on his digitally encrypted radio.

"How are we doin' in there?" he asked tersely.

"On our way," Special Agent Andrew Mathis replied. "We had a delay with discharge and prep, but we're rolling him out now."

"Rolling?"

There was a moment of silence before the receiver clicked in his ear. "Our friend didn't feel like cooperating. He started making a scene, so we had to give him a little something to relax him."

Woodley rolled his eyes. "How relaxed is he?"

"Very."

Woodley wasn't happy. They had planned on quickly escorting the shooter into the nondescript van and whisking him away with a minimum of fuss. Getting an unconscious 175-pound man into a white, unmarked van without attracting attention was much harder. He knew ASAC Simmons wouldn't be pleased either. The Jacksonville ASAC was coordinating with the U.S. Marshals Witness Security—or WITSEC—for transport, and the Chief Inspector and ASAC respectively from the Marshal and FBI offices in Atlanta were riding together in a silver Chevy Tahoe parked 100 feet behind the van. The white van had three Federal Marshals already waiting within, and Agent Mathis had another two Marshals with him.

"Who in the blazes ordered that?" shouted Carl Jones, the Assistant Chief Inspector for the U.S. Marshals WITSEC in Atlanta.

"One of the Marshals," Mathis replied.

Jones started to say something, but FBI SAC Atlanta, Joseph Wicks, cut him off. "We'll talk about this later. Just get our man out here."

"We're approaching the exit now."

The rain had cut visibility to a minimum in the pre-dawn dark, and the Bureau had instructed the hospital to dim the utility lights in the alley for the pick up. Wicks put the Tahoe into gear and eased up closer to the van. "Roger that. We're closing up to assist."

From his vantage point down the block, Woodley watched the Tahoe containing his ASAC and the other two supervisors begin rolling toward the waiting van. He suddenly felt an uneasiness he used to get as a Navy SEAL right before everything fell apart. He keyed the mic.

"Mr. Simmons, I think it would be best if you all held back for a moment."

"What's up, Woodley?" Simmons asked over the earpiece. The exit door opened, and two Marshals, dressed in the uniforms of maintenance workers, walked out looking like anything but Federal agents. They walked toward the van and opened the rear doors.

Woodley noticed a silver Ford pickup parked down the street start rolling towards the maintenance area. "Sir, hang back. We've got a silver pickup heading your way. Eagle-1, you see it?"

"Yes, sir," the sniper on the roof across the street replied. "The rain is making it real tough to see much right now, but he's definitely rolling towards the van."

"Do you have a shot?"

"Negative, repeat, I do not have a shot."

Suddenly the pickup accelerated towards the waiting van and the Tahoe rolling up behind it. Woodley shouted, "Go! GO!", and his own driver hit the gas. "Incoming! Incoming! Heads up!" The Suburban lurched forward as Woodley saw figures stand up in the pickup bed. They each held what appeared to be shotguns. "Shooters! Get us over there!" he shouted to his driver, a young agent named Malloy out of the Atlanta field office. "Simmons! Shooters!" Two of the men in the bed of the pickup opened fire on the two Marshals who had just emerged from the building, while a third tossed something underneath the white van. A moment later the van was engulfed in an explosion like a fist of fire which demolished the vehicle and those inside it. The two shooters then opened up on the Tahoe which was now rapidly accelerating in reverse. "Ram 'em, Malloy!"

Woodley braced himself for the impact, and the Suburban slammed into the silver pickup with sufficient force to send all three shooters flying through the air. The airbag whacked Woodley in the face, knocking him senseless for a moment. Malloy was already out of the driver's seat, weapon drawn. Woodley threw his own door open, shotgun at the ready, when he heard the sound of an engine wide open, and a crash. He glanced over to see the silver Tahoe slamming tail first into a docking bay at full speed with a sickening crunch of shattered glass and crumpled steel. In full combat mode now, Woodley looked back around assessing the situation, and saw the shooters sprawled out on the ground. None looked as if they would be shooting at anyone ever again. Woodley saw the driver sitting behind the wheel, and Malloy was shouting at the cab of the pickup for him to come out with his hands up.

Woodley aimed his shotgun at the driver's side window of the pickup, just above where the front of the Suburban's driver side headlight impacted, and fired three double-ought buckshot rounds into the cab. Malloy turned and looked at Woodley. "What are you doing?" he shouted.

"Shut up and cover this alley!" Woodley replied. "If anyone else comes in here who isn't one of us, you shoot first and ask questions later!" Woodley ran to the doorway from which the suspect and his escorts were to come through. "Mathis! You hear me?"

"Right here," Mathis' voice carried from down the hall. "The two Marshals almost got…"

"Just move! Get our boy out here now!" A moment later Mathis and two other figures appeared from around a corner, then Mathis snatched the unconscious Everett's wheelchair and began racing toward the exit. Unnoticed, one of the shooters from the pickup was still alive and was sighting in on Everett when a large caliber pistol thundered three times and the shooter dropped. ASAC Williams came running down the alley away from the wrecked Tahoe. "It's Williams!" he shouted. "Hold fire!"

"Nice shooting, sir. Are you alright?" Woodley asked, noting the blood on the ASAC's otherwise perfect white dress shirt. "How's..."

"He didn't make it," Williams said, "but we've got a job to do right now, and that's our immediate priority."

Woodley nodded and turned to Malloy, who was looking intently at the street. "Malloy! Get our 'Burb running!" The younger man jumped behind the wheel and turned the ignition. Nothing. He turned the key several times with the same result.

"It won't start!" Malloy shouted.

"Keep trying!" Woodley shouted, looking at the rooftops. "You see anything from up there?" he asked into his radio.

"Negative," replied the sniper. "Zero visibility."

"I've got eyes on the alley," Williams said, sighting down the barrel of his pistol and steadying himself against the side of the Suburban. "You get this thing started and get him out of here. I'll provide cover until you're gone and wait for backup."

Mathis charged out of the doorway, pushing Everett's wheelchair as fast as he could, two Marshals right behind with their MP-5s at the ready. "Throw him in the back!" Mathis snatched open the Suburban's rear doors and the two Marshals tossed the unconscious suspect into the back. Mathis climbed in alongside the suspect with one of the Marshals, and the other closed the doors and ran toward the front of the SUV. Two men ran around the corner into the alley with weapons in their hand, and ASAC Williams fired three rounds into each of them. They dropped to the ground, their guns clattering next to them.

A chime sounded in the cabin, and a voice began speaking through the Suburban's sound system. "This is OnStar, and we have been alerted that your vehicle's airbags have deployed. Is everyone alright?"

"You've got to be kidding me," Malloy managed to say.

Woodley ran to the driver's side. "Move over, Malloy. I'm driving." The younger agent clambered across the center console and Woodley hopped behind the wheel. He opened the large knife he kept in his pocket, and with several swipes cut away the spent airbag from the steering wheel hub. "OnStar, this is FBI Special Agent Mark Woodley, and you had better disable whatever is keeping me from getting this vehicle started."

"Sir, a program has been initiated which prevents fuel from flowing to the engine in the event of an accident..."

"I don't care what caused it, just get it running again!" Woodley shouted. He couldn't believe this hadn't been bypassed already. He was going to kick a mud hole in someone and stomp it dry for this. If he lived that long.

"Alright, Agent Woodley, try it now," the voice said. Woodley twisted the key, and the 6.2 liter V-8 coughed to life. ASAC Williams slammed his hand against the side of the Suburban twice in rapid succession and stepped backwards onto the curb.

"Thank you," he said dryly. "Now hang up and forget you had this conversation." He snatched the gear selector into reverse just as the last Marshal jumped in the back seat. Woodley floored the accelerator and the big SUV's tires howled in protest, the engine providing more power than the tires could transfer to the pavement. He spun the truck around in the alley, slammed it into gear, and headed for the street, his eyes searching every nook and cranny from which the next attack would come.

"Stay sharp. This isn't over," Woodley ordered over the roar of the engine. As if in response to his words, a blue and tan Ford Expedition fell in behind them, its engine howling as it sought to close in on the speeding Suburban. A figure leaned out of the passenger window, and opened fire from an Uzi submachine gun. The 9mm bullets peppered the back window of the Suburban, but couldn't penetrate the ballistic window tint on the inside of the windows.

Mathis was laying over the top of Everett, the Marshal next to him stuffing bullet-proof vests against the back doors. The thought of taking a bullet for this guy wasn't particularly appealing, but they needed him alive, and he would do his job. Special Agent Andrew Mathis was a rookie, just six months out of the Academy, and had graduated with Ronnie Malloy, who had jumped into the front passenger seat. There were a growing number of agents just like him, as the Bureau was replacing a large number of retiring agents in addition to bringing new ones on just to keep up. Years of hiring freezes and budget cuts had left the Bureau without needed agents—many times they fell behind attrition rates from retirement. Mathis thought briefly about the irony of the Bureau having to fill *his* position. He preferred to them to have to wait another 30 years or so for that.

Woodley glanced into the rear-view mirror to assess the situation, and knew exactly what Mathis was thinking. He hoped it wouldn't come to that, but he also realized their vehicle wouldn't hold out long against sustained automatic fire.

"Somebody make him go away!" he shouted, jerking the wheel hard to the left. The large SUV hurtled into a service alley behind a shopping center, and the Ford followed. The Marshal in the back seat unholstered his pistol—a Sig Sauer .45—leaned out the window and fired at the pursuing truck. Six slugs punched through the front window of the Ford and into the shooter in the front seat, shattering half the windshield in the process.

"One down," the Deputy U. S. Marshal said.

"Keep it up. Malloy, get dispatch on the horn and tell them we're heading to the airfield and we're coming in hot."

"What the...?" the Marshal said. Woodley glanced in the rear view again, and saw the Marshal watching out the window. He noticed movement in the front seat, saw the passenger door open, and the body of the first shooter was unceremoniously dumped out. It bounced and rolled until it stuck the side of a dumpster with a crunch Woodley felt even if he couldn't hear it. Another man moved into the front seat and prepared to fire.

"Give me a shotgun!" the Marshal shouted as he fired three more shots into the front of the Expedition. The other Marshal handed him the Remington 870 mounted to a rack in the rear cargo area, and he pumped several rounds as fast as he could fire —at the driver, the passenger, at the front grill in an attempt to take out the shooter, the driver, the radiator...at this point, he'd take what he could get. The rest of the windshield blew into the front seat like a crystal tarp, and the front grill shattered from two slugs. The Expedition twitched like a wounded animal then drifted slightly to the right. It struck an outcropping on one of the store's delivery areas, then jerked into the opposite wall. It slowed a little from the impacts before it struck a dumpster. The sound was like a bomb going off in the confines of the alleyway, and the SUV stopped in its tracks.

Woodley smiled as he looked in the rearview. "What's your name, Deputy?"

"Louis Carter, Agent Woodley."

"Well, Carter, if I ever get in another firefight, I want you with me."

"Hopefully we can wait until after our flight to Jacksonville," Carter replied.

"Amen to that," Woodley said as he punched the number for ASAC Williams on his secure cell. He was relieved when his ASAC answered.

"Sir, we're clear. Are you okay?"

"I'm fine. Paramedics are here and we're securing the area. Keep rolling. I'll meet up with you all later. Just get that man secured."

"Yes, sir," Woodley said. He was relieved his ASAC was relatively unharmed, but he knew others weren't so fortunate. Woodley had grown accustomed to death while in the military, and he was uncomfortably confident that unless these people were stopped, and fast, there would be much more to come.

CHAPTER NINETEEN

FBI Agent Thomas Hawkins sat in the rearmost seat of the Gulfstream V at Charles DeGaulle International Airport in Paris awaiting clearance to take off. He and Case Officer Land hadn't been able to verify his theory that the car detailer was dead, but he was missing, and in a case like this it probably meant the same thing. His body might turn up, or it might not, but the scapegoat had been sacrificed, and Seth Warrick likely felt confident he was in the clear. He was wrong.

Hawkins wanted to talk to William Matheson, the founder and president of BEAR, and that meant flying back to the States, New Orleans in particular. Land had called in to have the jet meet them in Paris, and it had arrived shortly after their helicopter touched down. She worked diligently on the computers, while Hawkins sorted through things in his head. He recalled the events at Xuffash's home in Monaco, playing out the events in his mind like a movie. He saw the shooter in silhouette, running across the yard. He tried to measure out the shooter's size in his mind's eye, and then compared it to Seth Warrick. He saw Warrick in his office, remembered his build. He then visualized the man in the video. It was possible, yes, but it was also possible Jimmy Hoffa was buried under the end zone at Giants Stadium.

Speculation was interesting, but didn't solve the case. Only hard facts could.

He took his phone out of his pocket and tried calling Mark Woodley again. He had been trying for the last hour or so, since he had found out about the attack on the agents and Deputy U.S. Marshals in Atlanta. The intel said there were injuries, but who and how bad he hadn't been able to find out. After three rings came a voice.

"Hey, Hawk, I just saw where you had called."

"Yeah, just checking up on you. Are you okay?"

"I'm not hurt. We got Everett on the plane a little bit ago, but we decided Jax was too hot, so the Marshals are going to put him up at one of their places out west for a while. Some of our people can grill him there."

"Good. So who got hurt? What's their condition?"

Woodley sat silent for a moment, and Hawkins looked at his phone to ensure he hadn't lost the connection. "The Marshals lost four, and we lost one—SAC Wicks. ASAC Williams got a little banged up but he's okay. He got the job done."

Hawkins couldn't believe what he had heard: four U.S. Marshals, the Special Agent in Charge of the Atlanta Division, killed during a prisoner transport. "Mark, I..."

"We should have had better coverage, but they knew where we were and how many people we had. They caught us with our pants down, Hawk. But they all got wiped. Not a one left for questioning, unfortunately."

"I don't think they would have told us much more than Everett might."

"We'll never know, but right now I don't care," Woodley said. "I'd kill 'em again if I could." Hawkins was angry as well, and he wasn't sure he felt much differently than his friend.

"Well, I'm glad you're okay, bud. Just keep your head down, huh?"

Woodley managed a chuckle. "We seem to do better when we're on the same continent."

"Let's remember that from now on, shall we? We're headed to New Orleans now on a lead. Going to talk to William Matheson, the guy who is the boss of our number one suspect in Ra's al' Xuffash's killing."

"Think he's connected?"

"Gonna do a little digging and find out."

"Right. Have a good flight."

"Thanks, Mark. Get some rest if you can." Hawkins put the phone back in his pocket just as Land turned from her computer console to face him. She could tell from the look on his face something had happened. He filled her in.

"This is going south fast," the CIA operative said.

"Then we had better, too."

SAC Robert Shear watched the FBI press officer on the television in his office. He couldn't recall the woman's name, but she was no Renee Cortez. The Atlanta Division's press officer answered questions as best she could, but looked a little flustered. Of course, Cortez would likely have been flustered under the same circumstances—standing in front of a group of shouting reporters while talking about the murder of your boss, an FBI official, couldn't be easy for anyone.

"Can you confirm several federal agents were killed this morning here in Atlanta, and was it related to the mass killing several nights ago?" a reporter shouted.

"At this time I can confirm several federal law enforcement agents were injured in the Atlanta area today. We cannot confirm anything that happened there is related to the shootings from several nights ago."

Another reporter shouted from the crowd at the press conference. "Can you confirm the Special Agent in Charge of the Atlanta Field Office was one of those injured?"

"I cannot confirm that at this time."

"It's also been said someone from the FBI's Jacksonville Field Office was killed."

"I cannot confirm that at this time," the press officer dead-panned. Shear knew they had bad information there—Williams had been injured but had still been able to take down targets. He had gotten word shortly after it took place that his ASAC, Walter Simmons, had been injured, but Atlanta SAC Wicks and the Assistant Chief Inspector for the U.S. Marshals out of Atlanta had died in the firefight. Three other deputy Marshals were also dead, and a fourth had apparently received a minor injury while being shot at. Simmons had demonstrated he was still a good Agent, not just an administrative desk-jockey. He had divorced, with no children and no other family. Simmons had maintained a cordial relationship with his ex-wife from what he had told Shear, so he felt obligated to call and inform her. She had responded emotionally, more so than Shear had expected. She was clearly relieved he was okay and insisted on speaking to him. She ended the call quickly. He didn't know how the conversation between them would go, but it wasn't the first time Shear had seen a close call help people to realize what really mattered. He had then spoken with the ASAC in Atlanta, as well as with Director Van Horn. There would be much to do in the next couple of days, even more than he had anticipated.

Shear shook his head and squeezed his eyes shut. *What a freakin' mess.*

He turned his attention to the TV once more, and the image changed. The TV host in the studio was introducing his current guests, one a prominent leader from a disgruntled splinter group out of the Coalition of Christian Churches, another a Bishop of the Catholic church via satellite from Rome, and the third a Rabbi from Jerusalem. Before the host could really begin, the disgruntled former CCC member—the Reverend Joe Mathers—launched into what he had to say.

"It is quite obvious the reason for all of this violence is the CCC's increasingly intolerant stance toward other viewpoints and other religions, and until they stop being so narrow-minded they will always be targets," Mathers said.

The Catholic priest immediately interjected. "The CCC has a right to believe as they choose, to stand for what they choose to stand for, and they should be able to do so without fear of violence. If they are not being violent or proposing violence, then it is irresponsible to say they have brought this on themselves."

The Rabbi then spoke up. "Welcome to the world of Israel, my friends," he said. "We are threatened with annihilation because our beliefs do not conform to others. We live with this reality each day, never knowing if that day will be our last. These recent attacks..."

"Are all the more reason we should stop trying to proselytize everyone and just let well enough alone," Mathers interrupted.

"It is not an issue of leaving violent people like this alone," the rabbi said from the other side of the world. "It is an issue of them trying to destroy anyone different from them, anyone who does not believe as they do."

The priest jumped in. "Violence, on anyone's part, is never the answer. There should be a peaceful dialogue to resolve our differences..."

"This country has used force for so long that violence is the only language we understand," Mathers said.

The host had heard enough by this point. "So what you're saying, Reverend, is not only are Protestants, Jews, and Catholics to blame for the violence, but they deserved it?"

"What I'm saying is..."

The host interrupted again. "Do you also think we deserved 9/11?"

"I think ..."

"Because it won't make you very popular in a lot of congregations if you feel that way."

"Well, if you'll give me a second to respond, I will," the angry man declared. "I believe the religious people in this country, and in other countries as well, are indeed bringing a lot of this on themselves."

There was a cacophony as both the priest and the rabbi exploded in response. The host was finally able to get control after a few seconds of saying "Gentlemen, gentlemen!" He continued. "Reverend, I'm sorry. I respect your right to have an opinion, but you are...you're just nuts. That is the most ridiculous line of garbage I have heard." The Reverend tried to interrupt, but the host wouldn't stop to give him the chance, and just continued talking over him. "People of faith in this country have been ridiculed and told they are unwelcome ideologically for years, and now they are actually experiencing physical violence like many already face in other parts of the world. And you, a self-proclaimed Christian, want to blame the violence on the *victims*? I'm not going to allow you to insult the memory of those who died simply because of their religious preference. You are gone, sir. You are gone. And we will be back to talk more with the Rabbi and the Bishop in just a moment. Stay tuned," and the bumper music began playing as the host's face faded to black.

Shear changed the channel to one of the other news networks and saw all of the panelists on this particular program were in the same studio, sitting around the same table. He didn't catch what was said, but suddenly a man in a suit and tie and a man wearing Middle Eastern garb were fighting across the table, pulling and swinging at each other while the host dove out of the way. It took several seconds before some of the others gathered around the table tried to get involved. The man in the suit got in a good shot to the nose of the Middle Easterner before security separated them. The host ran up to the camera, looking more than a little disheveled, as grown men screamed and kicked at each other behind him.

"And we'll be right back."

Hawkins' cell phone chirped in his coat pocket and awoke him from a light doze. He had spent several hours in the air wrangling with legal officials on both sides of the Atlantic in an effort to get access to Seth Warrick's sealed files. They had been able to determine Warrick had been in some trouble, but the files had been sealed by the court. Hawkins was beginning to think the Prime Minister, the House of Commons, and perhaps the Queen would have to get involved if there was to be any headway made. The number on the caller ID showed the call originated from the Jacksonville Field Office.

"Agent Hawkins, this is Delores, Mr. Shear's assistant?" Hawkins stifled a chuckle. Everyone in the office knew Delores, and yet if she ever called you, she always reminded you of her position.

"Mr. Shear is tied up on a conference call right now, but he asked me to contact you about the release of files on Seth Warrick. He suggested you check your email, as they should be hitting any minute now. They're sending them directly to you from England."

"Great," Hawkins said, and moved to the open console opposite from the one where Land worked. It seemed she had not moved since before he dozed off. He wondered if she ever slept. A few clicks later, and Hawkins had pulled up his email. There it was.

"Got it, Delores. Thanks, and be sure to tell Mr. Shear thanks, too." He clicked on the file to open it and began perusing. It didn't take him long to see why the file had been sealed, and why Warrick would want to keep it that way.

"Now this is interesting."

"What have you got?" Hawkins said, rising from his seat and standing behind Land at the computer console on board the Gulfstream six miles over the Atlantic Ocean.

"It seems William Matheson may have gotten his story somewhat mixed up regarding what happened to him a few years ago."

"Really?"

"Mmm hmm," Land said. "In this magazine article in June

2003, Matheson is quoted as saying he spent several years in the mountains of the Pacific Northwest searching for the elusive Sasquatch and was, at the time of writing, heading to Tibet looking for the Yeti."

"Let me guess: he has a home on Loch Ness."

"Possibly," Land chuckled. But then, in another article from November 2008, he mentions only the Pacific Northwest, but says he would love to be able to spend some time in Tibet."

"Could be a typo, or reporter error."

"Not likely. Matheson went into great detail in the one article about his planning for Tibet, and the writer noted he was there by the time of the article's publishing. Then he acts like he forgot about it 5 years later."

"So, where was he? Did something happen in Tibet he didn't want to be associated with?"

"Well, it seems like Tibet is the yellow flag, so we'll do a little focusing on that. Be nice if we had something to squeeze Matheson with when we got there."

"If there's something to squeeze," Hawkins said. "We don't want to get him spooked too early. We need to make him think we're just after Warrick at this point. Maybe get him to make a mistake we can use to our advantage."

Land nodded. "We need a little more on Warrick, though, too."

"Got that covered. Take a look at this," and he pointed to his monitor. Land stood and walked over to where Hawkins sat, and leaned over his shoulder to look at his computer screen. He caught the scent of her perfume—Obsession, he recalled—and had to refocus on what he was doing. He pointed to the digital images of court documents on his screen. "It seems Mr. Warrick has some dirty laundry."

CHAPTER TWENTY

The U.S. office of BEAR was located in Metairie, just outside of New Orleans. Although it carried a different name and a separate Zip Code, it was essentially a sub-section of the city. Traveling on I-610 there was no break from one city to the next, but it was clear Metairie was far more suburban with its non-descript office buildings, car dealerships, shopping malls, and restaurant chains. The BEAR office blended in with many others, a few blocks from the Lakeside Mall on Veterans Highway. Hawkins knew this side of town well, as he had once frequented the shopping mall and the movie theatre in its parking lot. He and Land drove past a few restaurants and car dealerships when Hawkins saw the building—there was no sign out front, not even a number, but it was located between two other clearly marked buildings which narrowed the possibilities down. He pulled the dark gray Dodge Charger he had borrowed from the New Orleans FO motor pool into a corner spot on the side of the building. A black sedan parked in the back caught his eye, and he started towards it.

"Where are you going?" Land asked as she climbed from the car.

"Just taking a look," Hawkins replied. He walked to the car

and admired it as he approached. It was a new BMW 7-Series sedan, similar to the one he had seen in Ra's al Xuffash's garage in Monaco.

"750 xDrive," he said to himself. "Haven't had a chance to check one of these out yet. Hot ride, from what I hear."

"That's not envy I hear, is it?" Land jabbed.

"Nah. I prefer domestic," Hawkins said as they began walking towards the front of the building." Give me a Dodge Charger Hellcat any day. But I can still appreciate it for what it is. Interesting that he, Xuffash, and Warrick have similar flavors of automobiles, black BMWs."

"Birds of a feather. Maybe BMW stands for "Bad Men's Wheels," Land mused.

"Ouch. I'll pretend I didn't hear that," Hawkins moaned as he held open the front door for Land to enter. The office offered nothing spectacular on the outside, but the interior appeared far more impressive. The floor was a polished charcoal-colored marble, and wrought iron-laced mahogany wood leapt from the baseboards to the dental crown molding. Elegant golden sconces wrapped in more wrought iron cast light upward and downward on the rich wood, and the receptionist sat behind a mahogany desk with a massive privacy shield on a raised semicircle that backed against a wall with "BEAR" embossed into the wood. Beneath the letters the company motto was likewise etched: "*Helping The World Become All It Should Be*". A security guard who looked like he knew how to hurt people sat to the right behind what appeared to be a stainless steel kiosk, looking somewhat incongruent with the rest of the room's modern, expensive décor. The guard looked up from his desk as Hawkins and Land walked in. Hawkins noticed the receptionist had been looking at them since they had rounded the corner and approached the door. She wore a practiced smile on her face as they approached her platform, and she spoke first.

"Welcome to BEAR International. You must be Agents Hawkins and Land."

She wasn't exactly right, calling Land an "agent", but Hawkins had merely said they were with the FBI so the woman assumed both were Federal Agents. The fact was Land probably shouldn't have been there, as CIA has no real jurisdiction on American soil. Since the case was international, and the company had greater holdings in France than the U.S., technically she was investigating a foreign company operating on American soil. Rather than go into all of that at this point, they allowed the mistake to pass unchallenged.

"Yes, we are."

"Very good," the receptionist replied. "Mr. Matheson is expecting you." She stood from behind her desk and descended two steps which brought her to floor level. They walked down a hall to the left of her dais, and the security guard eyed them closely. Hawkins thought about saying something to the man, then decided against it. The receptionist continued past numerous doors, most of which were closed. Hawkins was struck by the lack of activity. He saw names on a couple of the closed doors, but only one was open and actually had someone inside, and they were doing their level best to look busy. There were many offices which seemed to be completely empty. Perhaps BEAR had been here before moving most of the operations to France, and most of the personnel were now at the European location. He assumed there was nothing insidious about empty offices and continued on. They arrived at two large doors, and the receptionist gingerly knocked on the one on the right. After a moment or two, she stuck her head inside and spoke. She then turned to Hawkins and Land, opened the door wide and said, "Mr. Matheson will see you now."

The office was what Hawkins was expecting, based on what he had already seen of the inside of the building. It was opulent, and fairly large, probably forty feet square by Hawkins' estimation, and completely closed off from the outside world by massive walls and ornate bookcases. Rough-hewn stone and ornate iron covered the dark wood walls, and a massive desk of the same color wood squatted at the opposite end of the room from the entrance. Two dark brown leather chairs were positioned in front of the desk. Hawkins saw William Matheson seated behind it, apparently finishing up a telephone conversation. He hung up the phone as the two approached the midpoint of the room.

"Sorry about that," William Matheson offered. Matheson extended his hand, and after the normal introductions, motioned for Hawkins and Land to have a seat. "The head of Duke University's Cancer Research Center," he said tilting his head toward the phone now resting on the receiver. "I'm supposed to be speaking there at a symposium next week on advances in the treatment of melanoma and other 'untreatable' cancers."

"I'm familiar with some of the research your company has done in the area of cancer treatments. What you all have been able to do for melanoma patients, even at stage 4, is amazing."

"Yes, Agent Hawkins, we're very proud of what we've been able to accomplish. We've given hope and health to many who had neither. It's been a joy to be a part of making such strides for humanity."

"I'm sure," Land said. "As much as we'd love to talk about your company's successes, I'm afraid that's not why we're here. We do have a few questions about some of those involved in your company."

"Are you talking about Seth?" Matheson asked, leaning back in his chair and brushing the thought from the air with his hand. "It's unfortunate about what happened to that fellow in Monaco, but I'm quite sure Seth Warrick had nothing to do with it, Agent Land. He—or at least his car—was just in the wrong place at the wrong time."

"Well, it wouldn't be the first time he was where he shouldn't be," Hawkins said.

Matheson's expression didn't change, but remained placid. "What do you mean?"

"Well, after our meeting with Mr. Warrick I did a little

searching. And do you know what I found? A sealed record. Records are, generally speaking, only sealed when there is something in them to hide. Thanks to a federal court order, and the cooperation of the British government, Mr. Warrick's records were unsealed." Land pulled a file folder from her satchel and handed it across the desk to Matheson, who picked it up as if it were the Sunday comics.

"He was accused of raping multiple teenage girls at the church he volunteered at while attending Oxford," Hawkins continued. "He would coax them into a room, physically restrain them, then sexually assault them. He did it on numerous occasions to the same girls, escalating into outright beating them, then raping them. It was a compulsion, like a serial rapist developing his craft. The violence of the attacks increased over time. The police found out about it because one of the girls came forward. She told the authorities he had threatened to kill them if any of them told what had happened, but she was afraid he was going to kill her anyway and took her chances. Warrick was arrested but released on bond. The next day the girl disappeared. Her body was found three days later. She had been raped again, stripped naked, and hung by the neck from the top of a bridge. The other girls denied they had been raped, and the story began to circulate that the girl who accused Warrick was a prostitute and had committed suicide. The charges were dropped, and Warrick's record ordered sealed. Were you aware of any of this, Mr. Matheson?"

"How horrible." Matheson looked up at Hawkins. "I was aware Seth had encountered some...difficulties a number of years ago, but the charges were dropped."

"Even so," Land asked, "you felt Seth Warrick was the kind of person you wanted to head up your corporation?"

"Seth is an exceptional person, with exceptional abilities, a brilliant mind. He was exactly the sort of person I was looking for."

"I see," Hawkins said. He noticed something in Matheson's

body language as he spoke the last phrase. FBI agents were trained to observe everything about a person they were interviewing or questioning, from eye movement to posture to vocal intonation. They way Matheson had just said that, about Warrick being the kind of person he was looking for, had sounded as if it was an inside joke Hawkins and Land weren't privy to. Hawkins had a feeling Matheson was telling the truth, but it wasn't the positive traits which had drawn him to Warrick. "Good help is hard to find."

"Indeed it is," Matheson continued. "Anyhow, I'm afraid I can't offer anything else about Seth's involvement except to say I would be highly surprised, and disappointed, to find Seth had killed someone and gotten involved in a shootout with Federal Agents."

Yes, I'll bet you are disappointed—at least that we almost caught him, Hawkins thought. "That's all right, Mr. Matheson. We certainly appreciate your time."

"If anything else comes up, we'll be back in touch with you," Land said as they all stood.

"Come by anytime, Agents," Matheson said, smiling warmly and extending his hand. "Glad to be of any help I can."Hawkins and Land walked back through the building, out to the car, and got in.

Land spoke first. "He knows way more than he's letting on."

"Oh, yeah," Hawkins said as he put the car in gear and pulled out onto Veterans. "He's playing a game. He's smart, and he feels safe right now. But I'm convinced Matheson is the one holding the strings."

"So what now?"

"Start digging."

"They just left, and they know about your background."

"So what?" Warrick said over the phone, although he knew the significance of the revelation. The American agents had a scent now, and they wouldn't give up anytime soon. He needed to start taking some personal precautions. "They can't prove anything."

"No, but they're far more suspicious of you now that they know. You've brought down a lot of heat on me, much earlier than we had anticipated."

"The Americans caught a lucky break, nothing more," Warrick said, blowing the smoke from his cigar into the air. "They can't prove anything or you and I would already be in custody. They don't have anything on you. And they won't be able to find anything."

"*Hopefully*," Matheson added. "But you know the Americans don't give up. They have substantial resources with which to search for crumbs. And these two FBI agents who were here— well, they took it easy this time, but I know they suspect more than they let on. Find out what you can about them, Thomas Hawkins and Samantha Land."

Warrick scribbled the names on a piece of paper. "I'm on it. Important to know your enemies."

"You just make sure we're ready to go forward with the next phase at a moment's notice. The timeframe of events has been irretrievably disrupted, so we must be ready to act."

"I'll have our man be ready. He has what he needs."

"Good. Call me with you progress on the wider issue."

"Of course," Warrick said, and the line went dead. He pressed another button and dialed a cell phone held by a person on the other side of the globe. A woman's voice answered.

"*Oui*."

"Manon, my dear, I need for you to do a little research for me."

CHAPTER TWENTY-ONE

"Alright, Jim. Thanks for the update," the President of the United States said to Director FBI. He hung up the phone and looked up at Senator Valerie Keaton seated on the other side of his desk in the Oval Office. "Director Van Horn tells me one of his agents, Thomas Hawkins, has an interesting lead."

"How so?"

"It seems they believe William Matheson, the founder and president of BEAR, may be involved somehow. Agent Hawkins and his CIA liaison just finished talking to Matheson and they feel perhaps he's the central figure on all of this."

"William Matheson," Keaton stated in what was not quite a question, a contemplative look crossing her face. "I met him several years ago. Seemed nice enough, but I was troubled by something he said to me. And it may give that agent and the case officer some insight."

Thomas Hawkins and Samantha Land sat in Juju's eating red beans and rice with corn bread, along with a fried pork chop. While the cook and the food were the same, Juju's had been known as The Cajun Bakery, a place Hawkins had discovered while visiting New Orleans with his family when he was younger. Completely unremarkable if not outright unappealing on the outside, the ramshackle Cajun Bakery had been one of the spots all the locals knew about. The inside had looked like what the name claimed for it, an old bakery with display cases filled with fresh bread. All of the bread, however, was for the subs which were made there, some of the best such sandwiches in New Orleans. The remainder of the cases were refrigerated and contained all sorts of meats and cheeses. The Cajun Bakery had been one of the many buildings ruined by Hurricane Katrina in 2005, and Hawkins had been disappointed to see the old place boarded up and filled with mold and mildew. Hawkins had been pleased to discover the owner had relocated to the other side of town, out by Metairie, and the new place had been called Juju's. In addition to the incredible subs, they also had daily specials, two of which the FBI agent and CIA officer were eating.

A heavily built, bespectacled man named Koz ran the place, and had for years. Ray-Ban Wayfarer frames with prescription lenses rested on his nose, white t-shirt and shorts, and a stained white apron. He wore support stockings under his white athletic socks, which Land thought completed the ensemble nicely.

"Tom Hawkins!" Koz shouted from behind the counter. He hurriedly wiped his hands on a towel tucked into his apron strings and rushed around the counter.

"Hey, Koz!" Hawkins said as Koz wrapped him up in a bear hug. Land couldn't help but chuckle as Hawkins was picked up and shook like a stuffed animal in the arms of a child. "Good to see you too," he strained.

"It's been forever, Hawk. How ya been? How's the..." Koz hesitated, looked around, then continued in more hushed tones. "How's the FBI treatin' you?"

"Pretty well," Hawkins replied with a chuckle. "Let me introduce you to a friend of mine, Samantha Land."

Koz bowed and extended his hand as he introduced himself.

"Such a pleasure to meet you, ma'am. Welcome to my establishment."

"The pleasure is mine," Land said as she shook hands. "I've heard so much about how great the food is here."

"Well, if you two will take a seat, I'll be happy to personally prove that to be true." Koz said. "Drinks?" Hawkins and Land called out their sodas of choice. Hawkins pointed Land to a table and she headed for the seats. Koz leaned over and whispered something to Hawkins, chuckled loudly, then retreated to the kitchen. Hawkins walked over with a grin and sat down.

"I'm assuming that was for me," Land said.

"He told me I knew how to pick them," Hawkins said sheepishly.

Land smiled. "Nice to know he approves."

The burly cook brought the food to the table and hurried off to wait on the lunchtime rush. Land noticed Koz spoke animatedly to everyone who packed into the small restaurant.

"Does he know everyone by name who comes into this place?" she asked.

"He does if you come more than twice," Hawkins replied. "And most everyone who makes it past the outside and actually eats here does."

"Well, I'll be back," Land said. "The food is great."

"I always liked it, "Hawkins replied. "And I could always get Voodoo Zapp's chips here. I had to run a lot of those off when I went to Quantico, though."

"I'll bet." The two ate silently for a few moments before Land spoke again.

"So, is there a special someone in your life?"

"Me?" Hawkins asked then realized how foolish that had sounded. "No, afraid not."

"Why not?"

"If you think that's why I held back from kissing you, it's not. I...I had a special someone a few years ago."

"Didn't work out?"

Hawkins hesitated for a moment. "Not exactly." Land immediately regretted what she had said—she knew whatever it was, it wasn't good. She could see he was working himself up into telling a story his body language indicated he would rather forget.

"Her name was Anna. We had been together since high school, went to the same college. She was going through law school at Loyola while I pastored a church here in New Orleans. She was such a rock while I wrestled with the decision of whether or not to go into the Bureau. We prayed together about it, a lot. She knew I didn't want to chase down on the wrong road. When I felt like the Bureau was what I was supposed to do, she supported me one hundred percent. It took almost a year for my background check to get finished, and she would be graduating from law school about the time we estimated I'd be leaving for training in Quantico. I figured it was time to put up or shut up, so I proposed and she accepted." Hawkins paused for a moment. Land considered telling him he didn't need to continue, but he began speaking again before she could interject.

"We celebrated these events by going with my folks to Spain. We had always wanted to go, and my parents had just bought an apartment in Valencia as a vacation place. Dad was a big shot in the financial world. He had done very well for himself and had gotten very wealthy, so he and Mom bought this beautiful three-bedroom apartment not far from the beach. They were so excited for us that they took us to Valencia to show us the place and take us shopping. Anna's parents had died in a car wreck when we were in high school, so my folks were all she had. Mom took her to this fancy shop and had her fitted for a custom designer dress. We shopped and ate and had a great time. The last day, we were supposed to catch our flight late in the afternoon. I had someplace I wanted to go, and Anna was going with my parents to finish off some business Dad had, so I was going to meet back up with them for lunch." Hawkins paused.

"So what happened?"

He took a deep breath. "That was the day the Basque separatists detonated the truck bomb in the shopping district."

"Oh, Hawk." Land knew the event well. The ETA, a Basque separatist group, had been a thorn in the side of the Spanish government since the late 1950s. Starting out as a group dedicated to preserving Basque culture, they had transformed into a terrorist organization intent on organizing the Basque, scattered between Spain and France, into their own nation. They had increasingly turned to terroristic methods over the years, and hundreds of people had died as a result. The Valencia bombing was one of the final attacks before ETA effectively disbanded.

"I had just walked out of the lobby of our building when I felt the explosion, thought it was a garbage truck dropping a dumpster or something. Then I heard the sound, like a thousand cars crashing. I heard someone talking on their cell phone to someone who said a car had blown up in the shopping district. I started running. I was calling Mom, Dad, and Anna on their cell phones, but the system was already jammed with calls. It didn't seem real. It was like a dream where you know it's a dream and you're trying to wake yourself up, but you can't. People were running away from the area, and rescue workers were piling in. Everyone else was trying to leave, and I was going in. I had already been recruited by the Bureau at that point, and was still going through my background check, but I was telling people trying to turn me around that I was with the FBI so they might let me through. It worked. I wound up helping injured people get out of the area while I was searching desperately for Anna and my parents. I guess I breathed in too much smoke, because I passed out and woke up in a triage area several blocks away."

"Hawk, I'm...I'm so sorry."

Hawk continued talking. "Bob Shear, the SAC who recruited me, got me plugged in with the Legat out of Madrid. He got me the necessary clearances, and they treated me like a full agent. I spent several days in the zone, not doing much more than wandering around trying to help in the rescue and recovery. I never found them. No trace. But I was finally able to get my cell phone working after a couple of days and check my voicemail. There was one message. It was from Anna." He paused again. "She said she was having such a great time, that this all seemed like such a wonderful dream and that she never imagined she could be so happy. She told me she loved me, more than I would ever know, and the message ended. The bomb went off only a few minutes later."

Sam put her hand on Hawk's cheek and gently stroked it. "I am so sorry, Hawk. I can't imagine what you must have gone through."

"I was completely overwhelmed. It was so bad I just kind of shut down for a couple of weeks. Other agents had lost friends and colleagues, too, so they hooked me up with the Division's crisis counselor and told me to call if I needed to schedule for continuing assistance. I thanked them and went back home. As I said, Dad was very wealthy, and my brother and I split the inheritance. We sold a lot of the real estate and divided those proceeds, same with the stocks. He got the boats, and I got the cars. He and his wife wanted me to come and live with them in Texas for a while, but they have two kids and I didn't want to come in and mess up their life too badly. It worked out, because it was only about a week later I got called up for Quantico."

"Why isn't any of that in your file?" Sam asked, already knowing the answer.

"I wanted to work in CT, and SAC Shear knew my parents and fiancée being killed in a major terrorist attack might raise a couple of flags along the way. He went through channels all the way up and got it redacted from my profile."

Land had a wistful look in her eye, one Hawkins correctly took for sympathy. "You haven't gotten past Anna, have you?"

"You know, Sam, I haven't. I mean, it's been several years

now, and in some ways it's seems even longer. I've got a whole new life since then. But every time a friend would try and set me up, and I would try to go out with someone else, all I could see was her. It felt like...it felt like I was cheating on her, if that makes any sense."

"It does." She looked at her plate, then back at him. "I'm sorry I made you kiss me, Hawk. I never would have if I had known."

"No, no. I'm glad you did, Sam." Hawkins took a deep breath. "You make me feel like...well, I didn't know if I could ever feel that way again. But coming so close to being killed, to almost losing someone else...well, it was just a little too much at the time, I thought." He took her hands in his. "But let me assure you, kissing you was the best thing I have done in a long time. There are no guarantees in this life, for sure. I'm grateful for every moment Anna and I had together. But I'm not going to miss out on what might be, with you, because I'm afraid of tomorrow."

"Well, *that's* a big change," she said.

"I overstated my case there at the end, didn't I?"

Sam laughed. "Not at all. I was beginning to think maybe you didn't like me."

"Far from it," Hawkins said.

Land smiled, and Hawkins pulse accelerated slightly. "Nice to know I'm appreciated." She took a sip from her red plastic cup. "And in such fine settings."

Hawkins laughed. "Maybe when this is over I'll take you to dinner at Emeril's. We can wear something a little nicer than jeans and tennis shoes, if you'd like."

"I think I'd like that very much," Land said, and started to say something else when she was interrupted by the chirping of a cell phone. Hawkins reached into his back pocket and pulled out the electronic device. The caller ID showed "FEDERAL BUREAU OF INVESTIGATION".

"Hawkins."

"Agent Hawkins, this is Director Van Horn. I'm on a conference call with Senator Valerie Keaton, the chairperson of the Senate Intelligence Committee. I think she has some information you are going to want to hear about William Matheson."

Hawkins sat up a little straighter in his seat. "Yes sir. Can I help you, Senator Keaton?"

"No, but I believe I can help you. The President informed me you were looking into the BEAR Corporation, and possibly William Matheson."

"Yes, ma'am."

"Several years ago, when I first was elected to the Senate, I met William Matheson at a Washington dinner. He was trying to drum up support in the Senate for an exemption from FDA monitoring due to the nature of his company's research. He explained how some of the financial backing might be questionable at first glance, but the end result was going to be for the betterment of humanity, or something along those lines. I suppose he thought I was softening up, when he told me about what he claimed happened to him in Tibet, and it is very different from what he has told others."

Hawkins grabbed a legal pad a pen out of his satchel. Land looked at him inquisitively.

"Senator Keaton, I have CIA Case Officer Samantha Land here with me. Would it be alright with you if I added her to our conversation?"

"Absolutely," she replied. Hawkins punched in the codes that would connect his call to Land's phone and would allow her to hear the senator's story. Land's phone chirped, and he heard several clicks as her phone was relayed through the STE system.

"Go ahead, Senator. We're listening."

CHAPTER TWENTY-TWO

"What did you find?"

"The available information which could be easily accessed was very limited, as you could imagine," Seth Warrick said. "It seems Hawkins has been with the Bureau for a little over four years. He has distinguished himself in his duties in his time there. Interestingly enough, Agent Hawkins is a Seminary graduate."

"Excuse me?" Matheson asked incredulously.

"You heard right. He was a minister for several years before he entered the FBI." Warrick heard the silence in the line, and knew his employer was considering this. He loved the irony, and knew the other man would also.

"Appropriate," Matheson declared. "What about the young woman?"

"She is something entirely different. She served in the Army for a few years, nothing particularly significant in her records, then went to work for their State Department in the London station."

"CIA," the man pondered, more a statement than a question. She was obviously more than the sum of parts Warrick had found. Since she wasn't in the FBI, she obviously worked for someone else, some agency which prized secrecy even more than the FBI.

"Possibly, or NSA. Perhaps military intelligence from one branch or another, but she's apparently not FBI, although I can't be sure."

Warrick heard a chime in the background. "My assistant is buzzing in for me. Someone must be here. I'll call you back," then hung up the phone.

"Yes?" William Matheson said into his speakerphone.

"The two federal agents are here to speak with you again, Mr. Matheson."

That's quick, he thought to himself. *They were here only four hours ago.* He panicked momentarily, wondering if they had been listening in on the conversation. He had secured his phone lines as well as any civilian corporation could, but he knew there were ways around it if one had the technology and the determination, and the American Intelligence Community had both. He composed himself, banishing such pessimistic and paranoid thoughts from his mind. No, if he were to succeed, he had to play his role perfectly. "Send them in."

The two agents walked in, and all three went through the same pleasantries they had a few hours before.

"I must admit, I didn't expect to see you again so soon, Agents."

"Sorry to impose on you, Mr. Matheson, but we had some additional information come up on Warrick, his prior activities, and why you placed him as CEO of your company," Land said.

"I am not prepared to toss someone to the wolves because of a cloudy past, Agent Land."

"A person with a cloudy past, just like you, Mr. Matheson?" Hawkins asked. Land produced another file folder, this one with Matheson's name across the top. "We knew you had a period of years which were something of a blank slate. Your account of those times is public record, and has been reported in magazine articles more than once. But the reality is somewhat different, it seems." Matheson shifted in his chair slightly. His body language told Hawkins he was pushing the right buttons, so he continued.

"We found out your expedition party was trapped in an avalanche. Everyone but you perished, and the only reason you survived was because a group of Tibetan monks found you in the nick of time. They nursed you back to health over a period of weeks, and you came to be fascinated by them. You had thrived on material possessions and technology, and yet you had never found peace. These monks, however, living in a primitive village in one of the most remote parts of the world, had discovered true joy, true contentment. You remained there for years, until another group came upon the little village—Muslim extremist converts from a village a short distance away. They came to pros-elytize the monks, to convert them to the true way of Allah as they understood it, but the monks weren't interested. They were gracious toward the visitors, and listened to some of what they had to say, but they weren't interested in following the path of Islam. So the extremists returned a few days later and slaugh-tered the monks, the entire village. You escaped the carnage only because one of them hid you in a secret room in the floor of his hut. Not long after you were inside, the invaders murdered the one who had saved your life, and you were powerless to do anything about it." Hawkins paused for a moment, letting the revelation hang in the air. "Something like that can change a person, can't it, Mr. Matheson?"

Matheson held his expression the entire time, apart from a slight movement in his eyes. Hawkins continued.

"And that's what this is all about, isn't it, Mr. Matheson? Revenge? Striking back at *all* religions because of a few errant followers of one belief system? We were able to find the sources of some of your funding over the years, and there were several interesting names. I don't think some of the people on this list will like it when they find out the money and materials they supplied to you is likely going to be used against *them*, too. You got them to support your cause because you managed to convince them their assets were going to be used to strike at the 'Great White Satan.' Which is precisely the message Warrick gave in the video he sent to the networks wearing his Halloween costume. Little did they all know you were targeting *them* as well. Muslim, Christian, Jew—all the major world religions were your targets. You'd start the fire, get everyone at each other's throats, then hit while no one was looking. Because it wasn't just religion anymore that was the problem." Hawkins leaned in, his voice lowering. "You wanted a *purging* to take place, so civilization could be freed from the self-imposed dictatorship that is organized religion, and man could commune with nature in harmony. Or something like that, anyway. Sound close to the mark, Mr. Matheson?"

Matheson's expression had remained unchanged, but Hawkins noticed the man's forehead seemed redder. "I believe if you have anything else to say, Agent Hawkins, my attorney should be present to hear it. I think he would be most interested to hear you are attempting to besmirch my good name."

"I don't believe you have a good name, Mr. Matheson," Hawkins said. "I believe you're a coward. I believe you took the easy way out." He felt the rage rising up in his chest, but he squeezed it back down. "I've lost people I cared about at the hands of evil people, too. But I'm not killing innocent people to make up for it."

Matheson's lips were slightly pinched together now. "I'm going to have to ask you to leave."

"Gladly," Hawkins responded as he and Land stood and turned to go.

"You can keep those," Land said, pointing to the two folders lying on Matheson's desk, then they walked out. "We have more of them."

"You got him?" Land's voice asked over E. J. Niels' earpiece.

"Got 'em *both*," he said, his fingers flashing over his keyboard.

"Running hi-def ears and tracers on both lines. We'll be able to clip any other calls they make to anybody else, not to mention email and text message intercepts."

Niels was tied into the network over at NSAC, the National Signals Analysis Center, and had spent a fair amount of time over the last few days bouncing back and forth between Crypto City, Langley, and Bureau Headquarters. Director Van Horn himself had gone before the FISA—Foreign Intelligence Surveillance Act—judge and presented the case for allowing high-level monitoring of Matheson and Warrick. He had invoked United States Signals Intelligence Directive 18 (USSID 18), "Limitations and Procedures in SIGINT Ops of the US SIGINT System", which stated: "Domestic communications that are reasonably believed to contain foreign intelligence information shall be disseminated to the FBI (including US person identities) for possible further dissemination by the FBI in accordance with its minimization procedures." Further, it states: "Intelligence and Foreign Communications between two Americans can be retained and distributed at the discretion of the Director of NSA, providing that he determines that the intercept contains 'significant foreign intelligence or possible evidence of a crime.'" All of these criteria had been met, and the judge granted the warrant. Now the full resources of the FBI, NSA, and CIA were directed at two men on opposite sides of the globe.

"That didn't take long," Niels said as the windows on his screen changed color, signifying information was being transmitted along the intercepted lines.

Matheson typed furiously at his computer, entering the code which allowed him access to his encrypted computer. He opened the instant messaging program—he couldn't call Warrick as they would no doubt be looking for outgoing calls—but they wouldn't be able to track the encrypted IM network he and Warrick had established. Some of the best hackers in the world had been employed to provide secure communication between the two for fear of "industrial espionage", and it would serve them well this day.

WM: They're onto us. H and L just left, and they know everything. I threatened them with my attorneys, but they'll be back. We must act now. B is a go.

SW: Are you sure? This is advancing our timeframe considerably. I'm afraid some things may fall through the cracks.

WM: We need the advantage of a major distraction now. And I want the casualties. Don't think right now. Just do it. Give the order for B.

SW: Very well. Sending the order now.

Matheson sat back in his seat. The event happening today would buy him some time, but Warrick was right. This moved the timeframe up several weeks, but they had no choice now, their hand had been forced. The overall impact might now have to be lessened somewhat, but the devastation should still be enough to tilt the religious world into the chaos it deserved. And there was nothing the smug FBI preacher could do.

Matheson had struggled to be pleasant at all during the visit. Hawkins represented everything he hated: a Christian, a *preacher* of all things, joining the ranks of gun-toting killers employed by the American government. It wasn't just the American government he hated, of course; he hated most of those who had helped him get to this point with the same fervor. *All have sinned and fall short of the glory of God*, he thought. He knew their Bible said that. They were all guilty, all sinners, to use their own terms, and they would pay for their lack of vision.

Hawkins and Land were driving back to the CIA safe house

where they were quartered while in the Big Easy. Land had her hand-held computer out, looking at the live feeds Niels was sending her. Niels signed off to make sure Warrick and Matheson were being monitored in real-time at all times. They couldn't afford to let either of these men slip away now.

"'B'?" Hawkins asked. "Like 'site B'? 'Plan B?'"

"I don't know," Land said, "but we'd better figure it out soon. Whatever it is, it's not good. 'I want the casualties.' What kind of sick person is he?"

"We know what kind of sick person he is. Now we need to stop him, before we find out the hard way what B is."

CHAPTER TWENTY-THREE

It was a beautiful day in Boston, with clear skies and a pleasant breeze. People were walking along the waterfront, strolling through the park, and otherwise enjoying the mid-summer day. The students at the Muslim Center of Boston had finished another day of studies, and their families were joining them at the end of the day for a meal together and a time of prayer. Their Imam had urged them to pray daily for those who had suffered in the recent attacks, as well as to pray for those who committed such vile acts. None who had gathered here this afternoon advocated such violence for any reason; most couldn't comprehend how violence would accomplish anything worthwhile. Although they were all well aware of the senseless attacks against people of faith, it hadn't occurred to them to feel unusually threatened in their particular gathering place. After all, the two previous attacks had been in the south, and had been directed at Jews and Christians, both of which were to be viewed as sister faiths. There were certainly differences between the three, but none were worth killing for.

No one paid much attention to the exterminator spraying for bugs in the back hallway of the building. Nor did they pay attention to the fact he wore a bulky chemical suit—after all, he *was* spraying and working with pesticides. The man worked his way down the hall to the room where the large air handlers were located. He closed the door behind him, removed the metal covers, and placed a small metal canister inside each of the air handlers. A small timer attached to the latches would activate a detonating charge. The charge was nothing more than the equivalent of a fancy firecracker, but it would be sufficient to blow open the latch. Once the seal broke, the contents of the canister would be released into the air and pulled into the air handlers. The substance had no odor, so the people inside would not notice it. The exterminator finished spraying the contents of his small tank, then exited the building. The building's occupants never heard the pop which sealed their fates.

President Hathaway was having an afternoon snack of Diet Dr. Pepper and honey wheat pretzel sticks. His physician had given him a clean bill of health, but the President's cholesterol had been a little high, so the First Lady ordered the kitchen staff to cut out the salt and vinegar chips, cashews, and beef jerky he favored. Now he was relegated to diet sodas that tasted like battery acid—although the Diet Dr. Pepper was surprisingly good—and bland pretzel sticks without enough salt or taste. He nearly dropped the soda bottle when the National Security Advisor burst in.

"Karen, what the..."

"I'm sorry, sir, but this is important," she said. "We have a major incident in Boston. We're afraid this is biological in nature."

"What is it?"

"A Muslim center called 911, reporting several people had fallen violently ill. Seventeen seconds into the call, the caller began screaming and dropped the phone. The 911 operator had to pull her headset off, then started panicking from what she had heard. Her supervisor had the presence of mind to call the

Boston FBI Field Office, and they sent out their HazMat team. FEMA deployed shortly thereafter for quarantine, and CDC is on the way to the site."

"Did anyone leave the building? Do we have to worry about tracking anyone who may be contaminated?"

"Mr. President, there were no survivors."

Hathaway swallowed hard. "How many?"

"First estimate is over 140."

"Dear God." The President of the United States took a deep breath. "Get the Cabinet together."

"What have you got, Jim?" The Attorney General asked.

The Director of the FBI handed the AG a file folder marked GODKILLER. After Atlanta, the case had outgrown the CHURCHBOM moniker. Since people of faith were being targeted, someone made the comment that whoever was behind this was probably going to go after God next. While there was unilateral agreement God could handle murderous scum just fine, the title seemed to stick. It just had the certain ring to it FBI investigation titles needed to have. The AG opened the file as James Van Horn continued.

"As you can see, we have uncovered a significant connection between our initial suspects and BEAR. Ra's al Xuffash was a primary shipper for BEAR, and there had been money flowing both ways between Xuffash and Matheson. Funds were traced back to ISIS, as well as individuals and groups in Somalia, Syria, Lebanon, and Iran through Xuffash, who laundered it through the shipping company. He then donated large sums to Matheson's "research charities", and Matheson in turn cut a portion back to Xuffash. Xuffash was crooked, though, and would skim from the top of every deal that came his way. It was only a matter of time before someone whacked him. In fact, Matheson and Warrick might have bumped him sooner if they hadn't decided to use his son to do a little recruiting for the Jacksonville incident. When they became a liability, *poof.* Atlanta, on the other hand, was organized by a man Warrick had known in England, one Matthew William Everett. He has provided us with a wealth of information about financial transactions and recruiting, as well as confirming Matheson and Warrick using FOA to try and start a religious war."

"How'd you get him to talk?"

"We told him he's go down for all of it himself, and assured him we could make it stick. He bought it and began singing. He's a pretty nasty character himself—he killed the other assailants to cover his tracks, but couldn't get out of the room fast enough. So he laid low, waited on the cops to come in and planned on killing them to make good his escape. Didn't work out for him. Anyway, we've been able to follow the money trail back to BEAR out of France. We've got Matheson and Warrick by the purse strings. We also have Matheson's experience in Tibet which shows probable cause, if not outright motive. Someone could ask relevance on Warrick's past, but the Behavioral Analysis Unit believes it serves to establish sociopathic tendencies, something which comes in handy if you're planning mass murder."

"You've convinced me," the AG said, still poring over the files. "I'll get the warrants for you in the next thirty minutes."

"Thank you, sir."

"Excuse me, sir?" a female voice called from the door.

"Yes, Elise?"

"The President is on the phone."

"Hang on, Jim." The AG picked up the phone. "Yes, sir, Mr. President." Van Horn watched as the blood drained from the Attorney General's face. "I see." There was a pause. "Well, Mr. President, I can tell you than Director Van Horn has just presented me with actionable intelligence which tells us who is behind all of this." Another pause. "Yes, sir, we're certain William Matheson and Seth Warrick are primaries, and they're using BEAR as a front, possibly for the production of weapons of mass destruction." Van Horn looked at the AG, trying to read from his eyes what the President was saying. Elise spoke again, this time to Van Horn.

"Director Van Horn, SAC Boston is holding for you. He says it's urgent."

Boston. "B". In less than two hours it had gone from an internet instant message to deadly attack, and suddenly Van Horn understood the AG's comment about BEAR possibly producing weapons of mass destruction. He ran for the outer office, fearful of what he would hear from the Boston SAC. The AG covered the mouthpiece of the phone and called after the FBI Director.

"Jim, get these animals!"

CHAPTER TWENTY-FOUR

The security guard read the newest issue of Sports Illustrated for the fifth time today. He really needed to start bringing more reading material with him. He felt confident there couldn't be a place that needed a security guard any less than this BEAR office. After all, who would try to steal cancer stuff? He had been doing his job for months now, and had never seen more than the half dozen people who worked there come and go. He had taken special notice of the two visitors earlier today, and had been intrigued when he learned they were Feds. Not long after they had left, a Fed Ex guy had come in. *More visitors today than in the last month,* he had thought.

His thoughts were interrupted when he saw several cars and a Suburban wheeling into the parking lot at a high rate of speed. He dropped the Sports Illustrated as he stood from behind his metallic kiosk, his hand instinctively reaching for his pistol. Suddenly people wearing bulletproof vests with "FBI" emblazoned across the chest poured through the doorway, pistols drawn. He immediately realized having his hand on the pistol was a terrible idea. He raised his hands out to the side as the agents pointed 4 gun barrels at him. Two more agents secured the receptionist, while 4 other agents ran down the hallway. The man and woman he had seen earlier headed for Mr. Matheson's door. Then he couldn't see anymore, because the agents spun him towards the wall and forced him to his knees before he could think. He laced his fingers behind his head as he was instructed, and they handcuffed him. Moments later, the man and woman were back, standing on each side of him.

"Where is Matheson?" the man asked.

"I don't know," the security guard stammered.

"His car is here," the woman said.

"I'm telling you, I don't know. We never see him come and go. He always enters the back way. There's a door that leads out of his office to the parking lot. I don't know what to tell you." He could hear the sounds of drawers being opened, computers and peripherals being unplugged and carried away. What was going on?

"You'd better hope we don't find out otherwise, or you're going to be on the hook for a few hundred dead innocents," the man said, and then the guard was snatched to his feet and hauled out to a waiting van, where the other six people who worked at the BEAR New Orleans office were already seated. The van doors slammed shut, and the vehicle turned and sped from the parking lot.

"What do you mean, you're not going to cooperate?" Secretary of State Wilson Nelson asked the French Foreign Minister, Jacques Lupierre, over the secure phone line in his office.

"I'm afraid, Wilson, that you simply cannot waltz into our country and stick your noses into the business of corporations based in this country. If you are so interested in them, perhaps you should have encouraged them to stay there instead of moving here."

"Come on, Jacques. We've got a hundred dead Muslims

whose only crime was being Muslim. You've seen the same intel I have. Matheson and Warrick are dirty, and we think that plant is too. We need to check it out."

"Ah, so you *think* it is dirty. And if it is not, what will you search next? Will you take over our country until you are sure there are no weapons of mass destruction to be found?"

"Unwarranted sarcasm isn't going to accomplish anything, Jacques."

"And neither will this conversation," Lupierre said. "I am sorry, Wilson, but we are going to have to refuse your request. I will, however, see to it that a team of our own inspectors travels to the facility and has a look around."

"That's not going to be sufficient."

"It will have to be."

"You've got a lot of Muslim people in your country, Jacques. Do you really want them thinking you're protecting some who killed a bunch of their brethren?

"Have a pleasant day, Mister Secretary."

"And you, Minister." Nelson slammed down the phone. "If there was a way to bottle arrogance and stupidity and sell it, he would be a multibillionaire." He pressed the intercom button on his phone.

"Shelley, get me the President please. I'm going to need to see him in person if I can."

Mark Woodley had just aimed his Dodge Charger off I-295 toward the Jacksonville Field Office when his cell phone rang. He pressed the button on the touchscreen radio, activating the hands-free feature.

"Mark Woodley."

"Mark, it's Shear. Where are you?"

"Just about to turn into the parking lot."

"Well, turn around. I need you to get to JIA right now.

Everett just gave up a name—Dmitri Sergovich. Former Soviet bioweapons scientist. Matheson bought his services a few years ago, and Sergovich has apparently found a conscience."

Woodley spun the Charger around and launched back onto the freeway, lights and sirens going. "How so?"

"That's why you've got to get to JIA. He's coming in on a plane under a false passport and is due to arrive in the next hour."

"And Matheson's people are on to him."

"Right," SAC Shear said. "Looks like there is just one guy tasked to whack him. They didn't figure we would find out about him, so one low-key hitman was all they needed."

"Do we have a picture of this guy? Or at least a description?"

"CIA has an old photo of him from a few years ago. They're going to age it and send it to your phone."

"Tell them to hurry," Woodley said as roared past traffic at 110 miles per hour. "I'm going to be at the airport in 15 minutes. Do we know what airline he's coming in on?"

"Working on it. There're four flights coming in within that time frame, so we can narrow it down. But we don't want to spook the hitter, if we can help it. Be nice to grab him, too, if we can. I've got a couple other agents en route. I've also notified the Sheriff's Office, so their deputies are going to be there to keep an eye out, too. CIA is forwarding the same images to them."

"Big place to find one little Russian guy," Woodley muttered as he hit a clear stretch and accelerated to 130. "We're going to need a miracle to get him in time."

"We've had a couple of miracles to get us this far," Shear said over the speaker. "Maybe God can spare a couple more."

Dmitri Sergovich walked up the airway and into the terminal at Jacksonville International Airport. His ticket and passport declared him to be Igor Stravinsky, and that his country of residence was Romania instead of his actual home country of Russia.

Sergovich had lived in Moscow all of his life, until he moved to France 5 years ago to work for William Matheson and BEAR. In truth, he had wound up working for Seth Warrick, a man more warped and evil than Matheson himself. Evil was nothing new or shocking to Sergovich, as he had served in the Biological Weapons Development Program for the former Soviet Union when he was a young man, right before its collapse. He had helped design weapons meant to maim and kill soldiers in some of the most excruciating ways possible. Such techniques were considered psychological warfare in the days of the Soviet Union, but were considered taboo today by virtually all of the civilized world. Never mind the fact most of the civilized world had likewise had bioweapons programs at the same time. He had joined up with BEAR because of the money, but also because it offered him something he had not had since the USSR fell: self-worth. Sergovich watched as Russia had given in to its most corrupt desires, with little men grasping for wealth and scraps of power. This was different. He felt important, part of something significant.

It hadn't taken long before he realized his knowledge would not be used on soldiers at all. Some of the most infamous terrorists in the world had walked unafraid through the BEAR facility in the last few years, and Sergovich saw what evil truly was. When he learned of the plan to unleash the virus on a large scale into the civilian population of several countries through the shipments of supposed medical supplies, he knew he had to do something. Sergovich had done his part by engineering this latest iteration of what was known as BV-17 to be vulnerable to two things: high temperatures and high salinity. Over-the-counter saline solution would not be enough, nor would human perspiration, but the waters of the oceans would accomplish the task of destroying the virus. Now he just had to get word to the Americans so they could do something about it before the virus reached their shores. Once the it was loose, there would be nothing they could do. The earlier version, BV-16, was not contagious, and would only affect the individual to which it was applied, injected, or inhaled. This latest virus was highly contagious, although for just a few hours under ideal conditions, and it killed with the same speed as the other had. The intent was to kill the enemy quickly, then allow victorious forces to move through an area safe and unchallenged.

The thought of what would happen if Matheson and Warrick carried out their plan made Sergovich ill. Perhaps he was just getting weak and soft in his old age, but the thought of innocent women and children dying such horrible deaths was more than he could take. Yes, he had to reach the American officials, he thought as he walked into the main concourse. He hurried past the Starbuck's and failed to notice a man drinking a cup of coffee fall in step just a few feet behind him. The man held his newspaper under his arm, careful to conceal the poison-tipped plastic spike which resembled a coffee stirrer with a hilt. The man would get close to Sergovich, jab the spike into him, and walk away. The spike had a tip like a ballpoint pen which would release curare into the victim when stabbed. The poison would kill a grown man in less than 5 seconds. By the time the victim hit the ground the assassin would be gone, and a loose end would be eliminated.

The killer drew within five feet of his intended victim. The Russian scientist was trying hard not to stand out, but his concentration didn't allow him to sense the danger drawing near behind him. The assassin grasped the hilt of the plastic spike, turned it in his hand. The tip was sharp enough and the scientist's cotton shirt thin enough that it wouldn't require much pressure to pierce his flesh and inject the poison. The entire spike was filled with it, but a couple of drops into the man's body would be all that was needed. The assassin couldn't help but smile. This would be the easiest $25,000 he had ever made. He drew back his arm slightly as he fell in step directly behind the doctor.

Without warning a vise-like grip locked onto the wrist

holding the spike. He turned and saw a uniformed police officer swinging a black ASP tactical baton toward his face. *How did they spot me this is going to hurt*, was what flashed through his mind the instant before the metal rod struck him between the eyes.

He was right.

Sergovich turned to see the commotion behind him, and recoiled when he realized the American policeman had almost certainly saved him from death. He turned to run towards the front doors and ran straight into a massive chest covered in a dark blue polo-type shirt with "FBI" in yellow letters across the left breast. He panicked and started to run the other way when two strong hands grasped his upper shoulders.

"It's okay, Dr. Sergovich," Mark Woodley said with a smile. "I'm with the FBI. You're safe now."

"Safe," he repeated, as if trying to grasp the concept. It was likely Dmitri Sergovich had not felt safe in many years, if ever. He nodded and repeated the word. "Thank you. But we must hurry. There is much I must tell your superiors. We have little time."

"This way," Woodley said, and began walking Sergovich to the sliding glass doors which led to where his Charger was parked on the curb. He turned to see two large JSO deputies rolling the would-be killer's unconscious body over and cuffing him. A small crowd had attempted to gather, but two other deputies were shooing them away. A pair of FBI agents in regular clothes stood discreetly away from the action. If people saw the FBI grabbing someone at the airport it would garner far more attention than deputies subduing what most assumed was someone who had a few too many drinks in the bar. The deputy who had struck the assassin was a massive man, bigger than Woodley by a couple of inches in height and probably 50 pounds of muscle. The sleeves of his uniform stretched against his biceps as if they would shred at any moment from the pressure. Woodley gave him a salute. "Nice hit."

The deputy smiled and returned the salute. "That's why I'm here."

"Me, too," Woodley said as he led Sergovich through the doors and into the waiting Charger.

CHAPTER TWENTY-FIVE

"So how did Matheson slip away?" SAC Shear asked. He leaned forward in his office chair, the telephone gripped tightly in his hand.

"He had some luck, for one thing," Hawkins said, the frustration evident in his voice. "Niels told me they had a whole constellation which was supposed to be tasked on the building and the surrounding area, but a glitch kept all but one from being up at that point, and it was operating on a 2-minute delay due to a processing problem. They got the sats up 25 minutes before we hit. But Matheson's car never left. The only traffic which came and went was a Fed Ex truck. We didn't see any new packages that had been delivered, and the receptionist stated the driver said someone had called for a pickup. She told him she hadn't, and no one else other than Matheson would have called. She buzzed his office, and he didn't answer, not unusual in and of itself. She apologized, and the driver left. I think he got on that truck."

"Well, wouldn't Matheson leaving the building have been on the sat imagery?"

"That's where his luck came in. The truck pulled in on the side of the building near the covered walkway. Matheson could have come out the back door of his office and slipped into the truck without being seen. We had two agents across the street who didn't notice anything, for crying out loud."

"You're looking for the truck," Shear said. It wasn't a question.

"The driver has missed several stops and hasn't been heard from in the last few hours. We've got an APB out," Hawkins replied. "We have techs going through the files and computers we grabbed from the BEAR office, and the employees are being questioned, although they don't seem to know much. It appears Matheson was paying them well to sit there, file paperwork, answer phones, and watch videos. Most of the real work is done at the facility in France."

"And we're hitting a brick wall there," Shear said. "Director Van Horn informed me SecState was on the phone with the French Foreign Minister and he's being a creep. The President has put in a call directly to the French President but they're saying he's out of the office for a summit meeting with some regional leaders. CIA sats show he's sitting in his office watching dirty movies."

"Nice," Hawkins replied. "We could use some good news."

"Well, I can give you some of that. The good news is Dmitri Sergovich is singing like a canary," Shear said. "He's in with Woodley right now. They've got him talking with CDC also to give them the full rundown on this virus."

"And?"

"It's a nasty thing he had created when he was working for the Russians. A variant of the type that killed our original suspects here, only this one is highly contagious, albeit for a short period of time. Aggressive infection, accelerated death, and the virus is dead within a couple of hours. The area is clear for invading troops to come in or, in this case, whatever Matheson has in mind after the virus is released."

"I don't think he has any plans beyond that," Hawkins replied. "Right now he is simply interested in releasing the virus and killing as many people as he can. He's likely frustrated things haven't escalated with more violence between the religious groups, despite his best efforts, and he's frustrated because learned about his and Warrick's background. When he finds out we have Sergovich, he'll count his losses and go for the big hit, if he hasn't already."

"Sergovich seems to know a lot about that, too. We'll get back with you when we get more."

"Yes, sir." Hawkins replaced the handset into the receiver and updated Land on what he knew.

"He's going to go for the big show now," the CIA case officer said. "He's not going to wait. He knows if he does, he'll never be able to pull it off. He's going to do what damage he can while he can still do some damage at all."

"A cornered animal is usually the most dangerous."

"And we have *two* of them trapped."

"So you're clear," Seth Warrick shouted into his mobile phone. The loading docks were noisy, and he had to strain to hear the voice on the other end of the line.

"Yes, I'm fine," he said. "Leon Grimes picked me up in a package truck he acquired and I was able to slip away. Manon just arrived here as well." Matheson looked across the floor of the empty warehouse to see the tall, athletic French woman cleaning an Uzi submachine gun.

Leon Grimes was also there, hanging yellow jumpsuits on a rack mounted onto the old brick wall. Grimes was a mercenary with years of experience in killing people. It was a job he enjoyed, and one he did well. He had served in the United States Army years ago, but his loyalties now were to whomever could pay him the most. And William Matheson paid him a great deal of money. He had been on retainer with Matheson for several years, laying low by working at BEAR as supervisor of security. He had been forced to keep a low profile following an altercation with some American military and CIA operatives a few years back, but it seemed the winds of time had helped that storm to blow over. The mercenary walked over to the back of a Ford Expedition which sat in a service bay. Next to it sat a large Federal Express delivery truck.

"We're running a little late leaving with this last ship. The first one went out 12 hours ago, and we'll be leaving in about two hours ourselves. We'll arrive in Charleston a couple of hours after you, but the timing should still be adequate."

"That will be fine," Matheson said. "What about the plant?"

"The plant is in lockdown, no one in or out until the trucks leave. They'll be loaded and heading to their destinations within 6 hours, if all goes smoothly. Sergovich abandoning us complicated matters some, as we were having some storage and containment issues. We were able to resolve them, but it has just taken time. We are still several weeks ahead of our original timeframe..."

"Because we have no choice!" Matheson shouted. "If we don't act now this will all be for nothing! They've been able to completely unravel years of planning in a matter of weeks, primarily because of your botched killing of Xuffash!"

Warrick took a deep breath. "Regardless, we are going to accomplish the mission. Crying about it isn't going to do any good now, so we need to focus on the task at hand. I'll deliver my payload to Charleston, and we'll meet back at Calais in three weeks, just like we planned."

"Yes, three weeks," Matheson said. He had purchased a three-bedroom cottage a few miles from the shore in Calais, paying cash for it and using a false name to make the transaction more difficult to trace. The name was a full fake identity, one he had spent years and hundreds of thousands of dollars preparing for use following the release of the Battle Virus. That would be especially important now, as the American authorities knew of his involvement. BEAR would be finished, but it had served its purpose. The years of cancer research had only served to cover the perfection and manufacture of BV-16 and BV-17. Now it would be shipped to hospitals around the globe, packaged as disinfectant spray. It had been a brilliant move, he thought. They all respected BEAR because of the success in cancer research. When they heard BEAR was releasing a disinfectant, they all swarmed the company with orders for their newest product. The new product produced by BEAR had been ordered by hospitals in America, the Middle East, and Asia. The disinfectant meant to kill germs would instead release a germ which would kill them.

"You won't hear from me again until then. Good luck," Warrick said. He flipped his phone shut and threw it into the English Channel. He didn't need it any longer, nor did he need Matheson any longer. He grew increasingly furious Matheson had the gall to blame him for the disastrous turns their plan had taken. Matheson was arrogant and useless, and when this was all over, he and Manon would kill him. Then they would take what was theirs and spend their days as they chose. They could take advantage of the chaos which ensued and slip away. Matheson wanted to change the world by undermining its main religions, but Warrick and Manon just liked hurting people, and there would be plenty of opportunities to do that in the future. Warrick turned back to the massive cargo ship and walked up the ramp.

Mark Woodley stood in the corner of the small interrogation room, his arms folded across his chest. He listened intently as Dmitri Sergovich talked, while scientists from the Centers for Disease Control and the Defense Department took notes in the other room.

"The BEAR facility in France no longer producing anything but biological agents," the Russian said in heavily accented English. "It has been this way for several months now."

"How much have you been able to produce?" Woodley asked. He was afraid of the answer.

"Not as much as one might think. The creation of viable biological agent is somewhat easier than developing suitable method of introduction to target. In aerosol form, if it is too light, the wind will blow it away before sufficient quantities of virus can be taken in. If it is too heavy, it will not dissipate sufficiently to maximize infection. Contagion is not in and of itself solution either, because of number of factors. Suffice to say there was enough of Battle Virus produced to release in 30 cities."

"Any how many people would be affected in each city? What is the effective range of the weapon as it stands now?"

"Virus is stored in pressurized stainless steel boxes, approximately 12 inches square. Inside pressurized box is a 1 liter container of virus. When four latches are opened on box, two on front and one on each side, compression seal is broken. This causes rapid change in air pressure inside box, which in turn causes virus container to violently shatter. This will throw open top of box and propel virus into air. We were not able to accomplish Mr. Matheson's targeted goals for dispersion, but we have estimated dispersion in average city the size of New Orleans would be sufficient to cover downtown area, as many as 100,000 people. Viability time of virus itself is 15 minutes, and those infected will be contagious for approximately 45 minutes, perhaps less, depending on concentration of virus intake. Symptoms will occur rapidly, and death will follow in less than three minutes."

"Is there an antidote, and a vaccine?"

"Of course, but I did not reveal it to Mr. Matheson. It was my hope if he exposed anyone he would become infected."

"Do you have any of the vaccine?"

"Not enough to make a difference in short term. But there is a way to destroy the virus which I introduced into its genetic makeup once I realized what Matheson and Warrick were planning."

"And that is?"

"Salt water. If virus is exposed to water with certain level of salinity, it will destroy virus. High temperatures will also eradicate it. Remember, too, once virus is exposed to oxygen, it cannot survive for more than 15 minutes."

"So how is he planning on getting it to the target cities?"

"This is why I needed to speak with you. He is transporting virus to locations in Middle East and Russia by truck. Trailers containing virus will be loaded onto trains and carried to their destinations."

"Which are?"

"I only know of two: New Orleans, and Charleston. They will arrive by cargo ships, the *Talia* and the *Melina.*"

"When are they leaving, and when are they due to arrive?"

"The *Talia*, bound for New Orleans, left before I did, to come here. The *Melina* was still in port. That is ship bound for Charleston. They were trying to time ship's departures so that they would arrive in their respective cities at approximately same time."

Woodley walked to the door. "Thank you for your help, Dr. Sergovich."

"Agent Woodley," Sergovich said before Woodley could leave. "Believe me when I say I never intended for my work to be used for such purposes as this. That is why I am trying to help you now."

"Doctor, if you were so concerned about people dying, maybe you shouldn't have made this thing in the first place. Don't get me wrong. I appreciate your help. I just wish your conscience would have gotten a hold of you and everyone else who designs things like this before you ever created this stuff." Woodley started to walk out, then stopped and turned back toward the scientist. "When I was a kid, I used to worry big scary monsters like Frankenstein would get me. Now, my kids have to worry about tiny monsters they can't see, created in a lab just like Frankenstein, getting them. And the scariest part? Those little monsters are real." Woodley walked out into the room where the scientists had been writing notes. Several of them were now on the phone to their respective superiors. One who was not looked at Woodley. "Good work, Agent."

"Don't thank me," he said as he looked through the privacy glass and into the room where a small, old Russian man sat with his head in his hands. "Thank Dr. Frankenstein."

Secretary of State Wilson Nelson was on the phone once again with Jacques Lupierre, the Foreign Minister of France, and this conversation wasn't going much better.

"Jacques, are you looking at the same transcript I am?"

"Wilson, what I see are the angry words of a disgruntled employee. You can't expect me to allow a bunch of American cowboys to come in and tear up a major pharmaceutical production facility based on this."

Nelson's head was hurting, and he realized it was because he was grinding his teeth. He wondered if this was how Eisenhower felt when he talked with DeGaulle before the Invasion of Normandy in 1944. Nearly eight decades, and the world hadn't changed all that much.

"Jacques, this is going to the U.N. Security Council in fifteen minutes, and I can guarantee you they are going to side with us on this. The President has already spoken to the German chancellor, the Russian president, the Chinese premier...do you want me to go on down the list? They all agree with him."

"We will see, Wilson. I have my orders, and you have yours. I will speak with you again later, after the Security Council discusses the matter."

"You'd better believe you will," Nelson said. "And by the way."

"Yes?"

"Tell your President to turn off the TV and answer the phone," Nelson said, and he slammed the phone down.

CHAPTER TWENTY-SIX

Captain Steve Glosson glanced at his controls through the view plate of his pressurized helmet. His aircraft, a Lockheed SR-72A reconnaissance jet, soared at the edge of space at speeds which were beyond Classified. His surveillance officer, Lt. Robert Morris, sat in the space behind him carefully monitoring their present position in relation to their target. At the speed they were traveling, they would be on top of their target and beyond in a period of a few minutes.

Glosson glanced at the gauges monitoring the aircraft's outer skin and saw it was within normal parameters for their speed and altitude. The plane was covered with a titanium alloy hull designed to withstand the heat generated by the friction of an aircraft moving at well over five times the speed of sound. The engines required a special type of fuel which only burned at super-high temperatures and under certain conditions due to the unique requirements of the propulsion system. The Lockheed Combined Cycle Scramjet and turbine engines generated more thrust the faster they went, and had allowed the aircraft to achieve velocities which were only dreamt of among the general public. The small fleet of SR-72s had replaced the legendary SR-71 Blackbirds, aircraft which had absolute freedom to spy on whatever they wished from the 1960s until the end of the 20th century. Their incredible capabilities eventually began to be overshadowed by advancing technology and were retired, the idea at the time was that satellites had superseded their capability as the best eye in the sky and had therefore rendered the super-fast airplanes obsolete.

The problem was nearly every terrorist worth their salt knew the routes most of the platforms took in the sky and could schedule their activities accordingly. One of the first things Director Price had done upon his appointment as DNI was point out this fact, and insist that either the SR-71s be recommissioned or come up with something else capable of matching the aging craft's ability to be anywhere in the world at any time. The SR-72 project was conceived to be remotely piloted, with two such craft tested. The "A" variant was developed for a human crew that mirrored the tried and true SR-71 design. Operating relatively slow-moving drones remotely had been one thing, but a multi-Mach aircraft was another, and the SR-72A took the lead as the design of choice. One of the new SR-72A spycraft had just completed its final shakedown runs and was approved for full operational use, and Price had it flying days later. The second aircraft was ready a handful of months after that, with additional examples in varying stages of production. The IC and its allies were getting more than their money's worth from the new spyplane.

"We're 2 minutes out, Cap," Morris said. "Cameras are online and targeted on coordinates."

"Roger that," Glosson replied. "Stand by." Glosson eased back on the throttles, slowing the black aircraft to just over Mach 2 to allow for multiple high-resolution shots. The pictures would be sent via satellite relay back to CIA headquarters, where analysts would make sure what they wanted to see was indeed there. DNI would then advise SecDef when all was clear to proceed. Shortly thereafter F-22 Stealth Fighters would wing their way toward the target. Spec Ops people on the ground would paint the target with a laser device, giving the "smart bombs" a trail to follow to their final destination, and the headquarters for Biological Engineering and Research would vanish in smoke and flame.

Thirty seconds out, a warning tone sounded, and an icon began blinking on Morris' display.

"Couple of bogies," he warned. "Two Mirage's at 35,000 and climbing. SecDef will love to hear about this."

"We'll be gone before they can figure out what we are," Glosson stated calmly. "You just get the shots."

"Already getting them," Morris replied as the plane's high-res digital cameras clicked away. As the pictures were taken, they were immediately sent to Langley for review. Morris checked his radar display.

"Those Mirages are starting to climb hard."

"Let 'em," the pilot said. "We're gone," and he shoved the twin throttles forward to full afterburners. The plane rocketed forward at a startling rate considering its already mercurial speed, the scramjets engaged, and the SR-72 spyplane left its would-be pursuers wondering if they had just seen a UFO or joined the long list of pilots who had just been outrun by black aircraft from the Lockheed Skunkworks..

"So you've got Mirage fighters protecting the biological weapons facility of a known terrorist on French soil?" Secretary of State Wilson Nelson nearly shouted into the phone.

"We are merely ensuring the protection of our sovereignty," Jacques Lupierre, the French Foreign Minister, replied. "We are not some insignificant group which you Americans can shove aside whenever the need arises. You are flying surveillance aircraft over our country in direct contradiction to our denial of airspace privileges. We have a right...no, a responsibility to our people..."

"Don't give me that line of crap," SecState interrupted, not even bothering with the old scripted response of: *"What recon-naissance aircraft? We don't have anything that flies at 100,000 feet and Mach 6, faster and higher than the missile your idiot Mirage pilot blind-fired at it."* "You've seen the same evidence I have. You know what's going on there, and what needs to be done."

"And we feel we can deal with the situation ourselves, at an appropriate time."

"'Appropriate time?' There *is* no more time. We are going to deal with the threat that BEAR represents, and we are requesting you cooperate."

"And if we do not?"

"Then we'll wave as we fly over," SecState said, shaking his head and wincing as he visualized that statement being repeated in the press. "Look, Jacques. You know this needs to happen. Just do the right thing and give us the clearance."

"We will get back to you on the possibility of overflight rights," the French official offered dryly, "but we will not give you a license to engage in hostilities on our soil."

"The Security Council has been briefed, Jacques, and you're all alone on this one. If you want your government to have egg on its face, then you keep pulling this stuff. Otherwise, get on board and give us what we need."

"I will speak to my president on this," Lupierre said. "Until then, any further incursions into France's airspace will be construed as an act of war."

"Save the tough talk for somebody else, Jacques. I know your capabilities, and I know ours. You don't want to get into a spitting contest, do you?"

"That is irrelevant, Wilson. This is an issue of French sovereignty."

"This is an issue of global life and death!" Nelson shouted, exasperated. "Don't you know how many people are going to die if we don't erase this plant? Do you even care? Can you forget for a moment your antagonistic attitude towards the U.S. and see clear to do what's right?"

"We will get back to you on the possibility of overflight rights," Lupierre repeated, "but..."

"See you in the air, Jacques," Nelson said, and slammed down the phone. President Hathaway wasn't going to be happy about this. Nobody in the Cabinet—or the U. N., for that matter—would be. But the French government would like it even less.

"They're not wanting to play ball, sir," SecState said. "Lupierre told me he spoke for the entire French government when he denied our request for airspace usage for our fighters."

"They don't have a choice," the Secretary of Defense growled from a massive monitor above the one POTUS looked at which displayed the Secretary of State. "We've got to go in there and take that facility out right now, before they have a chance to move any more of those biological agents out." The President sat in the War Room, but only half of the chairs around the rectangular table were filled. The individuals who would ordinarily fill those seats were scattered around Washington in an attempt to fulfill their hectic duties and were meeting with the remainder of the Cabinet via video conferencing.

"I informed French President Granger that we were prepared to act without his government's permission if necessary," POTUS said. "His reply was we must do what feel we have to do, and so would they."

"Again, sir, we don't have a choice," SecDef declared. "We've got intel 15 minutes old from an SR-72 which shows lines of semi-trailers at the loading docks, ready to take off to points unknown with who knows how much of those bio-agents. If we don't take them out now while we know where they are, we'll never catch them all in time before some of it gets used."

"I must agree," the National Security Advisor interjected. "We have a clear and present danger to our country, as well as nations around the globe. We have full confirmation of actionable intel, as well as the support of the full Security Council, with the obvious exception of France. Even the Chinese and Russians are with us on this." No one was surprised about Russia's support..

"The Congress is with you on this, Mr. President," Vice President Kirk Talbert said, with both majority and minority leaders of the House and Senate seated around him. "Any required military action has been signed off on by an overwhelming majority." It was a rare thing to see such a display of non-partisan cooperation within the Beltway, but these were extreme times.

DNI Price cleared his throat and spoke up. "Mr. President, this is a difficult decision to be certain. There will be negative repercussions, particularly but not exclusively from the French. We are never popular with certain groups and nations when we act decisively as a nation instead of mumbling about as many do. But at the end of the day, Sir, our responsibility is to the American people, and no one else. We must do what is required to ensure the safety of our citizens, both here and abroad. If we understand this to be our task, with the full weight of the intelligence and data we have on the BEAR facility, there is only one course of action we *can* take."

POTUS sat pensively for a moment, looking at the pictures of tractor trailers being filled with one of the deadliest biotoxins the world had ever known, getting ready to be hauled off to any number of places. He thought of the people who had died in the attack in Boston, the men, women and children who had screamed in anguish as their internal organs liquefied, killing them with terrifying speed but also with agonizing slowness. He looked up at his Cabinet, those men and women whom he had appointed to help him in times just like these, each one knowing full well that the final decision rested on the President of the United States.

"Do it," POTUS said.

CHAPTER TWENTY-SEVEN

The F-22 Raptor Stealth Fighters hurtled through German airspace 25,000 feet above the ground at .65 Mach, their flat-grey stealth coating rendering them invisible to both radar and eye in the moonless night sky. The two aircraft had more than enough ordinance to reduce the BEAR facility to a pile of rubble, but their concern was on what kind of reception they could expect from the French military. The Stealth Fighters were all but invisible to radar and virtually every other means of tracking aircraft, but there was a chance, however slim, of being spotted. And the French were sure to be looking hard.

They had no sooner shot into French airspace than radar warnings chirped in each plane: Mirage fighters were patrolling the skies ahead, directly on their flight path to the BEAR plant. The French fighters were some 10,000 feet above them at the moment, but the F-22s would ideally have to climb slightly in order to acquire their targets and give the smart bombs time to lock on, putting them right in the midst of where the half-dozen Mirage fighters were now patrolling. The F-22 had effective countermeasures and was certainly more than capable of defending itself against attackers. It would be tricky if the

Mirages actually engaged the Stealth Fighters, as the Americans would have no choice but to defend themselves.

Captain Josh Sudduth checked his squadron's waypoints and compared it to the pattern being flown by the Mirages. No way around it—the F-22s would have to fly right through the Mirages' patrol pattern.

"Command, this is Spitter-One," Sudduth called into the radio headset. "We are picking up mosquitoes on our picnic site, advise."

"Spitter-One, continue on course. Continue through present waypoints and advise of contact."

The six Mirage fighters were flying in pairs, each duo covering portions of an invisible circle extending 15 miles out from the BEAR plant.

"Rembrandt, this is Spitter-One," Sudduth said, radioing the Spec Ops team on the ground a mile from the facility. "Are you in position?"

"Spitter-One, Rembrandt and Picasso are in position, brush at the ready. Awaiting your signal to paint," the voice replied. On the ground were two Army Rangers dressed as old women from the nearby village. If anyone had seen them, they might have wondered what two old women were doing walking around the French countryside at midnight carrying a picnic basket. They would never imagine the treats the basket contained: a laser device used to "paint" a target for bombs that homed in on data provided by the light beam, two MP-5S sub-machineguns with 6 magazines per weapon, 6 high explosive fragmentation grenades, and night vision goggles for each man. They both lay in the grass, their dresses and head wraps covering the night camos each wore. They weren't really needed—the F-22s targeting systems were more than capable—but they were an added layer to speed the process along. By the painting the targets it allowed the F-22s to basically fire-and-forget, enabling a faster exit from the hot zone for the aircraft.

"We are t-minus 3 minutes from the picnic area. Stand by to paint."

"Roger that," the old woman with a laser targeting device said.

Sudduth was hoping the Mirages would continue to ignore them, when two of the fighters suddenly changed direction on his radar screen and began vectoring towards them.

He cursed under his breath. *They're on to us.* "Command, this is Spitter-One. Bogies have spotted us, repeat, bogies are awake. Spitter-Two, this is One. Stay on target and stand by for strike. Rembrandt, paint, repeat, paint, do you copy?"

"Roger that, One. Brushstroke's a go." The targeting computer of Sudduth's aircraft beeped as it received targeting data from the laser beam. His comlink clicked in his ear.

"Spitter-One, this is Command. You are clear to picnic, repeat, clear to picnic."

"Copy, Command. All right, Spitter-Two, let's do it." He noticed the fighters were slightly off from his wings' vector. *They know we're here somewhere, they just don't know for sure. Must be only visual.* The aircraft's stealthy radar profile protected them, but it wouldn't prevent visual identification by the Mirage fighters stalking them.

"Open doors and get ready to rumble," he said, and pressed the button which opened the doors behind which rested four laser-guided high explosive cluster bombs, the four of which were sufficient to incinerate the entire facility and any bioweapons within. If the entire wing of Stealth Fighters were able to place their ordinance on target, it would be overkill. In a worst-case scenario, however, only one would be necessary to accomplish the mission. No sooner than the bay doors were opened on the two aircraft than all six French warplanes swooped towards the revealed Stealth Fighters like angry hornets whose nest had been disturbed. Warning lights and electronic warbles sounded throughout the cockpit as the Mirages rapidly locked their weapons on target. Sudduth thought to himself that if he survived, he would never buy a croissant again.

The French pilot nearly shouted for joy when the two American F-22 Stealth Fighters appeared on his radar screen. He had caught the movement of the two grey aircraft out of the corner of his eye—at least, he thought he had—and ordered his wingman to change course with him and fly towards what he had seen. The other pilots had mocked him, saying he was just seeing UFOs again. He grimaced at the cutting remarks, regretting he ever reported seeing what he thought was a flying saucer on the Mediterranean coast. It had in fact been a lighted blimp brought in for Spring Break festivities on the Riviera, but the bottom section of lights hadn't been functioning, leaving only the oddly shaped top to be lit with an eerie glow as it hovered over the water. If he could down an American F-22 Stealth Fighter, he could leave that embarrassment behind forever. He would be a hero! He had gotten a missile off at the American spyplane earlier, but he knew he had no real chance of hitting it. These sitting ducks before him, however, were a whole different story.

The French pilot pointed the nose of his Mirage at the lead Stealth Fighter who was now racing towards the BEAR facility. He knew the factory and warehouse indeed should be destroyed, but he resented the smug Americans and the fact they thought they were better than everyone else. He was tired of their jokes about his country and their military weakness. *Let's see what they think when they come and pick up the pieces of their precious Stealth Fighter after I have shot it down!*

As he prepared to fire a missile into the Stealth Fighter, a warning tone screamed in his own cockpit. Someone had a missile lock on *him*! How was that possible? His wingman began screaming he was being locked-onto by another aircraft, and then the other four Mirages joined in a similar chorus. He looked all around his craft, seeing nothing. Suddenly, a voice sounded in his ear.

"This is Colonel Bret Hunter of the United States Air Force. You will stand down now, or you will be shot out of the sky. We have missile locks on you, and we will not miss."

He looked at his radar in disbelief. There were no planes visible except for the slight blips given off by the presently unstealthy F-22s and his own wingmates.

"Last warning," the voice said again. "We have tone on you and will fire immediately unless you stand down and return to your base."

Hunter flew in arrow formation, three other radar-invisible F-22 Raptor fighter jets to his side and slightly behind. In an attempt to demonstrate restraint to the French the remainder of the squadron of F-22s had stayed at altitude, waiting in quiet reserve only to reveal themselves if needed. They each had the Mirages locked into their aircrafts' advanced targeting systems. One of the Mirage aircraft—the one in the lead—fired a single missile at the lead F-22. Hunter toggled his weapons to fire at the single Mirage.

"Fox 2," he said, and fired a Sidewinder missile. The projectile slammed into the Mirage, not more than a half-mile ahead, and the plane erupted in a ball of flame, pieces of the aircraft hurtling towards the empty countryside below. Hunter though he saw a silhouette of a parachute above the fireball, but he couldn't be sure in the dark. Hunter arced his craft well to the side, and resumed his pursuit of the remaining Mirages.

Sudduth swore as the computer screamed a warning at him that a missile had been fired. He stabbed the button releasing countermeasures, in this case a chaff-cartridge filled with material to draw the radar-guided missile off his tail. The enemy projectile veered after the chaff like a hunting dog after a new and stronger scent, and exploded a thousand feet from the target it had originally locked onto upon launch. Sudduth reoriented his aircraft and continued his run.

The Mirage pilot gripped the straps of his harness as the parachute burst up from his ejector seat. As he watched the fragments of his Mirage falling away beneath him, he saw the dark silhouette of a United States Air Force F-22 Raptor bank around the ball of flame and shattered metal that had been his multimillion dollar fighter, and he was certain he saw the American pilot inside wave in the light of the rapidly-dissipating fireball.

From the cockpit of his F-22, Hunter watched as the confused French pilots peeled off, two-by-two, and headed away from the area back towards their home field with full afterburners.

"Bombs away, boys," Sudduth said over the comm. "Get clear, and head for home." The squadron of F-22s pulled up and away, back towards Germany. Behind them, the BEAR research and development compound erupted into a paroxysm of fire, sixteen earth-shattering explosions ripping through reinforced concrete walls and metal tractor-trailers, destroying everything within the reach of their searing heat.

CHAPTER TWENTY-EIGHT

Been a long time since I've ridden like this, Mark Woodley thought. The grey and black camouflaged Navy Seahawk helicopter in which he sat bucked up and down in the torrential rainstorm, the twin Seahawk off to starboard carefully keeping a safe distance. Both helicopters were filled with Navy SEAL teams, equipped and ready to assault the cargo ship carrying the last major unsecured shipment of Matheson's bioweapon. It had been several years, back in his own time as a Navy SEAL, since Woodley had deployed from a helicopter onto the deck of a ship, but he had kept up his conditioning by playing with the HRT and SWAT teams when he could, and SecNav had given him the nod to be the FBI representative to go on board. He had been one of the lead agents in the case, and he had earned the right to be there when it all went down.

"Two clicks to target," the pilot said in Woodley's headset. "Everybody standby."

"Remember, people. Everybody on this boat is a terrorist. They know what they're doing. Consider each of them armed." The Charlie Team Commander, a tall, lean man named David Powell, spoke over the headset from the other Seahawk. He was the regular commander of the team, but the Attorney General and the Secretary of Defense had talked SecNav into putting an Agent with them for this op.

A short tone in Woodley's ear told him Powell was buzzing him on an I-call, an individual communication no one else could hear. "I know you're a SEAL, Woodley, but I also know you've been a cop for a while now. I need you to be a SEAL first, and an FBI Agent second while you're running one of these teams. Understood?"

"Roger that," he replied. "I know you don't like having someone like me along, but thanks for taking it so well."

"The only reason I let you on one of these aircraft is because you're a SEAL," Powell replied with a smile. "If you weren't, you'd have been swimming back to the *Reagan* as soon as we got off deck." He switched back the comm to the open channel to all the SEAL operators. "All right, ladies, let's get ready." Woodley stood, along with the rest of the SEALs in his Seahawk. They checked their weapons, ensuring everything was secure for the ride to the ship's deck. Woodley checked the fast-rope harness wrapped around him and, satisfied it was secure, got in line for his turn. "Thirty seconds," the voice said. He felt the helicopter flare, the pilot bringing the nose up sharply as it slowed. Lightning flashed, illuminating the backside of the massive cargo ship before them. The helicopters were up-fitted with the latest stealth technology, superior to the birds used in the raid that killed Osama bin Laden. They had come in low enough that the ship's radar would not see them regardless, and by approaching from the rear it was much less likely they could be spotted by visual sweep. Electronic "mufflers" emitted sound waves which nullified the frequencies generated by the aircrafts' engines, so they approached the ship in near silence, like dark vengeful spirits floating over the sea. The rain was so dense they could barely see the massive vessel tossed in the thirty-foot seas before them, so their comparatively small Seahawks would be invisible.

It was a challenging task to fast-rope onto the deck of a ship in conditions like this. On smooth seas it was easy, but in a storm of this kind, the deck of the ship could move thirty feet or more up or down in a matter of seconds. It made for an unpleasant landing when the surface leaped thirty feet into the air towards you. Stopping three stories sooner than you had planned could really ruin your day.

On cue, 16 men dropped from the two helicopters with a speed an observer would deem to be freefall. Woodley squeezed the clamp controlling the speed of his descent as the deck rose toward him. His boots barely made a sound as they touched the deck, and he undid the harness holding his rope. *Still got it*, he thought as he crouch-ran to a position behind a stack of cargo containers. His squad of 8, comprised of Alpha and Bravo Teams, was responsible for the tower that contained the bridge, living quarters, and other operations facilities. The other squad was responsible for securing the bioweapons and setting the charges which would scuttle the vessel. Woodley signaled to the other squad leader, crouched twenty feet away in the darkness, and Charlie and Delta Teams moved toward the bow of the ship. Woodley looked at his own group and held up two fingers. He then held up one and pointed to starboard, then two and pointed to port. He pumped his arm, and the teams moved for their respective entry points to the tower. His squad, Alpha, moved to the entrance on the starboard side of the massive tower. Jutting upward some eighty feet above them, the ship's command bridge sat at the very top of the structure, with levels of quarters, storage, offices, and galleys between the deck on which they stood and the conn.

One of the SEALs sprayed the latch handle and hinges of the white metal door with fast-acting penetrating oil, then gently turned the handle and pulled the door outward. He then extended a small mirror into the opening and looked to ensure no one stood nearby. When he was satisfied the hall was empty, he gave an "all clear" sign and the SEALs came in from out of the rain. Woodley said nothing, but double-clicked the "transmit" switch on his headset. A quick double-click in his headset told him Bravo had likewise entered on the port side.

150 feet beneath the ship, the SSN *Seawolf* glided soundlessly through the water, its electronic ears monitoring every sound on the cargo vessel above. Nick Rooney sat at one of the monitoring consoles, scanning the audio spectrum throughout the ship. A computer program he was running then placed the audio signals on a 3D diagram of the ship, allowing the SEALs a full inventory of who was on board and where they were. Rooney was the lead technician responsible for keeping Alpha and Bravo Team in-the-know, while Doug Keene was hooked to Charlie and Delta.

"Alright, Alpha, you're clear for level one. On level 2 we have 10 Tangos. Four seem to be asleep, four are playing poker, and two are flipping through magazines," Rooney said. "Level three has five more racking, and four seems clear. It's a little loud to hear much above that yet."

"Roger that," Woodley said. "We'll do a little clearing, then report back." This was very different than his time in HRT had been. In the Bureau, the plan was to bring them in alive. Teamed with the SEALs once again, he knew their mission was not to arrest people, but to put a stop to this terrorist threat by any and all means necessary. There was only one person on board who was preferred alive, and the person was Seth Warrick. That was Woodley's mission—to bring back Warrick alive, if possible. Either way, the Director of the FBI had made plain to Woodley that Warrick could not be allowed to roam free, and Woodley understood His orders clearly.

.   .   .

Rooney watched on his monitor as the two teams worked their way up opposite stairwells to the second floor. The sound of the storm outside masked any noise they made to the human ear, but the devices at Rooney's command were the most advanced ears known to man. They distinguished between sounds at levels most people didn't even know existed, and had no problem isolating the SEALs as they navigated their way up the stairs to deck 2. The sound each operator's heart made was distinctive enough to identify them. That signal was matched to the biofeedback device each team member wore, and so each dot on the display had the individual SEAL's name above it.

Woodley spoke softly into his comlink. "Status change?"

"Negative, Alpha-1," Rooney replied. "Tangos are status quo."

"Roger," Woodley said. The entry specialist moved up and stuck the mirror around the corner. He saw the small flash of his counterpart's mirror at the far end of the hall. The point man nodded to Woodley, who double-clicked his mic. A moment later, the double-click was returned, and both teams moved into the hallway.

"Alpha-1, your first targets are in the third room on your right," Rooney said. "Ambient noise levels in the hall suggest the door is wide open." As Woodley approached, he saw the door was indeed open. The room was dark, but light from the hallway revealed two sets of bunk beds, each bed occupied by one of Warrick's mercenaries. Woodley motioned the all clear, and two SEALs moved into the room. Four shots from their suppressed MP-5s ensured the sleeping terrorists would not be a threat again.

Woodley stiffened, despite himself. He had devoted several years now to the preservation of life, but he didn't think he would find it that difficult to switch gears once more and enter the world of a SEAL. He had been in situations before where the life of an enemy had to be taken, and he had performed his duty with precision and with excellence. He had set explosive charges on the hull of a ship that would send sleeping men to their grave, and he had plunged cold knives into the heart or carotid artery of an inattentive sentry. But all those events seemed like a lifetime ago now as he heard the life gurgling out of the four men who would never rise from their bunks again. He dismissed the thoughts running through his head, and his team continued down the hall.

Charlie and Delta Teams worked their way through the narrow passageway and into the main hold of the ship. Within its cavernous confines rested containers holding enough of Matheson's Battle Virus to kill most of the people living along the east coast of the United States. The SEALs had to place 8 charges at the main joints of the ship's hull, in addition to 20 high explosive packages throughout the cargo area. The explosive packs would shatter the containers holding the virus, destroying much of the weapon with their heat and flame. Anything that survived would be finished off when the ship's hull was ripped open by the charges and the ocean claimed it. But first, they had to get the charges planted.

"You've got some Tangos in the hold," Doug Keene signaled to the leader of the squad he was responsible for. "I've got 12 walking the area, and they are all armed."

"Roger that," Paul Powell said. "Where are they in relation to our position?"

"They're working in groups of two's, three groups around the perimeter and three walking random patterns throughout the containers."

Powell turned to his two squads. "We take the three couples on the perimeter first. Delta, that's you. We'll wait till they're down, then take out the ones on the inside." He pointed his finger, and Delta Team disappeared into the half-lit hold, Powell and Charlie Team hunkering down in the doorway.

· · ·

The suppressed gunshots sounded like 10-inch guns being fired from the deck of a battleship to the computerized ears of the *Seawolf*. Rooney kept a tally of the action thus far, and it had been desperately one-sided. Alpha and Bravo had taken out 15 terrorists without so much as a retaliatory shot fired. They were fortunate, because each Tango had been armed, from Beretta 92s to AK-47s. *What is it with terrorists and AK-47s? They really need to try something new.* He knew why terrorists favored the Russian assault rifle, of course; after the fall of the Soviet Union, many of the military's weapons wound up being sold to whoever had some cash. In addition, it seemed everyone was making their version of the AK-47, and while many were not as reliable as the original, they all fired the same deadly 7.62 round with reasonable accuracy. Cheap and powerful made for a fine terror rifle.

With the sounds of the rowdy poker game silenced by the SEALS, Rooney was more easily able to scan up through the remaining three levels of the tower. The only sounds the computer registered as coming from humans was on the top deck, the control bridge. There were five voices and heartbeats, and they were all classified in the display. One of the dots blinked for a moment, and then a sub-text box opened next to it. SUBJECT IDENTIFIED, it read. WARRICK, SETH. WANTED BY FEDERAL BUREAU OF INVESTIGATION AND CENTRAL INTELLIGENCE AGENCY. NOTIFY RELEVANT AUTHORITIES ASAP. "Woodley, I've got your boy," Rooney said. "He's on the bridge, sipping on Darjeeling and crying about the visibility. You're clear all the way up to the bridge. Copy?"

"Roger that," Woodley replied, and Alpha and Bravo made their way up opposing staircases once more. On the last deck before the bridge level, Bravo found their way up the stairs blocked by several metal crates which had fallen into a jumbled pile, likely not secured properly and then tossed about by the stormy seas.

"We've got an obstruction here," one of Bravo Team said. "No quiet way around it."

"Two of you stay there and keep an eye on it, just in case," Woodley replied. "Get out of the stairwell, and move into the hallway, but stay close enough to monitor the situation. The rest of you work your way down the hall and station at the stairwell below where we are."

Woodley turned to his squad. "Our boy is on the bridge. I'd like him alive, if possible, but he doesn't get off this ship under his own power."

The point man—Bertram was his name—moved to the bridge door. After spraying the hinges and latch handle, he eased the door open. He saw the five men, the bald one identified as their main target standing by the window overlooking the darkened ship deck. Bertram gave the thumbs up, and the SEALs stormed into the room. The two men closest to them at the radio controls never saw what killed them, 9mm rounds punching neat holes in their skulls. The one manning the helm turned towards the intruders, grabbing an AK-47 pistol off the panel in front of him, and Woodley put three rounds in his chest. The Tango closest to Warrick got his rifle up but never got a shot off thanks to another SEAL and his MP-5SD. Warrick dropped to the ground, striking a switch mounted on the wall as he went down, and a dull thud rolled throughout the tower. He kicked open the door, and ran out into a staircase filled with smoke.

"Warrick's coming your way, Bravo," Woodley said, then realized what had happened: the British terrorist had set charges in the stairwells for just such an emergency, and had detonated them. Woodley mind spun for a moment as he realized he had ordered some of his men to stay by the blocked stairwell, exactly where the explosion had likely occurred. "Bravo, are you all right? Do you copy?" No answer.

Woodley looked at the SEALs crouched around him. "Go

back down and check on them. Bertram, you come with me. We're going after Warrick."

Powell heard the gunfire reverberate throughout the ship's hull, and said to himself, *So much for subtlety.* He doubled that sentiment when he heard the muffled *whumpf* of an explosion somewhere above him. The Navy crewman in his ear said something about the sonic listening systems being offline, but Powell was busy distributing his men. Too late, two of the SEALs heard two pairs of guards coming their way. Having no time for subtlety, the SEALs opened fire on the four terrorists, dropping them before they could react. The sound of the suppressed fire was barely audible in the cacophony of the ship's hold. Even so, it wouldn't be long before the other guards would know something was wrong.

No sooner than Powell and his squad spotted the two isolated SEALs that two pairs of the terrorists did as well. *Better to be lucky than good,* Powell thought. He fired four three-round bursts, and two more SEALs opened fire behind him. The four Tangos in front of him dropped, and one of his men spoke into the headset: "Two more Tangos down behind us."

"That leaves four down here. Fan out and whack 'em so we can get our job done." Without another sound, the SEALs spread out and disappeared into the shadows.

Woodley and Bertram moved into the staircase Warrick had entered. They weren't sure what they'd find, as Rooney had informed them the explosion had disturbed the aural signature of the ship sufficiently to throw off their sensitive listening equipment. It would take a minute or two to get it recalibrated to its target, but they couldn't wait. Woodley saw the staircase go down normally to a deck, turn to go further down, and end there. The detonation charges had sent the remainder of the staircase down several stories to the main deck level. The section of stairs which remained—the ones underneath Woodley and Bertram's feet—was terribly unstable.

"This is Alpha-1," Woodley spoke into his comlink. "Everybody get downstairs to the extraction point. Repeat, everyone to extraction point."

Woodley turned to Bertram. "Go back onto the bridge and shut this baby down," he said. "Then rappel to the deck as fast as you can. This party's going to be over in a few minutes."

"Right," Bertram replied. "What about you?"

Woodley pointed to a hatch which led to the outside of the tower, nearly 10 feet below where the stairs had disappeared. "I'm going after our boy," he said. Without another word, Woodley pulled a length of decel cable from his pack and affixed a grapnel to one end. Bertram took his cue and went back inside the bridge.

The grapnel Woodley attached to the special deceleration cable looked much like a small harpoon—a stainless steel shaft with a hardened wedge-shaped head designed to puncture virtually any known material to a depth sufficient to carry out its secondary operation. He fed the decel line into his fast-drop harness, then locked the shaft of the grapnel into a small pistol-type launcher and fired it towards the ceiling above him. The head punctured the metal plate and split into three spiked arms that dug into the metal back in the direction from where it had come. Woodley tugged hard against the line and, satisfied the grapnel was rooted, stepped off into space. He arced his body so as to swing towards the wall opposite the hatch door, then kicked off towards his target. He reached the hatch on the first try, grabbing the wheel-lock with his left hand. He steadied himself by grabbing the wheel with his right hand also, then planted the toes of his boots as tightly against the door frame as he could. He twisted the wheel, then leaned carefully against the door to peer outside. The walkway to his left was clear, and the right-opening door would provide cover if anyone was to the right. He opened the door fully, stepping onto the metal grating of the walkway. He pressed a pad on his harness, which sent an electrical impulse through the decel line to the grapnel, which in turn retracted the head fully into the shaft. The grapnel fell free, and Woodley hurriedly tucked the line and grapnel into his pack. He gripped his MP-5 once more, and carefully pulled the hatch door toward himself to see what was on the other side of the walkway.

CHAPTER TWENTY-NINE

President Hathaway walked hurriedly into the Situation Room, his detail of Secret Service agents encircling him. "OK, people, what's the latest?"

"The target in France has been eliminated, with no possibility of any of the biological material surviving," the Secretary of Defense said. "We were fired upon by a French fighter, but we took him down without any casualties to our own."

"Nuts. How long ago?" POTUS asked.

"About five minutes ago, Mr. President."

"Well, we'll be getting a call about that shortly."

"SecState is already on the phone with Paris," the Chief of Staff reported.

"Well, I just got off the phone with the Russian president and the Chinese premier. They are in full support. The Germans authorizing use of their airspace didn't hurt our cause with most of the other European nations." The President shook his head. "I can't believe they would be stupid enough to fire on our planes while we're going to destroy a biological weapons facility!"

"We knew the French had been talking a big talk, but it was assumed to be posturing," Air Force General Roger Heberle, the

Chairman of the Joint Chiefs of Staff said. "It's a good thing we sent in additional fighter support or it might have been worse."

Army General John Crawley, one of the Joint Chiefs, interjected. "This whole thing stinks to high heaven. How did they lock onto the Stealths so quickly? They had to have been right over the facility for them to get a blip in the few seconds the Stealths were visible."

"Seems like an awful big coincidence," SecDef said.

"They weren't just protecting France's airspace," POTUS responded. "They were protecting that plant."

"What motive could they possibly have for protecting a facility confirmed to be producing bioweapons?" the White House Chief of Staff asked. "Is it possible this thing goes higher than we think?"

"Let's not jump to any conclusions," the National Security Advisor cautioned. "We don't know that, and we're treading a fine line of this being construed as an act of war, by *both* sides."

"This whole thing is starting to stink to high heaven," the President said. "Let's find out what they're saying to SecState, and we'll take it from there. What about our sea-based ops?"

"About the first ship, it was almost to New Orleans—we intercepted it 5 clicks out in the Gulf. The boat is being cleared now, and will soon be brought into a secure port. As for the one still in the Atlantic with one of our ringleaders on board, we're on it. We have confirmed deployment, but the sub monitoring them says there's some serious stuff going down onboard."

"That's what happens when you send in the SEALs," SecNav said proudly. "It won't be long till that ship is on its way to the bottom of the ocean."

Concern crawled across General Crowley's face. "I just want the bad guys going with it, not us. At the ship's current distance from shore it would have been easier to just pop it from the air, or have the *Seawolf* plink it with a torpedo."

"Yes sir, but we felt it would be best to try and take the terrorist leader alive," Director FBI explained.

"How likely is that sending in a bunch of SEALs?" the Chief of Staff asked.

The Director allowed himself a smile. "That's why we have one of our agents with them.". He's a former SEAL himself, and still has a good rapport with the teams. I'd rather HRT took it, but this is beyond our conventional operating parameters. I didn't say it was the ideal situation, but it was the best we could do in a short timeframe."

POTUS exhaled softly. "I hope the best we could do is enough," he said. "Especially where the virus in concerned. Now what about France?"

"Best we can tell, sir, they're going to scratch out a clean spot and have a fit," SecState responded, "but that's probably all."

"Probably is a big word, Mr. President," the Chairman of the JCOS said. "French President Granger has demonstrated some quirkiness as of late, and we need to consider the possibilities."

"What possibilities? France is all alone on this one."

DNI Price made a polite motion with his hand. "Not entirely, Mr. President. The new Spanish Prime Minister and he have become quite good friends since his election. Not to mention there is a growing influence of radical groups with a strong hatred of the United States within both countries. And we still aren't sure Matheson and Warrick are the sole proprietors of FOA, or whatever this really is." Price also had information on the French government's ties to Iran and other Middle Eastern terror states, not to mention a growing concern Spain was aligning itself too often with the wrong people, but he had no presentable information and held his counsel on those matters.

"France and Spain are hardly superpowers, but they could drum up support from our other enemies," the National Security Advisor said. "Most of whom are linked with other terrorist organizations. 'The enemy of my enemy is my friend'."

"In other words, the War on Terror isn't slowing down," the JCOS Chairman added.

The President of the United States let out a long breath. "It sounds like it's about to shift gears."

Woodley shut the hatch behind him and sealed it, satisfied no immediate threat hid on the walkway. Ahead of him metal stairs clung to the side of the ship's massive control tower like ivy on the side of a building. Below them another set of steps led further down the side towards the deck. Warrick wasn't stupid: it would be a tactical mistake for him to take the higher ground. It might seem reasonable at first—go high and snipe whomever came after—but Warrick had no idea how many men hunted him, and he could easily find himself outnumbered and overrun. Warrick and others of his ilk were cowards at heart, not willing to face someone unless they either had a sure upper hand or they had no choice. Also, Warrick was a cruel monster, but he wouldn't be a match for any of the operators on this boat coming after him. For Warrick, discretion *was* the better part of valor. Woodley glanced up the stairs through the driving rain and saw they led to another hatch, leading back up to the bridge. *Definitely down*, he thought. He squinted through the driving rain as he aimed his weapon down the stairs. Crouching low, he moved down each step cautiously, anticipating a spurt of gunfire to erupt at any moment. None came by the time he reached the next landing, which had yet another hatch, and a ladder that led to the deck below. He could see covered areas where two lifeboats waited, and Woodley felt certain that was Warrick's destination. Woodley, however, had no cover as he came down the 30 feet of ladder—he would be a sitting duck.

He slung the MP-5 over his arm, and pulled two flashbang grenades from his vest. He pulled the pin from one, aimed it as best he could so it would bounce under the cover, and tossed it down. *I must be living right*, Woodley thought to himself as it bounced directly under the covered area. A second later it went off: a flash far brighter than the lightning crashing all around them, and a noise likewise louder than the thunder. He counted to three, pulled the pin on the next flashbang, and repeated his action. The grenade bounced even further under the cover before it went off, and Woodley was already sliding down the ladder rails as it did. He hit the deck a second or two behind the second detonation, grabbed his MP-5 once again, and moved under the covered area. He spotted two lifeboats suspended in their stations, with one already being prepared to drop. He saw what looked like a pair of duffel bags inside the small craft before he noticed the form crouched in the shadows behind a crate near the rearmost lifeboat.

Woodley activated the small tactical flashlight mounted to his submachine gun and saw Seth Warrick on his knees, his hands covering his ears and his eyes squeezed shut. A large frame automatic pistol lay on the ground not far from the fallen man. *Whattaya know?* Woodley thought. *Better to be lucky than good.*

"Get up," he said as he motioned the flashlight up. He realized, in all likelihood, Warrick could neither see nor hear right now, but Woodley knew this man was too dangerous to approach unprepared.

He had no sooner thought this than Warrick suddenly sprang to life, spinning around and extending a hand towards Woodley. The Federal Agent reacted by firing a three-round burst, but not before a flash went off from Warrick's hand. Woodley felt as though someone had punched him in the right shoulder, and instantly realized he had been shot. The impact threw off his aim slightly, but two rounds perforated Warrick's right hand and the third punched a hole into the .22 Magnum Derringer Warrick had shot him with. Warrick cried out in pain, then charged Woodley, driving his left elbow into Woodley's chin. Woodley reeled, momentarily stunned, then Warrick put a left jab into Woodley's fresh wound. Stars filled Woodley's vision as pain registered from the bullet wound. The agent gathered his senses as Warrick moved for the automatic he had discarded to make himself appear more stunned than he really was. Warrick was fast, faster than Woodley expected, but the SEAL- turned-FBI agent was no slouch himself. His football days in Texas came back to him as he sprinted forward and tackled the thinner man from behind, ignoring the pain in his right shoulder, and lifting the English terrorist into the air. Woodley drove him into the ground with a satisfying "*Whoof*," and he was sure then Warrick had at least two broken ribs. Woodley swatted the gun off the deck and into the churning sea.

The maddened Warrick elbowed Woodley in the face, spun underneath him, planted both feet on Woodley's chest, and kicked him off. Warrick clambered for the lifeboat, but Woodley swept his legs out from under him. Warrick tried to catch himself instinctively with his right hand, grabbed the side railing, and screamed in pain. He fell against the railing, fire radiating from the broken ribs' impact against the metal tubes. Woodley stood and saw Warrick in the dimly lit area. Blood ran from both of his ears—the flashbangs *had* gotten him to some degree after all—and he squeezed his right arm up against his injured side.

"Give it up, Warrick. It's over."

"You're right, American," Warrick said, his breath coming in ragged gasps. "It is." He found another reserve of strength and vaulted over the railing into the lifeboat. He grabbed the release switch and smiled as he pulled it. He looked toward Woodley to give him a smug farewell, but Warrick's expression changed to one of shock when he saw the heavily built Federal Agent vault over the railing towards the now descending lifeboat. The former SEAL had his legs pulled up to him as if crouching, then extended his right leg just as he reached Warrick. The kick seemed as if it nearly took Warrick's head off, and the impact from the exploding charges ripping through the ship's hull threw the rapidly falling vessel off kilter. The boat rolled onto its side as it dropped, and unceremoniously dumped it contents, including both men, into the black, churning sea.

CHAPTER THIRTY

Thomas Hawkins stood at the bottom of the ramp leading up to the deck of the massive cargo ship. Marked and unmarked police vehicles covered the docks where the ship had been brought into port by the Coast Guard. Several vans were being loaded with suspects taken with very little incident from the ship, and HazMat crews scoured the cargo vessel in order to locate the remaining virus packages. The docks were cordoned off at the point of entry, with only local, state, and federal law enforcement personnel allowed within the perimeter. Hawkins thought to himself it didn't seem there were enough vehicles and personnel here for such a significant catch. The word had come down that the locals wanted to keep a low profile so as not to alarm people and draw unwanted attention to the fact there existed on board a quantity of a biological weapon sufficient to kill most of the population along the Gulf Coast. Hawkins understood the line of thinking, but he still would have felt better had there been a few more agents on scene. Samantha Land walked up next to him.

"The HazMat crew leader said they've found all of the big containers of the virus. They're going to haul the ship out to sea about 50 miles and scuttle her there after we finish going over the boat."

Hawkins relaxed slightly. "So we got all of it."

"Sure looks that way. I think we dodged the bullet on this one." Sam had barely finished speaking when the HazMat team leader, Kyle Horton, walked up.

"Agent Hawkins, we're finished. We've located all the virus containers, and they're secure. My team is going to stay behind on ship for a while to make sure everything *stays* secure. We don't need these suits anymore, but I'm going to keep my people in them for good measure. Better safe than sorry."

"Right," Hawkins said. "We need to be sure this whole area is locked down. Probably should put some SWAT or military on this in addition to the local PD."

"We don't want that much attention. I'm sure we're fine," Horton replied, then turned to walk back up the ramp.

"Wait a second," Sam interjected. "Didn't you say your people were staying on the boat with the virus for now?"

Horton stopped and turned to face her. "Yes."

"Then where are those two going?" Land asked as she pulled her pistol from the holster in her belt. Hawkins looked and saw two figures in yellowish-orange HazMat suits getting into a dark gray Ford Expedition, carrying a square silver box about the size of a bowling ball. Horton moved toward the men, no more than 30 feet away.

"Hey, where do you think you're going?" Horton shouted at the men. They climbed into the large SUV and shut the door. Hawkins had his own pistol out at this time and he and Land began moving toward the truck, several feet behind the rapidly moving Horton. Land was looking at the HazMat-suited man standing by the open rear door of the Expedition when she caught a glimpse of his face through the shielded helmet he wore, a face she recognized—the man she had seen at BEAR production facilities in France, the same mercenary she had seen briefly in Nice all those years ago.

He looked different now, she thought as she saw him once more, bald and shaven, but she knew those eyes. With startling speed, the man reached into the rear seat of the Expedition and emerged with an eruption of gunfire. Several 9mm bullets sprayed from the barrel of an Uzi into Horton, splotching his yellow suit with red. Hawkins and Land dove behind a car as bullets whizzed past them. The Expedition took off as the gunman fired into the crowd of police officers standing near their cruisers. Others scrambled to get out of the way as the massive truck slammed into one local police cruiser, then another, then another, before making its way at full speed for the dock's entry gate.

Hawkins dove behind the wheel of an unmarked Dodge Charger, and Land jumped in the passenger side. The car squealed off in pursuit as officers and agents on the boat ran to the side railing with their weapons drawn. Land noticed several police officers lying prone on the dock, with others scrambling to get into their cars as they roared in pursuit.

"One of the people in that truck is the guy I recognized in France at BEAR HQ," Land explained as they flashed past the guardhouse at the now shattered front gate. "I guess he didn't get toasted when the plant went up."

"Here's your chance to rectify that," Hawkins said. He spun the steering wheel to the right, then accelerated hard onto the street. He saw the fleeing Expedition heading for the ramp that would lead them onto the bridge crossing the Mississippi River. He suddenly realized what they were up to.

"They're heading for the French Quarter," Land uttered before Hawkins could.

"I'm not going to be able to outrun them in this, Mr. Matheson!" Manon shouted, darting past slower moving traffic on the bridge.

"You don't have to outrun them," Matheson replied calmly. "In fact, I want them to be there. Just keep us far enough ahead so I can accomplish the mission."

"What if our suits are compromised?" Leon Grimes asked from the rear cargo area as he reloaded his Uzi.

"Make sure that doesn't happen or you will die miserably. Then you won't be able to spend any of your hard-earned cash." Matheson resented Grimes and his loyalty to money alone. Manon, Warrick, and many others had been loyal out of belief in the cause. Of all his employees only Manon and Warrick were truly capable and trustworthy, and Warrick had to oversee the handling of the other ship. He had no way of knowing Warrick's fate, but the man had likely been caught or killed. Matheson hoped Warrick at least had the presence of mind to release the virus on the ship so there was *some* chance of contamination. If this container was the last viable release point...well, it would mean merely thousands dead instead of millions. All of Matheson's effort, all of his planning, would come down to one area of one city.

But perhaps that would be enough. He would release the weapon, right in the face of the FBI preacher and his CIA girlfriend. They would die horribly, gasping and shrieking at his feet as he stood in victory, safely isolated in his HazMat suit. Soon thousands of others would be doing the same. He, Manon and Grimes could escape in the confusion and live to carry on. Yes, yes, if everything went well, he could still salvage this, still make the point that needed to be made. He looked up from the stainless steel box in his lap and saw the Superdome in the distance. How nice it would have been to release it there at a major sporting event. But there was no time for that now. He had a destination, the symbolism of which made him smile.

The Expedition turned onto Tchoupitoulas, made a hard right just past Emeril's Restaurant, and raced for the river.

Land wondered aloud at their route. "Is he going for the Riverwalk? The casino?"

"I don't know," Hawkins replied as he wove the Charger through traffic. "It's almost dinner time, and the crowds will be big there for shopping and eating. I still think they're--Look out!" The door of the Expedition opened, and Grimes opened fire with his Uzi. Land and Hawkins ducked down as bullets sprayed the windshield and hood. Grimes smiled as he prepared to fire again when he found himself thrown against the interior with such force it dazed him momentarily. He looked out the window next to him and saw a New Orleans Police Department cruiser had nearly t-boned them as they turned onto Poydras Street and was continuing to bump into them as they sped past the Riverwalk shopping center and the Hilton Hotel. He smashed the window and fired angrily into the driver's side window of the police car. The officer jerked the wheel to the right and slammed on the brakes. He avoided being fatally shot by a split second, but he couldn't avoid the parking enforcement electric car and the minivan the other officer was ticketing. The traffic cop dove out of the way as glass, plastic, metal, and fiberglass shattered and crunched from the impact.

"He looks like he's okay," Land said as they shot past the wreck. She hoisted the MP-5 she had grabbed from the trunk and leaned out the window. Grimes was situating himself to fire on his pursuers again when he saw the CIA operative leaning out the window with the submachine gun in her hand. He saw the flash of the muzzle and felt a dozen angry hornets pierce his chest and neck, and he died full of anger at the fact he would never be able to spend the millions of dollars he had just earned.

Manon spared a glance back and saw the result. "Grimes is dead!"

"It doesn't matter! Drive!" Matheson shouted. Manon swerved past several cars waiting to turn into the valet parking area at Harrah's Casino, then raced across Canal Street and past the Aquarium of the Americas.

Hawkins had the siren wailing full blast, the LED strobes and wig-wag headlights blazing in the dusky light. There were just too many pedestrians for this sort of chase. *Somebody is going to get killed*, he thought as they approached Decatur Street, then shuddered at the irony of it. If they didn't stop Matheson, he was right—many people would die this night.

"Sam, we've gotta stop this now."

Land aimed for the left rear tire and opened fire. It took several shots before the tire was damaged enough that it broke apart. The Expedition twitched, swerved, then crashed into a parked tour bus in front of Bubba Gump's Restaurant. Hawkins came to a stop 30 feet behind, a crowd already forming around the wreck. Hawkins and Land jumped from the Charger, weapons drawn. Land caught a glimpse of movement on the passenger side, then saw a figure in yellow moving through the crowd.

"Hawk!" Land signaled towards the fleeing Matheson, silver container in his hand.

"I'm on him!" Hawkins shouted as he raced after the escaping figure. "You secure the driver!"

Land watched Hawkins run after Matheson, desperately fighting his way through the crowd. She realized the lives of all these people rested on Hawkins reaching Matheson before he could release the virus. Land was suddenly struck with fear, not for herself, and not just for the innocents enjoying a pleasant evening near the French Quarter, but for Thomas Hawkins. She knew what the virus did, and she didn't want to think about him dying that way. She didn't want to think about *anyone* dying that way, but especially this man she was quickly...

Her training and instincts saved her from the bullet which punched through her thoughts. The driver had managed to kick open the door and fired off a shot at Land. She dropped to one knee and fired the MP-5. One round fired before the action locked open—empty. The shot was a good one, aimed at the head, but Manon was also well-trained, and she spun and dropped. She had instinctively raised a hand to protect her face, and the bullet had struck the end of her gun barrel, knocking it from her hand. The hand stung badly, and for a moment she thought the bullet had struck her, had pierced her HazMat suit. She looked up and saw the CIA woman's submachine gun was out of ammo. Manon sprung up, grabbed a knife from the side pocket of the door, and threw herself at her crouching opponent.

Land threw the MP-5 up to block the thrust, and Manon kneed her in the abdomen. Manon slashed at Land again, this time cutting across her upper right arm. Manon managed a fair roundhouse kick for a person in a HazMat suit, and sent Land to the ground. She threw herself onto the prone Case Officer, ready to plunge her knife into the other woman's heart.

Land shook her head to clear it, then saw Manon coming at her with the knife raised. She waited until Manon started to come down, then put her boot into the other woman's faceplate. Land jumped to her feet and showed Manon how a roundhouse kick was done. The blow ripped open the front part of the French woman's HazMat suit. Land then delivered two hard punches into the center of Manon's face, blows which sent the woman stumbling backwards and falling over. Land paused for a moment to take inventory of her injury. Her right arm burned like fire where the knife had sliced her open, the cut worse than she had originally thought. *This could be a problem*, she thought. Her wounded arm wasn't going to do her much good in an extended fight.

Manon managed to stand, knife still in her hand, and turned to Land. Rage twisted Manon's formerly model-like face as surely as the blood which ran from her broken nose and the corner of her mouth. She didn't feel the pain, only dread. This woman had killed her. She had torn her suit open, and the virus would be released any second. There would be no way for her to survive now, not this close to the release point. Well, at least she would take this arrogant American woman with her. Her lips curled back to reveal gaps where her perfect teeth had been knocked loose by the powerful blows from Land. Manon raised the knife and a raw scream ripped from her throat as she charged at the Case Officer.

Land knew what was going through Manon's mind, knew what she was thinking as she came at her. Manon was taller, had an edged weapon, and didn't have a serious knife wound in her good arm. Land thought about it for a fraction of a second, then realized she had nothing to prove. She drew the compact 9mm pistol from the hidden holster at the small of her back with her left hand almost faster than the eye could follow, and fired two shots at Manon's bloody face. The other woman's head snapped back, and she fell to the street.

Blood ran from the wound in Land's arm and had spread onto her white t-shirt. It was really beginning to ache now, and would get worse as the adrenaline wore off. Reholstering her weapon she noticed dozens of people standing around, staring at her, not sure of what to do. She knew how they felt.

Several police units roared up, lights flashing and sirens wailing. She flashed her credentials, not wanting the arriving officers and agents to mistake her for a target. "I've got one suspect down here, but Agent Hawkins in in foot pursuit of the other who is the primary threat," she said to the NOPD sergeant who arrived first, a short dark-skinned man in his late 40s.

The sergeant saw her credentials and holstered his weapon, then looked at Land's arm and the blood spreading onto her t-shirt . "That's a bad slice. You need..."

"Sergeant, we've got to stop that other guy or this cut is going to be the least of our problems."

The sergeant pressed a bandage against the cut and began wrapping gauze around her bicep before she could say another word. She looked down in amazement. "Pretty impressive, Sarge."

He made an amused grunt as he finished the field wrap. "Lived in New Orleans all my life, then a Navy Corpsman. Plus, I been a cop here nearly 20 years. This ain't my first knife fight I've walked up on." He looked down at the still body in the hazmat suit lying nearby. He turned to a pair of other officers who had just arrived. "You two stay with this perp, I'm going with her."

Hawkins had Matheson in view. It was hard to miss a man in a bright yellow HazMat suit running down the street, even in New Orleans. As Hawkins ran past a seafood restaurant he thought about the times he had eaten dinner there with friends. His parents had gone there with him, years ago, when they had come to visit him. He chased Matheson past the entrance to the Jax Brewery, past the drug store and the gift shops, then turned and ran towards the Cathedral on Jackson Square.

That's where he's going to release it, Hawkins thought. *At the church.*

The crowd thinned out as they saw the two men running along the wrought iron fence surrounding the Square, but there were still too many people. As they neared the cathedral, Hawkins knew what he had to do. He stopped running, aimed his pistol though the crowd, and fired. Matheson stumbled and fell face first onto the ground near the steps of the cathedral. The crowd began screaming and running away, leaving only Hawkins and Matheson, who was bleeding from a bullet wound directly behind and below his right shoulder. He rolled over and looked at Hawkins, still 20 or 30 feet away. The FBI agent saw Matheson still clutched the silver box and was fumbling with one of the latch mechanisms. Hawkins aimed his pistol at Matheson's chest.

"Put the box down, Matheson. It's all over." Matheson continued to struggle. Hawkins couldn't tell if the gunshot wound or the bulky suit was hindering Matheson more.

"Don't do it," Hawkins said, with a calmness that surprised even himself. "No one else has to die today".

"That's the preacher in you talking now, isn't it, Agent Hawkins?" Matheson spat. "How very *Christian* of you," the word emphasized as if it were more poisonous than the virus in the container he clutched to his chest. "Well, in order to stop me, you're going to have to do exactly what religious fools like you always do to achieve your goals: resort to violence!" Matheson paused his struggling with the canister for a moment. "Don't blame me for what I'm about to do. It's *your* fault, and the fault of every religious zealot like you. Kill me, and you prove my point. And killing me is the *only* alternative you have, because you'll never reach me in time to stop me."

"We've both lost people because of what others have done in the name of politics and religion, Matheson. What you're doing..."

"Is what needs to be done!" Matheson shouted, frantic. He resumed struggling with the latches. "I've won, Christian."

"Stop," Hawkins said. Matheson continued. The latch clicked.

Everything seemed to go into slow motion for Hawkins. He exhaled and squeezed the trigger. The gun thundered in his hand, and a hollow-point slug punched through the HazMat suit and into Matheson's chest. A second shot immediately followed and struck Matheson just above his collarbone in the throat. The third shot struck him in the chin, the fourth at the bridge of the nose, and Matheson finally fell backwards. The metal box clattered from his hands onto the steps and tumbled down to the sidewalk.

Still sealed.

Hawkins took a deep breath. It was over.

He heard the sounds of sirens in the distance, approaching fast. *Just like the movies*, he thought. They always show up after the big showdown between the hero and the villain. Only he didn't feel like the big hero. He turned back toward Decatur Street and saw Samantha Land running toward him, a New Orleans police officer running with her. Her right arm was covered in blood, and much of the front of her white t-shirt was now a dark crimson shade. But she was alive. And so was he.

And so was New Orleans.

"You okay?" he asked.

She smiled at him, a wonderful thing to behold. "Never better. How about you?"

Hawkins turned and saw Matheson's body lying on the steps of the cathedral. The virus container, unopened, sat just below Matheson's fallen form like an obedient pet, waiting for his master's next command—in this case, a command which would never come. Several members of the HazMat team came running up along with a dozen Agents, their weapons all aimed at Matheson's prone form. Two of the HazMat operators immediately went to the metal box and carefully picked it up. Another member of the team opened what looked large a large metal picnic cooler. The two placed the BV-17 cannister inside the larger container and sealed it.

"I'll let you know later."

CHAPTER THIRTY-ONE

SAC Robert Shear sat in his office watching a cable news broadcast. The anchor was reviewing the events of the last few days.

"The architect of the anti-religious terror attacks, BEAR Pharmaceuticals founder and CEO William Matheson, was killed while allegedly attempting to release a biological agent in downtown New Orleans. Several of his accomplices were also killed in the pursuit and shootout. In addition the United States carried out an airstrike of the BEAR Pharmaceuticals facility in France where the biological agent was being produced. Sources indicate that a cargo ship in the Atlantic containing an unknown quantity of the biological weapon may also have been intercepted and destroyed. Authorities indicate that all of the biological weapons have been accounted for, but insist the investigation will continue to ensure all parties involved will be held accountable." Video clips from press conferences showed the President and other leaders declaring once again terror would not win the day, and that the United States and its allies would do what was needed to protect innocents of all walks of life from those who would do them harm. French President Granger was also shown, cursing the United States for violating their sovereignty, and swearing there would be consequences.

The news anchor and a recurring commentator with an opposing political viewpoint began discussing just how ludicrous the French president's statements were. For once, they agreed with each other completely.

This had been a costly case. Shear had nearly lost his ASAC, Walter Simmons, as good an agent as could be found. Simmons' ex-wife arrived at the hospital before he had been released, and he had requested a couple of days off now that the case was completed. It looked like some marital reconciliation might happen there, and Shear appreciated happy endings wherever he could find them. The funerals for the others killed in Atlanta were to be spread out over the next couple of days, and Shear had made arrangements to go to all of them. Woodley planned to head for Atlanta from Charleston the next day to be there as well.

Shear reached for the remote and turned the TV off. He straightened the stack of folders on his desk and reached for his jacket which hung on the coat rack. His people made him proud. Woodley and Hawkins, as well as the others, had done well. The Director told Shear they would all likely be getting promotions, and he said the President would certainly have something to say personally to the principals involved. For his own part Shear would likely be made an Assistant Director, and he would then recommend to Van Horn he consider moving Simmons up to SAC and Woodley up into the ASAC position. Shear felt confident the Director would agree. He had also recommended a move up the chain for Hawkins, as well as his choice of duty station.

Shear thought about the irony of a preacher saving the world. *Not in the way you might have planned, Hawk, but you did good, kid,* he mused as he turned off his office light and headed home for his first full good night's sleep in a long time.

"So where are you?"

"Charleston," Special Agent Mark Woodley said. "When they fished me out of the drink, they brought me and the other guys who had been injured to the Naval hospital here. Once they cleared me, Sarah and the kids came up to see her folks and have a mini-vacation. I'm heading to Atlanta in the morning. The funerals for the Marshals who were killed is tomorrow, and the Atlanta SAC's is the next day, so I'll be staying for it. Shear said Simmons was going to be there too. Did you hear he and his ex-wife have been together since the shootout?"

"Pretty cool, huh," Hawkins replied. "What was intended for evil can actually be for good."

"I think something like that is in the Bible somewhere," Woodley chuckled. "I'll head back to Charleston for a couple of days before going to Jacksonville. Sarah and I decided to sit here and reminisce about the good old days when I did safe things in the Navy, like ride around in a nuclear-powered tube under hundreds of feet of water, and plant underwater explosives and get shot at."

"I'll bet." Hawkins chuckled. "Yeah, I'm coming to Atlanta, too." He and Land had been debriefed in New Orleans at a secure office building at the corner of Canal and Decatur which doubled as a nondescript tax office. He was sitting at a table in Emeril's Restaurant, sipping on a glass of ice water and eating the best pepper cornbread he had ever put in his mouth. "I was glad to hear you were okay there, buddy."

"Same here, Hawk. I swear, I can't let you out of my sight for one minute," Woodley laughed. "But you didn't have to worry about me. SEALs don't *fall* off of ships, we *jump* off. And, sometimes, we take people with us."

"Of course. Too bad Warrick didn't make it back up with you."

"Right," Woodley laughed. "That dirtbag is so rotten inside the sharks wouldn't eat him. He got what was coming to him."

"Yes, he did," Hawkins said, and thought about the atrocities Warrick had been responsible for over the years. The rapes, the murders, hundreds dead...if ever there was anyone who deserved to die, he and Matheson would have been contenders for the top of the list. "Oops, gotta go pal. Dinner is about to be served."

"So, are you dining alone?"

"If I tell you, I'll have to kill you."

"Oooooh," Woodley said. "Dinner with a spy. Just watch your water glass. No telling what kind of drug she might drop in it while you're not looking."

"I'll try not to be distracted."

"Okay. You be careful, and I'll see you in Atlanta. Just remember to watch out for those CIA Spooks."

Hawkins smiled as he put his phone back into the inside pocket of his navy blazer. He was dressed up more than he had been recently, wearing a blue and white vertical striped Polo button down, tan dress slacks, and brown Johnston and Murphy laced ankle boots. He looked up and saw the waiter carrying a tray of food, and he also saw Samantha Land making her way back to the table, just in time. She was wearing a gray V-neck sleeveless shirt, a short black skirt, and black leather sandals with straps around the ankles. The lack of sleeves revealed a white gauze wrap which covered a bandage on the inside of her right arm across the bicep. It looked more like it covered a recent tattoo than a knife wound. Land was fortunate the knife had not cut lower and deeper or it would have more seriously damaged the bicep muscle. It was a broad cut, but it would heal fairly quickly without any long-term effects other than another scar. She arrived at the table just before the waiter, and another one of the wait staff was standing by to hold her chair in case Hawkins was too much of a ruffian to do so. He was not, and the second waiter stood by. The first set their plates before them and removed the domed stainless steel covers—Hawkins had ordered the bone-in ribeye with fried parsnips and garlic mashed pota-toes, and Land was having the roast pork tenderloin with collard greens.

"So, I'm wondering," Land queried as she took a bite. "Why

won't you consider coming to the Agency?"

"I didn't say I wouldn't consider it," Hawkins replied. "I just said I was very happy with the Bureau and wasn't really looking for anything else."

"Well, the DNI is very impressed with you. He says you'd be a great case officer at the Agency."

"I'm not sure how excited I am about spending another year of my life sequestered in some secret training facility learning to be a spy."

"Actually, it's 'facilities', and it usually doesn't take quite that long," Land said with a smile as she sipped from her water glass. "And it's not bad at all. Believe me, you'd love it."

Hawkins shrugged. "Be nice if I could transfer some of my credits, if you know what I mean."

"They usually don't make exceptions, but one never knows. Maybe you could be a permanent liaison or something."

"I think I'm content to keep my Bureau creds for now, thanks, but one never knows." Hawkins took a bite. "So, is it back to England for you?"

"Actually, I've requested to be brought in for a while. I'd like to spend a little more time stateside. I figure there's enough going on here to keep me occupied."

"So you'll be in Washington, then?"

"Working out of Langley, yes," Land replied. "What about you?"

"I'm not sure. Word's come down I have my pick of assignment, but I'm not sure where I want to go. I probably won't stay in Jacksonville, though. I might head for the mountains."

"Anywhere in particular?"

A grin crossed Hawkins' face. "I'll have to see what's open. I wouldn't mind being closer to Washington. There's someone I understand is going to be transferred there, and I'd like the opportunity to see her more often."

Land smiled, which was the reaction Hawkins was hoping for. "Lucky girl."

"Nice to know she feels that way." Hawkins paused, took a breath, and continued. "Seriously, Sam. I've had to work through some things, but with everything that's just happened, I've really had my eyes opened. I think it's time to put the past behind me and move forward. It's what they would have wanted." He paused for a moment, but only a moment. "It's what Anna would have wanted."

"You sure you feel that way?"

"Yeah. Yeah, I am. The last words I ever heard Anna say was how much she loved me. I think she was trying to tell me goodbye without telling me. I think it's time I told her goodbye, too. And now? Well, I've found someone who makes everything seem okay again. Shows how God does everything for a reason, I suppose."

"Not only would you make a great Case Officer, you're sweet."

Hawkins took another bite. "So, you really think I'd make a good Case Officer?"

Land pointed her fork at him. "If I didn't, I wouldn't be trying to recruit you. That would make me look bad."

"So, is that the reason you agreed to let me take you out for a night on the town? Just trying to soften me up?"

Land leaned slightly across the table, a sparkle in her emerald eyes. "Agent Hawkins, I am here with you tonight because I want to be with you. Ultimately, I don't care who you work for. I wanted to have some time with you when we weren't being shot at." Her eyes twinkled. "And I'd thought I'd give you another chance to kiss me."

"I think I'd like to have more time than just tonight," Hawkins said.

"Northern Virginia and D.C. are very pretty this time of year," Land offered.

Hawkins looked across the table at the CIA Case Officer, who smiled back at him radiantly.

It was a beautiful sight to behold.

GLOSSARY OF TERMS AND ACRONYMS

AG—Attorney General

AO—area of operation

ASAC—Assistant Special Agent in Charge

BUCAR—FBI-issued automobile; also refers to SUVs, etc., used by FBI agents

CCC—Coalition of Christian Churches

CIA—Central Intelligence Agency

COMINT—Communications Intelligence; information derived from electronic signals
that contain voice and/or text

Constellation—several satellites working in union

Crypto City—NSA Headquarters

DNI—Director of National Intelligence

DNSA—Director of National Security Agency

DIN—Defense Intelligence Network; top secret news gathering agency of the U.S.
intelligence community

DSS—Diplomatic Security Service

ELINT—Electronic Intelligence; information derived from electronic signals that do not
contain voice or text

ENPS—Electronic News Production System

FBI—Federal Bureau of Investigation

FCI—Foreign Counterintelligence

FDLE—Florida Department of Law Enforcement

FISA—Foreign Intelligence Surveillance Act; court issues secret warrants to target U.S.

citizens or permanent resident aliens; subject must be "an agent of a foreign power or involved in espionage or terrorism"; FISA does not cover US citizens outside US borders; No warrant needed to spy on foreign embassies and diplomats within US, only an okay from the AG, which is good for a year (James Banford, *Body Of Secrets*, New York: Doubleday, 2001.)

FLIR—Forward Looking Infrared

FO—FBI Field Office

GBI—Georgia Bureau of Investigation

GSW—Gunshot wound

HRT—Hostage Rescue Team

HUMINT—Human Intelligence; information derived from actual human personnel in the

field, either overt or covert

INTELINK—Secure Intranet used by U.S. intelligence community

IOSA—Integrated Overhead Signals Intelligence Architecture

JCOS—Joint Chiefs of Staff

JSO—Jacksonville (FL) Sheriff's Office

LEO—Law Enforcement Officer

MI-6—British Intelligence Agency

MOSSAD—Israeli Intelligence Agency

NCTC—National Counterterrorism Center

NSA—National Security Agency

NSAC—National Signals Analysis Center

OILSTOCK – High-resolution interactive geographic based software system that can store, track, and display near real-time and historical SIGINT related data over a map background

Operator—Individual member of special ops team; i.e. SEALs or HRT

POTUS—President of the United States

ROE—Rules of Engagement

SAC—Special Agent in Charge

SCS—Special Collection Service; cover joint NSA/CIA organization that specializes in

worldwide covert operations

SEAL—Sea, Air, and Land; Navy Special Forces group

SecNav—Secretary of the Navy

SIGINT—Signals Intelligence; information gained by electronic surveillance (ELINT) or

communications intercepts (COMINT)

Spook—slang term for a spy, particularly a CIA operative

STE—Secure Terminal Equipment

SUSLO—Special United States Liaison Officer; NSA representative in foreign countries

Tango—target

TTIC—Terrorism Threat Integration Center

Wetworks—term used for covert assassinations

ABOUT THE AUTHOR

Marcus Buckley has been a pastor and police chaplain in Florida and South Carolina for over 25 years. He is a graduate of Stetson University and New Orleans Baptist Theological Seminary and earned his doctorate from North Greenville University. He lives in Florida with his wife and three children.

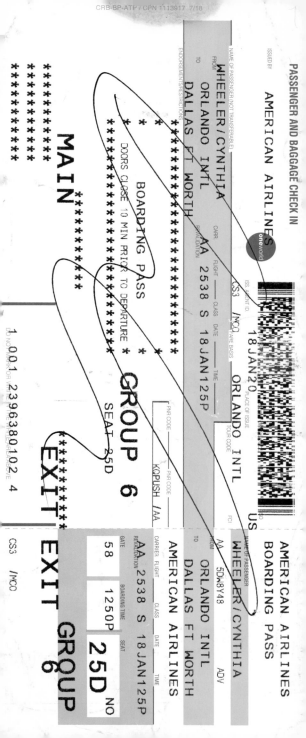

PASSENGER AND BAGGAGE CHECK IN

ISSUED BY

AMERICAN AIRLINES

oneworld

NAME OF PASSENGER (NOT TRANSFERABLE)

FROM
WHEELER / CYNTHIA

TO
ORLANDO INTL
DALLAS FT WORTH

ENDORSEMENTS/RESTRICTIONS

CARR.   FLIGHT   CLASS   DATE   TIME
AA   2538   S   18JAN   125P

BOARDING PASS

DOORS CLOSE 10 MIN PRIOR TO DEPARTURE

MAIN

* * * * * * * * * * * *
* * * * * * * * * * * *
* * * * * * * * * * * *
* * * * * * * * * * * *

* *
* * * * * * * * * * * * * * * * * * *

GROUP 6

SEAT 25D

ISS. ARPT ID.
18JAN20 PLACE OF ISSUE

VALIDATION   DATE

/MCO FARE BASIS   ORLANDO INTL

PNR CODE

PNR CODE
KQPUSH /AA

FCI   US

AMERICAN AIRLINES
BOARDING PASS

NAME OF PASSENGER

TO
WHEELER / CYNTHIA

FROM
ORLANDO INTL   ADV
DALLAS FT WORTH

AA   5DM8Y48

CARRIER FLIGHT   CLASS   DATE   TIME
AA   2538   S   18JAN125P

AMERICAN AIRLINES

GATE   BOARDING TIME   SEAT
58   1250P   **25D** NO

EXIT EXIT GROUP
6

* * * * * * * * * *

CS3   /MCO

THINK AVIS AND BUDGET.

Receive **up to 35% off** base rates with **AWD # K817167** for Avis rentals. To reserve, visit **avis.com/aacomfort** or call **1-800-331-1212**. Save **up to 30% off** base rates for Budget car rentals when you use **BCD # U072412**. To book, visit **budget.com/aaexplore** or call **1-800-527-0700**. Plus, earn American Airlines AAdvantage® bonus miles when you rent with either Avis or Budget.

AVIS **Budget**®

For full terms and conditions, visit www.aa.com/carpromo.
©2018 Avis Rent A Car System, LLC
©2018 Budget Rent A Car System, Inc.

FSC
MIX
Paper
FSC® C101637

This document should be retained as evidence of your journey.

CPSIA information can be obtained
at www.ICGtesting.com
Printed in the USA
FFHW021853010120
57439886-62878FF